The Closing Days

The Closing Days

Isaac Kovach

PARALLEL GREY PRESS

New York

PARALLEL GREY PRESS

ISBN 9798-9902867-0-2 (paperback)
ISBN 979-8-9902867-1-9 (ebook)

Book cover design by Kamil Rekosz - rekosz.com

Printed in the United States of America

Some characters and events in this book are fictitious. Any similarity to real persons, living or dead, is coincidental and not intended by the author.

To Katarina

I

When our plane banked right, pulling the city and the Bay into view, everything that had happened in the past few months felt escapable. Everyone that knew me was down there, and everyone at my destination was a stranger. I had a long flight in front of me, and I wanted to use the hours well. Maybe I could start a conversation with the woman beside me and practice my German. Maybe I could finish reading my book or plan my first days in Vienna. Five hours later, as we passed over the ragged edge of Greenland, none of those things had happened.

Instead, I just stared forward, fidgeting with the beige plastic clasp of my tray table while I listened in on my rowmates' conversation. The man sitting by the window pointed his finger up and whispered in German, "I have visited two crematoriums in my life. Inside the concentration camp at Dachau during a school field trip, and in Santa Cruz this past week to collect my uncle's remains. He's stowed in my hand luggage."

The man was wearing a heather-grey UC Santa Cruz Banana Slugs sweatshirt. The woman beside him gazed upward and replied, "I'm very sorry," which in German is said literally, "It does me great suffering." He, a middle-aged father of two from outside of Hamburg, and she, an unattached thirtysomething Austrian, had connected during the seatmate ingratiation window that exists between the clicking of seatbelts and liftoff. Now, twenty-eight thousand feet up on an arc between San Francisco and Vienna, they revealed themselves to each other, their conversation softly moving between death and triviality. Past and present. It appeared that I would spend the flight in silence. Not that I had much to add. I've never been to a crematorium, Nazi run or otherwise. If given the opportunity to speak, I would probably find a way to grasp their conversation and redirect it into a soliloquy about getting expelled from Stanford and the way my girlfriend, Janet, had dumped me via a crisply folded letter slipped beneath my door about a month before. She'd spelled my last name wrong on the envelope. We'd dated for almost a year.

As the man by the window detailed the various illegalities present in the unregistered, international transference of the ashes that were once his Uncle Karl, a flight attendant stepped down the aisle with a bottle of red wine wrapped in a white cloth napkin. Her cheekbones held an Eastern European lift, her black hair pulled back into a ponytail. When she reached my row, I lifted my glass and our eyes met. She poured the wine and held my gaze for longer than necessary.

"Sir."

"Yes?"

She leaned in close. I felt her warm breath on my neck. "Sir, I believe your mouth is bleeding."

I reached to the corner of my mouth and then pulled my hand away. A bead of crimson shone back from the tip of my index finger.

"Here you are, sir." She handed me a stack of thin cocktail napkins.

"Um—thanks," I said, as I fumbled out of my seat and walked towards the rear bathroom. Halfway there, an arrhythmic rock of turbulence sent my shoulder into the meaty arm of a sleeping bald man. His eyes flashed open, two white orbs glistening from the middle of his tanned head.

"What the fuck?" he said, in English. He looked like one of the golfers who would yell angry shit at my friends and me if we took too long to finish a hole at the par-three course in Golden Gate Park.

"Sorry, man," I replied, steadying myself on his headrest. I gave his shoulder a friendly pat and kept walking. A few seats farther, I turned back. He was leaning out into the aisle and staring at me. A chunky, silver Rolex glimmered from the thick wrist of his hairy arm. Definitely a golfer. I considered returning to apologize further, or to murder him, but elected to trudge on.

Humming fluorescents and the scent of urine greeted me inside the restroom. I tossed the soiled napkins towards the toilet. Thin and speckled red, they fluttered like dismembered butterfly wings down onto the seat. Leaning close to the mirror, I examined my face.

There is a tender, worn spot in the left corner of my mouth that never fully heals. It first tore about a decade ago. My body tries to scab it over and stitch it up, but each time I yawn or eat, it ruptures, producing a jab of pain and a dot of blood. I've grown something that resembles a beard, so it isn't too noticeable from a foot or so away. I try like hell not to touch it, lick it, or draw attention to it. I washed my face with water scooped from the aluminum sink and blotted myself dry with pungent brown paper towels.

When I returned to my seat, my rowmates were still talking. As I sat down, the man was saying to the woman, "Yes, flying on a plane *is* an act of surrender." They spoke to each other like actors, emotions accentuated for an unseen third party; although, I suppose I was their third party. Their conversation slowed into a fallow period following a long diatribe on the ideal season for potty training, and after a few minutes of shared silence, I closed my eyes and began to drift between consciousness and sleep.

An hour or two later, as most around me slept with mouths agape, I became very awake. I massaged my knees and stretched into the aisle, tapping my white and navy Nike Air Pennys onto the floor. It gave a little, providing an unnerving sense of hollowness. The closer I examined any area of the plane—the seams in the fuselage, the pale lights running down the aisle—the more the complete shabbiness of our flying bus emerged. Every surface was scuffed or threadbare. If our aircraft sheared open right there over the Atlantic, releasing us and our belongings into the saltwater, nothing would ever be found. At my mom's insistence, my suitcase contained a photocopy of my passport sealed within a Ziploc bag. She took great comfort in this preparation. I am assured it is watertight, as she chose a bag with yellow and blue seals that press together into green. The bag might float to the surface, informing birds and turtles of my age and birthplace. Family and friends waiting at our arrival gate would be unsettled when our flight switched from *On Time* to *Delayed* to—I'm not sure what exactly. For those who dropped passengers off at the airport, the shock would come easier. They saw loved ones leave, and they were prepared for an absence. Only the date of return would be modified.

I closed my eyes and imagined shooting three-pointers during an NBA Finals game. I'd stand in the corner, toes tucked behind the line, and receive a pass. With one motion I would rise, flick my wrist, and propel the ball towards the basket. This image calmed me. I approached the precipice of sleep, but I struggled when my mind shifted to the contours of my mom's face. I have no ability to recall faces in my mind. If I can't see someone in front of me, I begin to lose my memory of them and they begin to feel like a ghost. If I dwell on the sensation, I begin to feel like a ghost as well.

I took a deep breath and held it. Metallic cabin air stung my sinuses. I released the breath and tried a Hail Mary, an Our Father, and a Glory Be—a slightly different sequence of prayer than normal. It didn't help. The more I shifted and stretched, the more my calves tightened, so I stepped out into the aisle and walked to the rear of the plane where a yellow light illuminated the flight attendant from earlier. As I passed the row of the once-again-sleeping bald man, I considered flipping his tray table and showering him with his half-empty cup of tomato juice. His black Greg Norman polo confirmed he was a golfer. It's unclear why all golfers wish to always appear as golfers, even on flights to Europe in fall, but this man was no exception.

By the galley, the flight attendant sat in a jump seat, happily chatting to one of her colleagues, who was standing next to her. Alongside them was a tray with glasses of apple juice and Halloween-sized Toblerone. Their conversation continued as I entered beneath the light. I rehearsed in my mind the best way to interrupt them in German, but at the last moment I grew nervous and spoke English.

"Mind if I?" I asked, reaching for the tray. The liquid in each glass shifted in unison, holding level while the plane made otherwise imperceptible movements. The sitting attendant nodded. I drank an apple juice in one long swig. Just seeing anyone awake, even strangers, reassured me. Little silver nametags dangled from their shirts—Sandra and Melanie—and they spoke about shifts not lining up with what had been promised. Midway through an exchange about the bangs-dominated haircut of their boss's boss, they paused and looked over at me.

"Yes?" the one standing, Sandra, asked me, not unkindly.

I shrugged. "Nothing really. I can't sleep, and I'm just happy someone else is awake."

She smiled. "Care for some brandy?"

"You know, I think I already had too much wine."

She placed her hand on the plastic counter beside her. "I could give you a new in-flight magazine?"

"Sure, thanks."

She took out a plastic-wrapped stack of magazines from a cabinet, peeled it open, and extended the top one towards me. On the cover, a man wearing scuba gear over a business suit waved back at me. It looked like the scuba gear was added in postproduction.

"How much longer do you think this flight will be?" I asked.

"About four hours."

"Ok. Do you have any coffee?"

"Of course." She reached above her and pulled a blue, rectangular plastic coffee pot from a shelf and poured me a cup. I took a sip and pretended to enjoy it. Glassware matters. It matters deeply, and the waxy paper cup did this acrid liquid no favors. We had reached the point where I should return to my seat and let them continue their conversation. I lingered. I struggled to think of anything to say that would allow me to pass some of the remaining four hours in their company. Maybe Sandra would fall in love with me, and we'd get married and fight over her career flying around talking to lonely men late at night. The thought of our future arguments was starting to piss me off when the sitting flight attendant, Melanie, broke in.

"Sir. We do kindly ask that passengers remain in their seats, for safety, during the flight."

I'm only twenty-three. Before this flight I'd never been called "sir" in my life, and when she said it, it felt like code for, "You poor American bastard."

"Yes, of course," I replied and slunk back to my seat, coffee, magazine, and Toblerone in hand. I unwrapped the chocolate from its foil, broke off a triangle, and let it melt in my mouth. It went well with the coffee, and I savored it and slipped into a haze as I flipped through page after page of advertisements for United Airlines–emblazoned travel gear. The fleeces weren't terrible.

Four months before my flight, I had been fumbling through the end of spring quarter. I was supposed to write a paper about Tito, the former Yugoslav dictator. But no matter how early I woke up to write, or how bad I made myself feel for procrastinating, I couldn't make much progress. I loved the course, Central Europe since 1945, but my time was eaten up by a lab class about how to use sensors to measure heat transfer phenomena. My major was mechanical engineering, which I hated, but I was too far along to change. I had chosen it during my first week at Stanford based on five minutes flipping through a brochure at the student center. I liked cars I guess, and I knew Dad wouldn't have been happy with a liberal arts degree.

Instead of my paper or my lab work, I mainly focused on the NBA. The Bulls had won a record seventy-two regular season games and the playoffs were on. Night after night, I watched Jordan—a little thicker after his baseball sabbatical—back down his man on the block and then spring into the air, twisting, fading away from the basket and launching a shot just clear of his defender's fingertips. It was a new move, and though at first it wasn't as thrilling as when he sprang towards the basket in his wiry youth, its inevitability was intoxicating.

The Bulls won the championship on Father's Day. In the locker room after the game, Jordan writhed on the floor and cried uncontrollably. His father, James, had been murdered three years before on the shoulder of the highway in Lumberton, North Carolina, and this was Michael's first championship without him. They clinched at home in their stark white uniforms with broad and vivid red letters. That's an image I can clearly resurrect in my mind. I'm not a Bulls fan. I like the Warriors, and we are terrible. But I'm drawn to Michael. I started the Finals pulling for Seattle—Shawn Kemp is my guy in NBA Jam—but after the Bulls dropped two straight, I started cheering for Chicago. At the close of Game 6, I felt relief. The series had to end that way. My paper was due the next morning, so I took a dissertation about Tito written in German, translated an entertaining portion, and turned it in.

Exactly three months after the Finals, my professor called me into his office. Unfortunately, he loved the paper and wanted to put me up for an award. When rereading it to bask in my wordplay, he realized my use of endless paragraphs and excessive commas suggested that the original text might be German. He called a few former colleagues in Bonn and they located the paper that inspired me. If I left the university of my own accord, he wouldn't report the fraud. I could stay and fight and maybe get probation, but he thought it best for me to exit without the stain. I was unquestionably at fault. I don't believe in plagiarizing. I just couldn't seem to write, and I had been certain I would get away with it. The following morning, I went into the registrar's office when they opened at eight a.m. and withdrew from school. Then, I went to a travel agent at the Town and Country strip mall on El Camino and bought a one-way ticket to Vienna.

I chose Vienna because my Grandpa Charlie had spent nine months there immediately following the war and mentioned, without much detail, that it had been a formative period for him. I thumbed through his snapshots of the period on many a Sunday afternoon after church, intrigued by the stone buildings, the unsmiling faces, and the rubble. His grandfather had emigrated alone from Passau, a town near the border between Germany and Austria, in 1893. My grandpa's only illumination on the intersection of his lineage and the war came from a comment one afternoon while I looked at a photo of a river lined with oak trees.

"That one's of a forest near where my grandfather was born. Wish I could have visited under different circumstances."

Though I was only fourteen at the time, the comment lingered. The photos weren't the only thing he brought back. In a trunk in his attic, I found a silver German sword, an officer's saber. Across its handle was a *Reichsadler* perched on top of a swastika. Seeing those familiar crooked lines outside of a television screen raised the hairs on my arm. Grandpa Charlie became my personal Indiana Jones. I went downstairs to ask him about it, but I had no courage at all, so instead I asked if I could have something from his attic. He told me I could have absolutely anything I wanted, so I found a box big enough to hide the saber and covered it with random books and old yellow copies of *National Geographic*. Grandpa could never throw away an issue. We ended up selling a few at an estate sale the year after he died of prostate cancer. The rest are in a dump now, somewhere around Colma. The saber is still under my bed in my room at my parents' place. When I opened it that first night, a dark, tangy-smelling residue covered the bottom of the blade. I now realize this was grease, spread to ease friction with the scabbard. At the time, I assumed it was blood.

My interest in our family's history inspired me to learn German, which I hoped to improve in Austria. Our last name is Vogel and my dad was impressed to have a son who could teach him to pronounce it correctly. I explained my plans for going abroad to my parents in our kitchen in the Outer Sunset of San Francisco at 2:17 a.m., three days before the flight. I wanted to tell them at a better time, but my mom is a doctor and is never at home and awake. The kitchen was dark other than a dim bulb glowing beneath our microwave. The window behind the sink was cracked open. It had been painted over so many times it never really shut all the way, and the smell of fog and wet eucalyptus filled the room. I phrased things the best I could.

"I'm not 'expelled' exactly, but my professor asked me to leave so he wouldn't *have* to expel me."

"So, they kicked you out," stated my dad, rubbing his forehead. He sat across the table from me. My mom stood a few feet behind him, arms crossed, leaning against the doorway to the living room. Dad owns a small hardware store on Divis and has never been to college. He always ran down private schools until the day I got into Stanford. Then, without a word, he started wearing a Stanford ballcap to work. He must have picked it up from a gas station, though, because the typeface of the *S* was all wrong. The curves were too smooth.

"Basically, yes. But I can transfer somewhere else, and it will be like it never happened."

"But it did happen," answered my dad.

"Yeah. But I'll transfer to Cal next fall, and I won't ever do something like this again."

"We didn't raise you to cheat."

"I know."

He stood up. "You do realize that you are in an incredible amount of debt, right? Paying for three years of Stanford to graduate from Cal is an absolute fucking disaster."

"I know. I'll figure it out. I called the loan people and they have a grace period, so I only have to come up with the money for a couple payments as long as I get back in school next year. It's in my name so it won't affect you."

"It won't affect us, huh?"

"I mean financially, I guess."

From the doorway, my mom asked, "What was the paper about?"

"We had to write about a patriotic tradition in Europe, so I chose this stupid relay that they ran through Yugoslavia on Tito's birthday every year. It started in his hometown, wound through the whole country, and ended in Belgrade."

"I thought you liked history?" she asked in a sad voice.

"I do, I just, I couldn't—I don't know. I actually wrote some of it—just not enough."

My dad sat back down, placed his hands on the table, and said, "You should stay, work at the store, and save money. You do not deserve a vacation to Europe."

I bit my lower lip and picked at the fragile corner of my

mouth. I hadn't slept much since withdrawing.

"I know. I feel terrible, but I need to change something right now. I can't stay home for a year. I have enough savings to get to Vienna, and I'll find a job there. It's going to work out."

My mom walked over and pulled my hand away from my face. Then, she sat down next to Dad and put her arm around him. She's a pediatric surgeon at UCSF, where she got her doctorate. Her view of academia is transactional and rooted in experience. Dad's conceptions are from television. I wasn't sure who this news hurt more. She looked over at me, her eyes bright, and in an artificially kind voice asked, "Alex, you didn't cheat a lot, did you?"

"No, it was just this one time."

"It's better to fail than to cheat, ok?"

"Ok. Please. Let's—ok."

I didn't speak much to either of them in the days before I left. The longest exchange was with Mom about how much Pepto Bismol to take on my trip. I took three bottles.

After finishing my in-flight magazine, I flipped through *Rick Steve's Europe Through the Back Door*, dog-earing pages of interest and marking up a map affixed into the back cover of the book. When we began our descent into Vienna, the Austrian woman beside me placed her hand onto my wrist. On the other side of her, our rowmate was asleep.

"Excuse me?" she said in German. Her face looked colorless, her posture rigid. She rubbed at her eyes, which sent a tear sliding down one cheek, leaving a solemn track.

"Yes? What's wrong?"

She laughed. "I'm just really afraid of landing. Very afraid."

I nodded and put my hand atop hers. She twisted towards me, laid her head on my shoulder, and closed her eyes tightly. She smelled of peppermint and unbrushed teeth.

"I'm so sorry. This is so embarrassing," she said.

"It's fine, don't worry—I'm studying to become a therapist, actually."

"Really?"

"No."

She laughed.

"I'm Alex," I said.

"I'm Stefanie. I'm sorry. I hate flying. I . . . I can leave you alone."

"No, no. I'm happy to help. Let's talk about something light to distract you—maybe that guy's uncle above us?"

She laughed again. "Were you listening to our conversation?"

"Only all of it."

"Oh, I don't know why I talk so much on planes. I guess because I'm nervous."

We stayed in that position, whispering small talk to one another as the plane descended. It was my first time speaking German in a noncontrived situation, and it was my first exposure to Austrian phrasing and rhythm. When most Americans talk about the German language, they focus on how it sounds to nonspeakers and suggest that the strong, throaty vocalizations are emblematic of the German character. What they misunderstand is that once you are within the language, its sound melts away.

Stefanie's shoulders stiffened when our plane touched down and the pilot hit the brakes, sending screeches and vibrations throughout the cabin. Once the braking eased and our plane began to taxi to our gate, she released me, and we instantly became strangers once again. I tried to keep the conversation going, but she went back to speaking with her now awake, ashes-smuggling friend. We nodded goodbye to one another at the baggage carousel.

Though in a haze, I managed to find the train from the airport into the city. I spent the ride pulling lost strands of her long blonde hair from my black Nike sweatshirt. I got off at a stop in the fifth district and worked my way through the biting late October air to my hostel. Inside, I took an empty bunk in a room filled with Australian guys who were very tall and unseasonably tanned.

Leaving my bag in a flimsy plywood locker, I stepped out to explore with my passport and my entire life savings thrust down into my right front pocket: six hundred dollars in twice-folded American Express Travelers Cheques and five one-hundred-schilling bills. I headed in the direction of the city center down a long, twisting street lined with shops. My pulse buzzed, and my steps were effortless, almost manic. I had made it to Europe, alone, and I had a new country to explore.

Compared to home, the city was flat and clean, transit was everywhere, and all the buildings were stone. I didn't see a single wooden structure. I noticed that at intersections, pedestrians stopped and waited for the signal to change, even when no cars were approaching. They spoke softly to one another, and I listened in and practiced replies in my head, careful with my sentence structure, moving verbs to the end of sentences where appropriate, not rushing through the longer words. Eager to engage someone, I stepped into a bakery and walked up to a glass display case.

"Grüß Gott," said the woman behind the counter.

"Hello, may I please have two of these?" I responded in crisp German and pointed down at the first thing I saw: puffy balls of beige dough dusted in sugar.

"These or these?" she asked.

I couldn't see what she meant, so I just replied, "Yes, exactly."

"Ten schillings," she said, sliding over to the register. Ten schillings was about a dollar.

I held my money hovering above the counter. Dark marks, almost bruises, underlined her eyes. She didn't reach for the bill, and after a harrowing moment, I realized I was supposed to lay it down into a small, curved plastic tray built into the counter. I did so, and she scooped it out and put a few coins in its place alongside a small white bag containing my order. It was a strange ritual, the dish serving as an intermediary between us, no opportunity for the brushing of fingers or the notion of contact. Eager to speak a little more, I asked, "I'm new to Vienna—would you mind pointing me towards Stephansplatz?"

Without expression, she pointed to her left.

"Ah, thanks. Goodbye."

"Auf Wiedersehen," she replied in a muffled monotone.

I walked outside and examined my purchase. They were two jelly-filled donuts. I had anticipated my first meal in Europe being more elegant and refined.

As I progressed down the street, the spires of distant cathedrals peeked out above the skyline. I reached the Ringstraße, a broad, four-lane avenue running where Vienna's medieval walls once stood. I sat on a bench to eat, and although I tried holding my donut with the tips of my fingers, I still spilled powdered sugar on my sweatshirt. Halfway through the second donut, a man sat down on the far edge of my bench and smoked a cigarette. My body tensed. He leaned back, legs splayed, and gazed out over the passing cars. Was it obvious that I was an American? Did anyone care? Before I could attempt contact, he stood up and left.

I finished the donut and crossed the Ring into the first district, an intricate blend of pedestrian streets, stately architecture, and tourist schlock. A cobblestone road led to Stephansplatz, a large, open square that contained Stephansdom, the alleged jewel of the city—a hulking, coarse, Gothic cathedral. Calling Stephansdom ugly might be too much, but it stood incongruous to the clean lines of the buildings surrounding it. Clearly much older, with its tower three to four times higher than any nearby rooftop, it was an anachronism within the anachronism of the first district. I paced around its periphery with my neck twisted upward, trying to feel whatever one should when encountering a building first consecrated seven hundred years before California became a state. Formed of stacked beige limestone, its walls had been shaded black by the passage of time, accentuating their roughness and placing the cathedral in a permanent shadow.

Around its entrance, tourists clustered in small groups, continuously forming and then breaking up and moving along, like bacteria beneath a microscope. Most were underdressed for the cold in wrinkled, brightly colored clothes. A few sported makeshift layers of newly bought hoodies with *Vienna* written in script across the chest. Their mouths hung open and their hands clutched crumpled maps covered with ads. The cathedral apparently had an entrance fee, although not during Mass, and many seemed unsure about paying it or pretending to be believers. Men sporting shabby Mozart wigs stepped up to thrust binders in their faces, imploring them to buy tickets to some symphony, somewhere. It wasn't quite as sad as Fisherman's Wharf, but it wasn't *not* shitty. Clouds settled overhead, the temperature dropped further, and I walked off without a destination.

That night at the hostel, I sat at a small bar and nursed a pint of fizzy yellow beer while I thumbed through my book, a paperback copy of Heinrich Böll's *The Clown* due back at the main branch of the SF public library months ago. At some point during the evening, I met a fellow American, a Chicagoland suburbanite named Jake, and we had a standard-issue conversation about what he was hoping to find in Vienna. Hearing a guy openly vocalize banal goals absolutely identical to my own, goals I could never state aloud, felt like running into someone wearing the same outfit as me. He drifted into a feature-length monologue about his "passion for glassblowing," and I just stared forward, without an exit plan. Eventually, he left, and I sort of missed him. To his credit, he did tell me about a bulletin board at the University of Vienna's campus where apartments and jobs were listed for students. I ended the evening with a short phone call to my parents on the hostel lobby's pay phone. My mom picked up, the connection wasn't great, and I let her know I was alive. I'd planned to apologize again for everything, but in the moment, I wilted and we hung up feeling further apart.

The sky was overcast the next morning, which seemed to fit the city. Though the sun was fully obscured, its light vibrated through the clouds and reflected off the wet streets, casting everything in an arresting clarity as I walked across town towards the university. Down narrow, winding streets, I passed alongside commuters walking to work. They were prepared for the morning chill with leather boots and long coats that fit well. I was not. The wind bit through my jacket and worked its way above my Nikes, stinging my ankles. Coming from San Francisco, I knew damp and chill and sunlessness. But real autumn was new.

Set on the grounds of an old hospital, the University of Vienna campus was a maze of low-slung, ivory-colored buildings lining wide courtyards. I wandered into the large foyer of a building that resembled what Jake had described. I sensed it was the right place to be, but I couldn't find the bulletin board. It was forty-five past the hour, presumably during class, and the halls were empty. I leaned back against the wall at the base of a staircase and waited for someone to walk by.

Two sets of footsteps broke the silence. To my left, a woman walked down the stone steps. She didn't look overly friendly or overly concerned with being unfriendly. Although I had been in Vienna for less than one full day, a look of empathetic indifference had emerged as the standard Austrian expression. To my right, an old man ambled towards me, leather briefcase in hand. As I waffled over which of these two to interrupt, a voice spoke.

"Excuse me?"

It was the woman. Lithe and confident, she stopped a step above me, our eyes aligned.

"Yes?" I answered.

"Do you need any help?"

"How did you know?" I stammered out, my German flimsy, my commitment to the curve of an umlaut incomplete.

A slight grin appeared on her face, revealing the notion of a dimple in her right cheek. "I thought you looked confused—and American," she responded, switching from German to lightly accented English.

I offered a grin back. "How do you know I'm American?" I asked, responding in English. She stepped down from the last step on the staircase. Her green eyes studied mine and then looked down. She pointed at my shoes.

"Those."

I examined my chunky Air Pennys. She wore a pair of svelte, midrise lavender Pumas that I had to admit I could never imagine anyone back home wearing. She probably didn't even know who Penny Hardaway was. I shrugged.

"I'm looking for a bulletin board that lists places to rent, jobs, that sort of thing."

Her eyes darted off to the left. "Yes, that's right over here."

I followed her down a long, ivory hallway and turned left, then right again. Along the marble floor ran an inch-wide grey, bumpy inlay. I stopped and rubbed it with the toe of my sneaker.

"That's to guide blind people," she said. I'd never seen anything like it. I didn't know how blind people navigated back home. She continued walking, I followed, and one final turn led us into a well-lit corner of the building. On the far wall hung a tired, brown bulletin board covered with white, pink, and green papers.

"So. Here it is," she said, gesturing with an air of finality.

Then, looking down at her watch, she mumbled a word to herself in German.

Planning the words before I began, I spoke in stilted but flawless German. "I really appreciate your help in locating this information. If you are late for something, please don't let me keep you."

An unabashed smile grew on her face. "You speak German well!"

"I speak a little."

We looked at each other for a breath or two, and I caught a whiff of apricot from somewhere. Maybe her hair. She made the faintest of turns, beginning to withdraw. Her lips parted to speak, but before she could say anything, I extended my hand. "Alex."

"Johanna."

She pronounced it, of course, in the German way, "Yo-han-na." I'd known a number of "Joe-annas" back home—my mom's friend, the travel agent, for example—but the name from this woman's lips was different. It held a clean verve. She took my hand and gave it a gentle shake. The light in the room poured in from windows on two sides and was amplified by the white plaster walls. It cast Johanna in a warm sharpness, and I really saw her for the first time. Her dark brown hair hung past her shoulders, just a touch wild. She wore a tan scarf wrapped around her neck and a snug, black leather jacket.

"And you're a visiting student here?" she asked.

My shoulders tightened. I hadn't figured out how I was going to answer questions like that.

"No—I'm just exploring Europe for a while on a break from school."

"Well, it was nice to meet you, Alex. I have to go see my professor now," she said.

"Sure."

She took a half step back, then turned, the heel of her

Pumas tapping on the stone floor. I was so absorbed by her presence that I almost let her slip away.

"Maybe we could grab a coffee sometime?" I asked.

She turned back. "Ok," she said, and smiled, pulling her hair behind one ear then looking again at her watch. The sound of doors opening echoed through the halls and students began streaming past.

"Do you remember numbers well?" she asked.

"I'll remember this one."

She blushed a faint but perceptible scarlet. An amazing scarlet. "01-319-82-87, got it?"

"I've already forgotten it."

She laughed and then looked away for a moment. "How about this—Café Westend. Eleven tomorrow morning. It's across from Westbahnhof."

"Got it."

"*Tschüß*," she said, in a light birdsong.

"Bye."

With that, she turned and walked away. After an inspection of the bulletin board only revealed apartments I couldn't afford and jobs I wasn't qualified for, I stepped outside into the morning air and repeated the terms of our engagement. To-morrow. Café Westend. Eleven a.m. I spent the rest of the day walking the city. I ventured out past the first district into ran-dom, everyday neighborhoods. It was striking that although there were people everywhere, the streets held the tenor of a small town. Nobody rushed around. No place was over-crowded. Other than the stations of the U6 line, the city was impossibly clean. Although it was different than home, I felt I could manage. Austria was like Pepsi to America's Coke. The same flavors, just combined at odd ratios.

That night, back at the hostel, I unfolded my map of the city and tried to connect its patterns to paths I had traveled. From above, Vienna's streets are a series of concentric circles wedded by wandering lines. I plotted a path to Café Westend, whose address I found in a green phone book by the hostel's front desk. I went to bed that evening with the goal of sleeping as late as possible to avoid any extra waking hours with my mind spinning about Stanford, Johanna, and everything else.

I awoke around 4:30 a.m., heart racing, calves wooden. I lay there in near blackness surrounded by at least twenty other beds, each occupied by a sleeping stranger. The linoleum floor magnified their breathing into a throbbing wheeze. I tried to fall back to sleep by picturing my third-grade teacher, Mrs. Treadway, teaching us the multiplication tables. It didn't help. She was too attractive. I took out my book and tried reading by my Timex's Indiglo light, but it wasn't bright enough. After an hour of rubbing my neck and flipping from one side to the other, I gave up and went to take a shower in the hostel's drafty bathroom. I couldn't find my soap, so I used an orphaned green bar stuck to a tray in the last stall. The hot water lasted ninety seconds. I remembered reading in my travel guide about a market, the Naschmarkt, open on Saturday mornings near the U-Bahn stop, Kettenbrückegasse. After getting out of the shower, I spent some time aimlessly staring at myself in the mirror, then headed out towards the market.

A persistent drizzle hung in the predawn sky. The streets were empty as I walked east, making a few wrong turns before finding an alley that opened into the market. Row upon row of tables lined its edges, and I made my way down the main thoroughfare. At the beginning, the displays were little more than old blankets covered in a mix of disparate items: mismatched shoes, cassette tapes, tangled wires. The vendors were as disheveled as what they sold, sitting cross-legged on the ground with distant looks. As I progressed deeper, the order of the wares gained structure. Lumpy piles on the pavement gave way to tables with sorted cardboard boxes and locked glass cases.

I scanned the nicer tables. Most contained a classic assortment of flea market junk: old plates, scuffed books, broken cameras, cracked leather briefcases. I found a grey porcelain mug with a solid weight to it. Years of use had left a roughness in the glaze of the handle. It wasn't just a mug. It was a European mug. I confirmed this by checking the bottom: "Made in Germany." Why they wrote "Made in Germany" and not *"Hergestellt in Deutschland"* troubled me, but maybe I could give it to Dad. I'd broken his Super Bowl XVI mug last summer emptying the dishwasher, and he'd refused to let me try and find a replacement. The seller of this mug, a tall guy with thick, nicely brushed hair, was having a discussion with a man from the next booth over. Their language was smooth, Slavic, and incomprehensible. I cleared my throat and uttered "Excuse me" in German. He waited until he completed speaking with his friend, then turned towards me with a look of incredulity.

"Fifty schillings," I offered, gruffly.

With an appalled face and a dismissive wave of his hand he answered, "150."

At a store, new, the mug was maybe worth eighty-five. Dad could do without it. I put it down and continued on. I made two other timid attempts to buy something. First, a blue ten-dinar bill from Yugoslavia that was labeled in each of the country's four official languages. Then, a postcard from 1912 written to a soldier at war. In the corner sat a crisp, pink Kaiser Franz Joseph stamp. Each seller appeared reluctant to sell. One seemed annoyed that I had the audacity to disturb him. The other ignored me entirely until I waved the postcard in front of his face.

Somewhere between the junk at the entrance and the professionally organized tables of kitsch near the food stands, I came across a stretch of quality, unfiltered items. I began to linger and dig. I opened and read through boxes of intimate documents one might keep tucked away in a dresser drawer beneath underwear: a birth certificate here, a death certificate there, photos and letters scattered throughout. Many lifetimes lay before me. The rain picked up and fell onto much of it, wrinkling paper and smearing ink while sellers stood and stared, unconcerned. It clearly wasn't their stuff, nor the stuff of anyone they loved, so what pipeline led the personal items of presumably dead Austrians onto these tables?

As I worked through a set of bright-orange binders containing stamps from the DDR, I came across a battered photo album the size of a paperback novel. Opening it released the scent of ink and raisins. Inside the cover, written in pencil, was an illegible word followed by "1940, July 7th to July 21st." The photographs were phenomenal. Forty-two black and white images, expertly exposed, documenting a group of twentysomethings on vacation in the Alps. The photos ran the full gamut of possible Alpine elevation and weather: one-piece bathing suits worn beside a sunny lake followed by fully coated poses amid snowy peaks. It was clear that in midsummer 1940, these Austrians spent a vacation far from the international concerns of their homeland. They didn't look as though they feared the arrival of my grandfather on his tank a few years later, although maybe they didn't live to see it. Each photo contained depth and texture with a haunting, almost three-dimensional clarity. Making eye contact with the table's vendor, I held the book up with my left hand and extended two one hundred schilling bills with my right. The vendor paused, then accepted the money. I had my first purchase. The buzz of acquisition gave way to thoughts of Johanna, and I left for Café Westend.

I walked awhile along the Gürtel, a dirty, busy road that surrounds the inner districts of Vienna. With the openness of the road beside me, the soft light of the morning warmed my face. Just before the café, I stopped by a darkened window to inspect myself. Instant regret. My eyelids were puffy and the skin of my forehead dry. The found soap of the hostel had been a poor decision.

I continued on, and when I reached the block of the café, I saw Johanna leaning back against a stucco wall. Hair down, faded black jeans, white Chucks.

She looked towards me and smiled as I approached. "They had a fire in the kitchen last night, so they've closed," she said, turning and motioning to the window beside her. As she pointed, her jacket sleeve pulled back, revealing a delicate wrist.

Peering inside, I didn't see much more than chairs on tables and empty space. "Damn. Ok."

"Maybe we could try a different place nearby? Have you seen much of Vienna?"

"I'm new. I'm down for anything."

She shifted her weight from the wall. "Ok—this way."

She turned left, and we set off down the street. She led, and I followed. We reached a stoplight and a spearmint Volkswagen Golf screeched by. As she took a step off the curb, I had a sliver of a moment to glance at her. She wore no make-up. The sun picked up the different shades in her dark hair—auburn and chestnut at the outer layers, underneath almost black. Something about her matched the city.

"Are you okay speaking in German together? If it's too hard—" she asked.

"No, it's great, I want to. If I say something that sounds super nuts, just ask me about it because maybe I didn't mean it like it came out."

"No problem."

"Are you from here?"

"Yes. Well, my family is split between Vienna and the Innviertel, so I'm mixed up by Austrian standards. But I completed my *Matura* here."

I nodded, with no clue what or where the Innviertel was. We continued silently for a few blocks, turning down a side street, our feet plodding rhythmically as the street arched downhill. She stopped abruptly, and our eyes met. Yesterday, hers were olive. Today, something closer to hazel.

"This is the place," she said, pushing open the door of Café Jelinek.

With hardwood floors, lace curtains, and smoke-darkened walls, the interior of the café brought to mind the living room of a chain-smoking grandmother. We took a green velvet booth in the back next to a sunlit window. Johanna unwrapped her scarf and opened a menu in front of me. I inspected it, scanning various words I recognized. Colors, ingredients. There seemed to be the expected pattern and progression to the menu, but the specifics were confusing. A waitress in a formfitting black skirt and white button-up appeared alongside us with a folded notepad and a pertinent gaze.

"Could you order for us? I'm still learning my way through a menu," I asked Johanna.

"But your German is wonderful."

"Well—thank you, but I'm finding I learned *German*-German names for food. *Hochdeutsch* I guess."

She rolled her eyes and smiled.

"We do not say *Hochdeutsch* in Austria. We call the official German *Standarddeutsch*, because *Hoch* implies superiority, of which the Germans have none. The food in Austria is far better than Germany by the way."

"Ok, but these names make no sense. Like, what the hell is a *Verlängerter*?"

The waitress cleared her throat, unamused. Johanna raised a solitary finger, and she quieted. I was impressed.

"Would you like a snack as well?" Johanna asked.

I nodded. Tracing the edge of the menu with her finger, she ordered in a soft, lilting voice. Then, she stopped and looked up at me.

"Should we order too much or too little?"

"Too much, no question."

She spoke a few more words, and the waitress lowered her pad and backed away, leaving us alone. I took a deep breath and smoothed a ridge in the white tablecloth. There wasn't much I felt compelled to discuss. I already liked her.

"A *Verlängerter* is an espresso with more water than a normal shot. *Ver-längern*: to extend. Nothing could make more sense." She smiled, showing fully the dimple from the day before. "I ordered you one. They're ok. It's what my grandfather drinks, but I prefer café latte." She stood up, removed her jacket, and placed it on a wooden coat rack standing beside our booth. She extended her hand, and I took off my jacket and handed it to her. She placed it alongside hers. They looked good hanging there together.

"And what is your impression of Austria so far?"

"I'm a little jet-lagged and out of it, but it seems amazing. It's super ornate, like a royal wedding cake or something—but, this is my first time anywhere really, so I don't have a lot of expectations."

She laughed.

"I mean my first time in Europe. I'm from San Francisco, but even in America, I haven't traveled much. Have you been to the US?"

"No."

"It's different."

She took a band from her wrist and pulled her hair back into a ponytail. She had cute ears, a little big, and I immediately missed how her hair looked when it was down.

"How is it that you speak German so well?"

I shrugged. My interest began with my grandfather, but I was afraid to mention his wartime connection to the city and broach the subject of Austria's sins.

"I took it in school, and I guess I liked learning it. Do you study at the University of Vienna?" I asked.

"Yes."

"What's your major?"

"Philosophy and pedagogics."

Knowing little of philosophy and unsure of what pedagogics even was, I nodded silently with reverence for the European liberal arts. It must be refreshing to study without a path to a career. Dad had said Europe would be like that.

"What is pedagogics exactly?"

"You don't know pedagogics?"

I shook my head.

Her eyes narrowed. "It must exist in America."

I shrugged.

"Ok. Pedagogy is the theory of teaching. So, you study the history and ideas of teaching methods, but you do not learn to become a teacher. For example—I'm researching how exhibition design affects visitor education within children's museums."

"Do you like it?"

"This research or the field of study?"

"Both."

"I love it. The nurture of thought within a child's mind is magical."

"Awesome. I was studying mechanical engineering. I didn't love it."

"Then why study it?"

"Well, I chose the wrong thing. It seemed practical and maybe interesting from the outside. My school was really expensive, so you can't just pick whatever. I mean, some people do, but I don't think my parents wanted that. You guys don't pay for school, right?"

"Of course not."

"Oh, well, we pay a lot. I paid—it's better not to say—but I did think I might like engineering. Once I started, though, I didn't. Everyone told me that intro classes are dull and later ones are better, so I stuck with it. But then I hated the later ones even more, and now changing would mean starting over."

"That is problematic."

"Yeah. It's my fault. At least I've enjoyed the classes I've taken outside of my major."

The waitress soundlessly reappeared and laid before us a series of plates and glasses. A small coffee rested in front of me on a silver platter with an even smaller glass of water. Baskets contained bread, and plates were set down with cheese, meat, tomato slices. Even a radish. I don't think I'd ever seen a radish in a nongarnish situation before. It was quite the spread.

"*Mahlzeit*," the waitress announced, then walked off. Taking my lead from Johanna, I took a piece of bread and assembled an open-faced sandwich of sorts.

"I do feel a little disoriented here. Just boarding a plane and then suddenly being submerged in a different language and culture is—I think I'm still processing everything."

She nodded as she took a bite into her sandwich. We made eye contact, and as I waited for her to respond, she smiled, putting her hand in front of her mouth as she chewed and tilted her head from side to side.

"Makes sense," she said, then took a sip of water.

"You wouldn't find a place like this in California. The fact you can go into a restaurant and grab a table and just order a coffee from a waiter is awesome. And all the old decor—look at this thing!" I pointed at a framed print behind her on the wall. A rough sketch of a group of men and a horse beside a domed cathedral, it hung ten degrees askew, and a dead fly lay feet up, entombed between the glass and the print. Scribbled in pencil in the corner was the year 1895. "That's charming. I mean, it's decrepit, but with authenticity."

She gave the frame a long look, then nudged it level.

"I like it."

"Yeah, I like it too."

"I used to work here though. It's not that charming."

"You worked here?"

"Yes. In summers when I was in Gymnasium. I lived with my grandfather not too far away, just down the Mahü and up Kirchengasse, in the seventh. He knows the owner, Antonín, and he convinced him to give me a job." She mimed her hands through the air as she spoke, the right moving up and then over, tracing the streets.

"So you have a lot of memories here?"

She looked over my shoulder.

"Yes, actually. Over there, at that round table, is where I broke up with my boyfriend," she said, pointing down near the entrance.

"Ah, ok." I took a cursory glance at the table. "Recently?"

"A few weeks ago."

I nodded, took a deep breath, and exhaled slowly. I wondered if their breakup was the end of a dying relationship or just another chapter in a cycle of splits and reconnections. I wondered if he was smarter than me and if she'd ever dated an American.

"How did it go? The breakup, I mean."

"Oh, well—we arrived here together, then we left separately." She said, with a half grin. "By my choice," she added.

I considered follow-up questions but passed.

"Is there a particular goal for you here, on your trip?" Johanna asked.

The truth was my goal was to have moments like this. Or at least, whatever this moment had been before she'd mentioned her ex.

"Am I prying? I hope not. I'm not usually so direct. It's only that you are American, and I heard that's how you are."

"Really? Who is out there labeling my people?"

She laughed. "My roommate. She spent a summer in Chicago. She liked it."

"Well—I've never even been within a thousand miles of Chicago, but no, of course you're not prying. I guess I'm here to take a break from goals, other than getting to know the culture."

"That sounds nice."

I closed and opened my hands, stretching their tendons. I have my mom's hands. Slender, with long fingers. Mom uses hers to slice open the bodies of children, remove things that shouldn't be there, and sew them up again with blue nylon thread. I use mine to spread butter and to hand in plagiarized papers.

We continued to eat and the conversation flowed, some about Vienna, pieces about Johanna. We brushed along the edges of personal information and subjects of emotional consequence, but only just so. She projected calm and self-assuredness, and yet, I could sense sadness within her. I didn't think she'd had an easy, meaningless life, like mine. The ex-boyfriend didn't come up again. After our plates were cleared, she pulled a box of cigarettes out of her leather purse, opened it, and extended it to me. I paused. She gave the box a light tap and raised her chin. I took one and gingerly rotated it. I'd only smoked a handful of times. She lit another one in her mouth and then handed it over to me, taking the unlit one from my hand. I thought of the faint dew from her lips as I placed it between mine. I drew a trace amount of smoke into my lungs, the smell of fire and figs flooding my nose as I exhaled.

She raised her eyebrows again—they followed a perfect, natural arc—took a drag, and pulled a leaded glass ashtray from by the window over into the center of the table. I took a deeper pull, drawing heat into my lungs, and exhaled, watching the smoke pause, then fade. Beneath the table, our knees touched, and the distance between us lessened. Being with her quieted my thoughts, which is the greatest gift someone can provide. Then, she leaned back, and her knee was gone.

"You don't smoke, do you?"

"Not really. As of last year, you can't even smoke in restaurants in California."

Her eyes widened. "I thought America was about freedom?"

I shrugged. "That's all just marketing. I'd like to smoke, but I have a hard time disassociating smoking from death."

She rolled her eyes, kindly, and we smoked in silence, my

head lightening. We finished our cigarettes and then stood and collected our things. She mentioned that she needed to travel to some faraway district to meet an aunt visiting from the countryside. At the door, we paused, and she turned her left cheek towards me. I had yet to take part in this ritual. I leaned in and lightly kissed one cheek, catching her scent—apricot again? Had she worn perfume? I retracted and turned for the other cheek, catching the blur of her eyes for the second we were aligned as lovers, then continued to the far cheek and mimed a soft peck. My lips brushed the down of her face. The scent was definitely apricot. Had she worn perfume for me? Or was it just shampoo? I stayed close longer than I should, then withdrew, slightly dizzy. Somehow, during the process my hand had taken hers. She gave it a tender squeeze as she said, "Tschüß, Alex." Then she stepped out the door and took a brisk step up the street.

I followed, calling out, "Johanna!"

She turned towards me.

"I still don't have your number."

She looked into her purse and produced a ballpoint pen, holding it up like a conductor's wand.

"Do you have any paper?" she asked.

"I do not."

She took my hand and wrote along my left pointer finger, "0 1 3 1 9 8 2 8 7." She drew the funny line through the seven that Europeans like to do. Beneath the numbers, she put a *J*. With a flash of a smile, she turned and headed up the street, leaving me with her pen in my hand. The press of her fingers on mine lingered. Once she turned the corner, her presence ebbed, I felt a haze of jet lag, and my thoughts began to tumble over one another. Was that a date? Should I have asked more about the ex-boyfriend? I examined her pen. It was electric blue and had the words *Rieder Brauerei* written down the barrel in a thick black letter typeface. My eyes welled. There is an intimacy in holding the pen of another. Her thoughts had flowed from her mind down into her hand and rolled out through the ballpoint tip. If she died on the way to see her aunt, I might have to consider giving the pen to her family, although I suppose they'd have plenty of her things. If I died walking to the hostel with it in my pocket, my parents wouldn't know the significance. They'd probably have to fly to Austria to get my body washed and sanitized and mailed back to San Francisco. It would be cheaper to cremate me and stuff me down into the inner pocket of a carry-on suitcase, like the German guy did on my plane, but I've told them I don't want to be cremated. I want something of myself to remain. I'd rather melt into the soil than be blackened into ash and scraped into an urn. I hope my belongings don't end up for sale at a place like the Naschmarkt.

I set off with no destination in mind. It was Saturday, and I shouldn't call her until at least Tuesday evening. That left about eighty hours for me to replay the events of the previous ninety minutes. I paced the city for hours before ending up in the last car of a *Straßenbahn* ambling in circles around the Ring. Depending on one's persuasion, you could travel the Ring clockwise or counterclockwise on the number one or number two line. I sat in a cluster of four seats, two facing two, with a yellow can of cold beer balanced on the hardwood seat next to me while I flipped through the last pages of *The Clown*. It's not an uplifting book. Through the large glass windows, Vienna hobbled by at six miles per hour. The charms of the city followed one after another—the Hofburg, Parliament, the Rathaus. Flood lights illuminated each structure, casting a sterile artifice over their beauty. I finished my book, got off, ate a sausage from a *Würstelstand*, grabbed another beer, and hopped back on in the other direction.

With each passing loop and each can of beer, my ability to eavesdrop on Austrian German sharpened. A group of people about my age climbed aboard: three women and one dude. I cleared the seat next to mine, brushed the crumbs from the front of my shirt, and straightened my shoulders in hopes the group might engage me with life-changing conversation and invite me to wherever they were going. It worked, sort of. They sat and stood around me, and a redhead in the group began a story about a fight with her boyfriend. The man among the women nodded somberly as the redhead detailed the audacity of her soon-to-be ex-boyfriend. His principal transgression was either always being around or never being around. I missed a few words in translation but am pretty certain she was a bitch. A half dozen stops later, they all stomped off, leaving me alone with my now lukewarm beer.

I lay my forehead against the cool glass as we stopped once again in front of the Rathaus, Vienna's city hall. Its five-towered facade and rows upon rows of tall, thin windows loomed in the night, slowing my breath and taking my focus. As the doors began to close, I stepped off into the evening and walked through a park weakly lit by streetlamps. When I reached the Rathaus, I ran an ungloved hand over its porous, limestone base. Like Stephansdom, black dirt tinted its sandy color, but it wore its age better. In comparison, the other grand structures along the Ring failed to resonate. Parliament was a Greek cliché, the Opera too broad shouldered and tense. The Rathaus appeared fragile and alive and wounded in some invisible way.

I saw a pay phone nearby and felt a pull to call Dad. It would be one p.m. in California, nine hours behind Vienna. The morning fog had probably burned off already, leaving a few hours of clear sky before it would return and envelop our neighborhood. Dad's favorite thing to do on Saturdays is to walk the eleven blocks from our house to Ocean Beach and drink his coffee on the dunes before going into the store. He's up at five, shovels his Folgers into our beige plastic Mr. Coffee machine, and is at the beach by 5:35. He makes it into work with plenty of time for the seven a.m. open. By one p.m., he's usually sitting behind the counter, eating donuts, and listening to the start of a Giants game on the radio. He and his store smell of oiled metal and freshly cut keys, a smell so strong I could taste it even in Vienna, six thousand miles away. I wanted to tell him about Europe—he's never been abroad—but as I considered the possible paths our conversation might take, I became certain a call wouldn't go well. His disappointment in me would bleed through, packaged within a terse sentence. "Well, I hope you're enjoying your time off," or "I would love to chat, but I've got to get back to work." The cool night air began to seep past my jacket, and I wondered if Johanna was thinking about me. Almost certainly not. She knew hundreds of people in Austria, and I knew one. I didn't have anything to offer her other than, I suppose, my time. My time was very available.

Later in the evening, I waited at the Michelbeuern U-Bahn station for a train back to the hostel. The station had black concrete floors, white painted walls, and an open roof revealing a cloudless night. It was quiet save for a persistent hum from the nearby Gürtel. Across the tracks on the opposite platform, a couple began to argue. Without warning, the man hit the woman flush in the face, twice in rapid succession, knocking her down onto all fours. She wobbled up to her knees as a cut opened below her eye, blood dripping down her face. From my side of the tracks, a group of people called out in anger. A brief, subdued yell of alarm came out of me as well. Suddenly, the man who had struck the woman jumped down from the platform and ran towards us. The gravel around the train tracks crunched beneath his feet. A male accomplice, previously unnoticed, followed a step behind. Both effortlessly hopped over the tracks and a center divide, scaled onto our platform, and began to hit one of the men who had yelled in opposition at their violence. The attacker's accomplice kicked the man. The muffled thud of knuckle on forehead sang out. I looked on, completely still. A moment later a train arrived, people stepped off, and I stepped on. The doors closed and we pulled forward into the darkness. As we passed alongside the fray, I could see the bystander who had yelled laying on the ground curled into a ball, arms bent around his head in protection. Blood and thick spit hung in a web from his face onto the floor beneath him. A group huddled a few feet away. No one intervened.

As the train accelerated, I lost sight of them, and the veins along my temple throbbed. Not only had I not helped the man, I hadn't considered it. Something had led me onto the safety of the departing train. When we reached the next stop, I sprinted up the stairs and back towards the previous station, frantically searching for any sign I was headed in the right direction. By sheer dumb chance, I found it. The beaten man lay in the same spot on the platform, surrounded by crouching bystanders. I pushed through, knelt down next to him, and put my hand onto his arm. His jaw lay open, heavy and crooked, definitely broken.

"Are you ok?" I asked.

He didn't respond.

"What's your name?"

"Thomas," he mumbled.

"Help is coming, Thomas."

He had pissed himself, and the pungent odor stung the air. I sat there with him, rubbing his shoulder until the EMTs and police arrived twenty minutes later. I'm five feet, ten inches, 160 pounds, and uncoordinated. I maintain no illusions that I am a tough guy, but the meekness of my response saddened me. I'm not sure how long it should take to arrive at true empathy for another, but I know it took me too long. As I described the assault to a disinterested police officer, some thirty-five minutes after the attack, I looked down at Thomas and understood his despair. It bolted through me and revealed that what I had mistaken as empathy to that point was only fear and self-pity. It was strange to give a statement to a German-speaking cop standing beside a Volkswagen hatchback cop car. It was strange to see an injured man loaded into a minivan-sized ambulance barely wide enough for a gurney. It was very strange to think that in the same day, I had been drinking coffee with Johanna. I reached into my pocket; her pen was still there. Eventually, the scene wrapped up, and I walked back to my hostel through the black night. Certain that I would be unable to sleep, I slept better that evening than any night since I had withdrawn from school.

II

The next few days were a relentless sequence of errands, walks, unknown faces, and expenditures. I rented a furnished, one-bedroom apartment eleven floors above a square from a student, Philip, leaving to study kinesthetics in Florence. Why Italy and why kinesthetics, I don't know, I didn't ask, I just handed him the schilling equivalent of $450 in exchange for a thick and dimpled silver key. No contract, little discussion; just a direct money for key exchange. The flow of capital can be beautiful. I sat behind the register of our hardware store an entire summer accepting cash for goods—usually light bulbs or batteries—and a small fragment of the wealth of those living within walking distance of the intersection of Divisadero and Fell Street ended up in the store's account, of which a splinter became my salary, and now found its way to Florence, care of Philip, wearer of thick glasses and owner of seven plastic house plants that he left behind to beautify the apartment. While I only had enough cash left for a week or two of food, I now had my own place to sleep for the next four months and a thirteen-inch television set with six different German-language channels, five of which featured soft-core pornography from ten p.m. until five a.m. each night. The lone non-nudie channel showed recordings of early eighties concerts. The crown jewel thus far was a performance of "99 Red Balloons" by Nena. Only, it wasn't "99 Red Balloons" at all, it was the original German version: "Neun Und Neunzig Luftballons." The video fixated me, and I was certain that if I considered it fully, it could reveal a lot about Nena and maybe everything about Europe.

The opening line, "Hast Du etwas Zeit für mich" translates to, "Do you have time for me?" Yes, Nena. I do. A lot of it. Her armpits unshaven, her teeth slightly asymmetrical and off-white, Nena sang directly into the camera. She had no discernible rhythm, and yet, lips curled, hands clapping off beat, she danced and it all worked. Her cheeks flushed the perfect cherry as she sprinted around the stage. It took a few viewings before I realized Nena was singing about an accidental ninety-nine-year-long war that ends with civilization in ruin. This is pop music for Germans. The professional dynamics of her support band raised other questions. They were all male and wore Hawaiian shirts: a drummer, guitarist, bassist, and keytar player. Did they feel like legitimate musicians? What had their dreams been and did they align with being ancillary gears in the Nena machine? At one point in the song, they were given an extra two measures to riff on their instruments—was that the highlight of their night? Weren't they all trying to sleep with Nena? Was it better to be them, superfluous but on television, or me: essentially nonexistent? When viewed alone on the opening nights of a Viennese winter, the video resonates.

On late Tuesday afternoon, I walked across the square beneath my apartment to use the pay phone to call Johanna. It rang differently than home; an odd half-note staccato pairing replaced the familiar single, whole-note pulse. The air of the phone booth was still and warm and didn't settle right into my lungs. Perhaps the previous occupant had consumed all of the oxygen. After five rings, someone answered. I knew it wouldn't be Johanna. I imagined a roommate emerging from the shower and reaching for an orange handset, hair wet, body wrapped in a towel.

"Hallo." A female voice. Stern. Not Johanna.

"Hi, is Johanna there?"

"What?"

I repeated my question, sharpening the opening and closing of each word. On the journey to foreign language comprehension, talking on the phone to a stranger comes last, if at all. I hoped Johanna hadn't given me a fake number.

"Excuse me, could you speak a little slower?" I asked, still in German.

"Johanna is not here. Could I take a message?"

"That's ok, I'll call back. When will she be home?"

"You are the American?"

"Well, yes, I am *an* American. Alex."

The voice on the other end of the phone laughed.

"Try in an hour."

"Ok."

It wasn't a bad sign that Johanna had told the voice on the phone about me. With time to kill, I walked in a loop around the square, stopping to stare into shop windows and look up at my apartment, curious what was visible from different angles on the street. I couldn't see much; a plastic houseplant, my desk chair. For a moment I thought I saw a man in my apartment, but the moment passed. The square itself was uninspiring. Overhead Straßenbahn wires stretched in from each corner and converged around Franz-Josefs-Bahnhof, a boxy, glass-walled train station that looks like an insurance office from the 1970s. I can't imagine it's anyone's favorite building. The Austrian penchant for naming everything after the curly sideburned Franz Josef was troubling when one considered he presided over the country's collapse from a broad, Central European power into a landlocked afterthought.

I entered three different stores and bought nothing. Within

each store, only a cashier was present, their eyes following me up and down the narrow aisles, the only noise the squeaking of my sneakers. I kept my hands outside of my pockets lest I be taken as a shoplifter. I missed the space, crowds, and anonymity of American shopping. After some time, I returned to the phone booth. Inside, a mustached man hunched down with his elbows on the tiny stainless-steel counter beneath the phone. The handset nestled into his shoulder. His left hand held a cigarette while the other rubbed at his forehead. He whispered, low and steady, like a wave lapping at the shore. I liked his voice, and though I couldn't make out any words, I hoped things were going better for him than it looked. With a sigh, he laid the phone down, paused, then stepped out, avoiding my glance. I entered the booth and dialed Johanna. The man's warmth remained in the handset.

"Hello."

"Johanna?"

"Alex, hi."

"Hey. How are you?"

In my time anticipating this conversation, I hadn't thought to prepare material. We spoke in German, hers too soft to hear, mine too halting and fumbled.

"Good, you?"

"Good."

"How are you finding Vienna?"

"It's good. It's cold." I was already repeating myself.

"Yes, the grey daytime is difficult. I prefer once the sun goes down completely."

"Absolutely." We'd covered weather. "Did you want to meet up, maybe grab lunch this week?" I asked.

"I do, but I can't. I have too much work for school, although possibly on a short break. Do you have a number I could call you on?"

"Yeah, I actually rented an apartment on Julius-Tandler-Platz. It has a phone but I have to go somewhere and pay to get it switched on."

"Oh, wow! That's very close to my apartment. How long are you renting it?"

"Four months."

"Ok."

"Do you know any other places where jobs are listed? I looked at that bulletin board you helped me find, but there wasn't anything that fit."

"Well—for students of the university, yes. Do you have a work visa?"

"No, it would have to be unofficial. Maybe a restaurant or something?"

"Are you allowed to stay in Austria for so long?"

"No, but the stamp in my passport is hard to read and I've heard they don't look too closely at Americans. A friend of mine overstayed in Paris for years."

"Interesting." A long silence passed. Maybe the fact I would be living nearby Johanna for an extended time obliterated my ephemeral appeal. Outside the phonebooth, a few drunks lay on the steps of the train station, sprawled out in the sun. One looked over at me, and I returned his glare. Johanna and I continued talking for a few minutes, interminable pauses followed by us both attempting to speak at once. We hung up with the arrangement that she would call if she was free.

I spent the rest of the week working through the remainder of my guidebook, broadening my understanding of the Habsburg empire's eight hundred years in power. I jotted down the names of heroes I found cast into bronze or carved from marble around town: Schwarzenberg, Prinz Eugen, Maria Theresia. One couldn't help but notice that on the city's official tourist paths, the Habsburgs received far more coverage than Austria's more famous and recent son, Hitler. I only found Adolf's name mentioned in my American guidebook in a short section on his Vienna years spent as a struggling artist. I had a coffee at a supposed favorite hangout of his, Café

Sperl, and walked by the art academy that rejected him twice. It says something about art that the worst man in recent memory wanted to be an artist.

The next Monday, Johanna called. She wasn't able to meet up until she finished a paper about Kierkegaard's ruminations on Abraham and Isaac. She read me a section where he explains how Abraham might have acted as he unsheathed his blade to sacrifice his son. The Old Testament is opaque to me, especially this story. Kierkegaard believed Abraham would have tried to appear wild and unhinged in order to force Isaac to believe that the murder was Abraham's will, not God's. If his son had to die, he wished for him to die with his faith intact, and without hatred of God. The parallels between this abandoned sacrifice, and what happened to Jesus, were evident. It was a lot to discuss over the phone, but she was into it, and her voice hummed with the joy of stumbling on illumination. At the end of her reading, I wanted to ask what she believed about the whole Christ thing, but I couldn't get the words out. I'm a Catholic floating on a thin plank of belief atop an ocean of nihilism, and I'm afraid any movement might send me plunging below. Her excitement for her paper surpassed anything I had ever felt at Stanford. For me, the only goal of an assignment had been to finish it, and most of my hours had been spent calculating the forces required to destroy engines that didn't exist. Johanna mentioned the need to get back to work, cleared her throat, and said,

"Are you free tomorrow, at seven p.m.?"

"Yeah, why?"

"Would you be up for meeting my grandfather, Heinrich? I spoke with him, and he might be able to help you find work. He's retired now, he used to be a journalist, but he knows almost everyone in Vienna. You could meet at Café Weimar near the Volksoper."

"Wow. Yeah. Definitely. Thank you."

"No problem. He'll be expecting you. He likes to sit in a booth facing the entrance, to the right of the piano."

"Got it."

"Goodnight, Alex."

I hung up and walked over to my window overlooking the square. What an end to the conversation. I guess my plans for a long stay in Vienna hadn't scared her off. I spent the evening imagining which features Heinrich's face might share with Johanna's, and which anecdotes of life in America would charm him. I decided to keep things simple. There's a sign by the driver at the front of every bus in SF that says, "Information gladly given, but safety requires avoiding unnecessary conversation." I think of it often, and it sounded like the right approach for a European grandfather.

It was a few minutes before seven p.m. when I arrived at Café Weimar, a vaulted-ceiling, white-tablecloth type of place. Piano music echoed about, provided by an old woman at an upright, jet-black Bösendorfer in the center of the room. In a booth to the piano's right, a grey haired man sat eyeing the door. Our eyes met and I walked over, deliberate with my steps, slowly inhaling the heavy, smoke-filled air. I repeated my goals to myself: find a job and charm this guy. Don't fuck up.

"Herr Trost?"

"Alex."

"Yes."

"I'm Heinrich. Please, take a seat."

I slid into the red, upholstered booth across from him. On the table lay a white porcelain cup containing what looked to be espresso. A tuxedoed waiter approached, hands clasped behind his back, and gave me an attentive look. I motioned to Heinrich's cup.

"Verlängerter, please."

The waiter nodded and backed away. Heinrich's eyes settled on me. I saw no clear trace of Johanna in his face, although, maybe something in the bridge of the nose.

"What brings you to Austria, Alex?" he asked.

"I'm taking some time off school to travel through Europe, and Vienna seemed like a great place to start."

"And you and Johanna are close?"

"I've only, well, we're actually just getting to know each other, but she's been very kind."

He reached out and smoothed a wrinkle in the tablecloth with his right hand. The sleeves of his navy wool sweater were pulled back to his elbows, revealing firm, strong forearms.

"And how is she?"

"Johanna?"

"Yes."

"She seems well—why?" Would he have known about her breakup—or was there something else?

"I worry about her." The waiter arrived with my coffee, a glass of water, and a small carafe of cream on a silver tray. As he arranged things before me, I glanced at Heinrich. He had recently shaved, perhaps immediately prior to our meeting. He had a clean jawline and bright, grey eyes. Beside us was a large window, through which blinked the red hazard lights of a champagne-colored Audi sedan.

"Your German is quite good."

"Thanks."

I took a sip of my espresso. A little too acidic and over extracted. I added a splash of cream.

"Have you ever been to America?" I asked.

"No," he answered with a shake of his head. "A friend of mine visited once and enjoyed it. California and New York. He spoke often of the large Fords and Chevrolets. He said they were magnificent, but one isn't allowed to drive them fast, so they were like caged eagles." He paused and looked down into his cup. "And how do you find Viennese coffee?" he asked with a soft smile. He spoke in a strong baritone with a rasp at its edges.

"I like it, although I'm still learning my way around the menu. My plan is to try everything at least once."

He leaned over and held his left hand in the air, two fingers extended.

"Franz. Two *Fiakers*." he shouted towards our waiter, standing near the door. "A fiaker is wonderful in the cold weather," he said, then sat up straight, smoothed his brown pants, and placed his hands in his lap. "And you are looking for employment?"

"Yes."

"Of any particular kind?"

"I'm pretty open so long as it doesn't require a visa."

My grandfather's sense of law and order would be offended by such a requirement. Hopefully Heinrich wouldn't hold it against me. Something about him, maybe his clean style, made him seem like a man comfortable operating past the fringe of legality. No man in my family, myself included, owned an article of clothing that fit as well as the pants and sweater he was wearing. No man in my family brushed their hair as well either. The waiter appeared once again, handing each of us a tall glass containing black coffee topped with thick whipped cream. The scent of hot alcohol wafted about.

"Rum?" I asked.

Heinrich nodded. He reached over and laid his hand onto the wrist of the waiter.

"He's my granddaughter's friend, an American."

The waiter nodded towards me with a blank look of disdain. I don't think Americans were a unique or welcome sight to him. I'd never been served by a waiter in a tuxedo before. It had its charms. Heinrich smiled and the waiter walked off.

"His father and I were friends. An interesting man, very resourceful. Unfortunately, he was an alcoholic. He was hit by a car while drunk and died right down there." He pointed towards the window.

"Oh, that's terrible." I wasn't sure of the correctly weighted adjective to speak of death in German.

"Yes, it was terrible. So—for work—what I have to offer you is simple. I am a retired journalist, and my office is a catastrophe. I have years of writing and research strewn about, and much of it might be useful for reporters working at my former employer. I'd like to have it all put into order and indexed into an accessible system. This is more work than is endurable for any one person, but you could attempt it, and I will pay you if your performance is sufficient. Perhaps starting at one hundred schillings per hour for four hours per day?"

I ran my hand through my hair and then rubbed the back of my neck. It sounded perfect. No commitment and enough money to enjoy the city while saving a little towards my loan. I took a spoon and tapped on the side of my Fiaker, knocking whipped cream down into the coffee. Coming from a background of Cool Whip and other industrial, dairy-like products, the heft and tang of actual whipped cream was at once unsettling and delicious.

"It sounds perfect. I would love to do it."

He clasped his hands together.

"Wonderful, Alex. And you can read German as well as you speak, yes?"

"Yes."

"Wonderful."

He took the demitasse spoon that lay by his glass, mixed in the whipped cream, and drank the rest of his Fiaker in one gulp.

"Do you care for the drink?" he asked.

I followed his technique and finished mine. The rum made my eyes water and burned on the way down.

"I do, although I think I prefer beer."

"I try and drink what fits the season," he said with a kind grin. "If you don't mind, I should be heading out. I'll see you tomorrow morning, seven thirty a.m.?"

I nodded. Seven thirty was very early, but at least I'd have the afternoon free. He raised his hand in the air and motioned to the waiter.

"Check please, Franz. I'll cover it, Alex."

The waiter arrived by our side and looked over the indecipherable scribbles on his small notepad.

"Two Verlängerters, two Fiakers—170 schillings, please."

"One hundred and eighty," Heinrich said, handing him two hundred-schilling bills.

"Thank you, sir."

The waiter handed back a twenty-schilling bill and then stepped away. Heinrich reached down and picked up a well-oiled, dark leather messenger bag. From within, he pulled out a green notebook. He opened it and wrote down his address and phone number in an even, controlled, cursive script. He ripped out the page, folded it, and handed it over.

"I'm in the seventh district, near Sankt Ulrich, back behind the Volkstheater. Do call if you have any trouble finding it."

"Sure."

He rose to leave. He was taller than I anticipated. Taller than me.

"Until tomorrow, Alex."

"Goodbye."

He turned and walked towards the exit with a relaxed, upright gait. A whiff of bar soap and rum trailed behind him. I stared out the window and watched a woman gaze down into the open hood of the Audi that still had its hazards on. Beside her, a man stood, hands on hips, face blank. Their night wasn't going well. I gathered my things, flipped a fifty-groschen coin into the piano lady's glass bowl, then headed down the hill towards my Straßenbahn stop. Snow flurries fell and stung my cheeks. When I reached the corner, a wave of exhaustion rushed through me. Things seemed to have gone well with Heinrich. Although he spoke and moved in a subdued fashion, he had an intense presence. The Trost family shared an emotional receptiveness and ability to connect with lonely, confused Americans. A Straßenbahn arrived, and I took a seat in the first car next to two elderly women in thick brown fur coats.

Back at my apartment, I sat down to write a letter to my best friend, Hank. His actual name is Zhang Yong, but when we met as kids at a playground in the city, Hank is the closest pronunciation I could come up with. It stuck. Like most of my friends from the Outer Sunset, he's Chinese American. His parents are first-generation immigrants from somewhere rural in southeastern China; I think Guangdong Province. I've asked many times about their family history, but his parents don't speak English well and Hank is reluctant to go into it. During senior year, Hank didn't get into Stanford, or Berkeley, or SF State, and things between us grew strained when he settled for City College and I moved down to Palo Alto. I was probably a dick—Stanford doesn't instill humility—but I tried to invite him down for parties and to perform the most impossible of all social projects: friend mixing. We endured my first two years, our connection reduced but alive, and then Janet became involved. She was a history major at Stanford, it was her book on Tito that I had borrowed for my plagiarized paper, and she, Hank, and I started spending every weekend together. We had an occasional fourth, Rose, but she didn't say much.

One night, when I was back up for the weekend, Hank laid it out for me. I sat on his parents' overstuffed lime green sofa while he stood in the center of the living room, arms crossed. He's tall and thin, like a corn stalk. He's definitely cooler than me, and dresses like Kurt Cobain in loose T-shirts and cardigans. He loves Nirvana, but I prefer Pearl Jam. Nirvana was too depressing before Kurt fired a shotgun into himself, and afterward, well, I can't listen to it. Hank and I fought about it, and we agreed that I wouldn't bitch when he had it on as long as he didn't play "Polly" or "Heart-Shaped Box." Hank claims he hates Eddie Vedder's voice, but I'm not sure that's truly possible. That night, at his parent's house, we were listening to *Throwing Copper,* which we both adore.

"So, who is going to go for Janet?" Hank asked.

"What do you mean?"

"What the fuck do you think I mean?"

I laughed. He raised his shoulders up and then back to stretch them. He has scoliosis and complains hourly about his back being tight. We wore our suede-bottomed JanSport backpacks over one shoulder for three years of middle school, which exacerbated the rightward slope of his spine.

"Who do you think she likes?" I asked.

"You, of course. I think she's the type of Chinese girl that only dates rich white guys, but I still want to go for her."

"I'm not rich. Your family's house has one more bedroom than ours."

"Yeah, but you're down in fucking Shallow Alto now. You're rich, even if you're not yet." It stung. Though only a fifty-five-minute drive from the city, Palo Alto couldn't feel further away. When I drive back and hit the crest of Dolores Street just past the intersection with Jersey, my eyes well at the long arc of palms. Hank and I are city kids. It's our identity.

"Well, what the fuck do you want me to do?"

"Tell her you're seeing someone."

"Wouldn't she know if that was true? We hang out all the time."

"Tell her it's someone from up here."

Janet is from Orange County and never comes to the city. It must be stated that under no circumstances should someone from San Francisco ever attempt to meaningfully connect with someone from Southern California. There is an existential unease in our fog that is imbued within us. It's the opposite of the cultureless, forcefully irrigated, windswept desert void in the core of Southern Californians. This difference cannot be overcome. Hank and I didn't fully grasp this at the time.

"What if that makes her like me more?"

"Alex, I don't care how you do it. Just give me a shot."

"Sure."

And I did give him a shot. Janet was nice, but I got tired of listening to her complain about her parents and their alleged favoritism towards her younger sister, Hannah. In her stories, her parents didn't sound that bad, but any attempt to probe deeper or question her conclusions was met with exasperated anger, flushed cheeks, and the threat of tears. A couple of nights when we were all together, I bailed early so Hank and she could be alone. One Saturday, we had a plan for the three of us to go bowling and I didn't show up at all. Hank called me from a pay phone to say thanks, the unmistakable crash of pins echoing in the background. He ended up sleeping on her couch that night. Sometime before dawn he tried to kiss her, she turned away, and it was over. He stopped coming down to PA, Janet and I kept hanging out, and we ended up slipping into a relationship. I think she pushed it on me. She has an affected, industrious narcissism about her, and the concept of me must have fit into her brand somehow, like a pair of jeans, or a summer internship. I told Hank about the relationship over the phone.

"I've got something to tell you."

"Rose told me already."

"Ok. Are we cool?"

"We are not."

"Ok."

We didn't talk again. Janet and I dated for ten months and eleven days and she dumped me via a letter slid beneath my door. She had sealed the letter into an envelope: the business kind with the scribbled shit so you can't see through it. There was a new guy, Charles, and didn't I consider it "just" for them to be together since their connection was more vibrant than our bond? Her letter was long, indulgently long, and I wished she'd workshopped it with a friend and cut it down to two or three sentences. Janet has a few sublime qualities—a great laugh and a precise memory that almost lets you re-enter the past with her—but she's not as interesting as she thinks she is. At least, not to me. We broke up a few weeks before I left school. The worst part about it was that I'd introduced her to my parents over lunch right before she dumped me. Although she must have already known Charles, and probably had his sweat on her body, she prettied herself up and put on a charm offensive for my parents. They were enamored—she had that effect on strangers—and they were glowing when they left campus that evening to drive back up to the city. When I told my mom about the breakup, she offered to call Janet and help me win her back. I declined. I ran into Rose the weekend I moved out and asked her to say hi to Hank.

I wanted to write Hank a long, restorative letter, but after a few dreadful first lines, I put my notebook away and switched to a gold-foil, Klimt postcard with a miniscule span of available writing space. No, not *The Kiss*. I was saving that one for my aunt. For Hank, I chose a painting of Judith, a topless lady holding a dismembered head.

> Hank,
> I got kicked out of school and moved to Austria.
> I'm not sure how long I'll be here, but the beer,
> sights, and vibe are all promising. I'm sorry
> about how it went down with Janet. You were
> a dick about it, but I was a dick too. When I get
> back, let's hang out.
> —Alex

I didn't like how it looked, so I ripped it down the middle and placed it into my trash can. My chest filled with the realization that Hank's and my friendship was on an inevitable decline. Any positive interactions between us might slow the descent, but reversing the trend was not going to happen. A ring interrupted my frustration; I had an incoming call and only Johanna knew the number. I waited halfway into the following ring, then picked up.

"Hi," I answered.

"Hey, Alex? It's Johanna."

"Hey, what's up?"

"How did it go with my grandfather?"

"Great. He's super cool."

"You think so?"

"Definitely. His clothes fit well, he offered me a job, and he bought me a coffee. That's all you could want from a grandfather."

She laughed. "He does have a few nice outfits, I suppose. He told me that he's asked you to put his research into order. That's great. He's an incredible writer. His politics are far too conservative, which comes out in the subjects he focuses on, but I enjoy his prose. It's distinct."

"Cool."

"Among journalists, he's well known in Vienna." When she spoke about him, her voice became confident and childlike. "I don't know how much of the family Trost you can handle in one day, but would you like to meet tomorrow and go for a walk? Maybe at one p.m.? I have ninety minutes between lectures."

"I'd love to. I have to be at your grandfather's at 7:30, so I might be tired, but I'm in."

"Let's meet at Schwedenplatz by the canal. We can walk the second district, if it's nice out."

"Ok."

A long silence followed. I thought of the phone line running from my handset down through the brick shafts of my building, under the city in cold concrete tunnels, through dark junctions, up to her apartment, and finally, to the phone she cradled to her face.

"Ok, Tschüss. Bis Morgen." She said, breaking the silence.

"Johanna?"

"Yeah?"

"Thank you for looking out for me."

"No problem."

III

I arrived at Heinrich's apartment five minutes early, freshly showered and carrying a bag of assorted *Gebäck* from a bakery near my place. Gebäck are hard to explain. They're essentially tiny loaves of bread that offer their consumer the ability to enjoy different styles of starch without the commitment of slogging through an entire, full-sized loaf. Whole wheat, white, pumpkin seed, sunflower seed; there are a multitude of varieties, and they are incredible. I grew up eating slices of Iron Kids, which had the taste and texture of folded Kleenex. Heinrich buzzed me in and was waiting at his doorway on the second floor in an ironed, white button-up shirt, brown slacks, and navy house slippers.

"Alex, welcome."

"Good morning."

He lived in a two-bedroom apartment with stark white walls and twenty-foot-high ceilings that arced inward at the top. The architecture was bel étage, so his floor was the showpiece of the building and borrowed its height from the shorter, cramped ground floor. He thanked me for the bread and gave me a brief tour. We didn't enter the bedrooms, so I only caught a glimpse. He slept in a twin bed, and save for a closed armoire, his bedroom appeared empty. The kitchen was clean and sparse. The only thing visible on the counter was a shining chrome espresso machine. A yellow, compact Miele refrigerator sat in the corner. The tour ended in his large living room. The white walls amplified the sunlight that poured in from rows of tall windows on two sides, giving the room a glowing, precise clarity. On one end was a sitting area with a small couch, a coffee table, and two chairs. The rest of the room served as his office. Bookshelves and filing cabinets lined the walls. There were no photos, no posters, no personal effects. Just books. His desk looked out into the room, so when sitting at it, watery sun warmed your face, and you felt in command of your surroundings, like the captain of a ship. Around his desk waited an arc of seven metal rolling file cabinets, each a different drab color, each filled to absolute capacity.

"This will be your beginning. This is my research from the 1950s," he said, tapping his palm on a brown, three-drawer cabinet that came up to his hip. "This navy cabinet here contains my articles from the same period. The goal is to pair the research with the articles, and to create an index with a labeling system so it's easy to retrieve, for example, articles about Theodor Körner, or work on labor disputes. We once had a system like that, inefficient but functional, in the basement of our newspaper, but a flood destroyed it."

"Ok. Got it."

"I suggest working through one drawer, or even a portion of a drawer, and creating a basic plan. Then, present it to me for approval. It may take you up to a week. There's no need to hurry."

"Has anyone tried this before and failed to get your approval?"

He sighed.

"Yes, a friend of Johanna's, Valerie. She used too many different colors to organize things. There were, I believe, more than five different shades of green."

"Oh my."

He laughed and said, "I will leave you to it," then took a chair from beside the couch and carried it over to a window. He picked up a book, sat down, and began to read with the sun on his face. The window had a deep sill, on which rested a notebook and a glass of water. To even remove a single file from his cabinets required a firm push with one hand while pulling with the other. I worked a few inches of files free from the navy cabinet and opened the first folder, releasing the dry smell of dust and newsprint. It contained handwritten notes on grid-lined paper followed by typewritten drafts covered in various proofreading and correction marks from, I assumed, his editor. After each series of drafts was a newspaper clipping, flat, thin, and brittle. I supposed the initial one was his first ever byline: a three-paragraph blurb about the reconstruction of a church in the first district. At first, I couldn't make out his handwritten notes at all. They were written in a cryptic German shorthand, but when I read them along with their final publication, I started to put it together. He wrote with looping, beautiful letters, especially his lowercase *e*, which leaned back, almost fully vertical. I spent the first hour flipping and reading in silence. My hands began to sweat, and after a drop slipped down onto an article from 1952, curling the yellowed paper, I started to rub my palms on my jeans to keep them dry. The research material from the brown cabinet was esoteric and stunning. About half was notes scrawled into countless small notepads, and the other half was a blend of truly everything: an interview transcript on hotel stationary from Prague followed by a napkin with an unlabeled phone number followed by a page from a Russian novel, written in Cyrillic, with two sentences underlined. Photos of the dead at crime scenes, photos of graves. It was a broad expanse of cultural detritus with limited chronology, not unlike what I'd seen at the Naschmarkt a few days before. I loved it. Everything was so delicate and so dry, the strike of one match would consume the entire apartment.

Periodically, Heinich would shift in his seat, lean forward, and jot notes onto the pad in front of him. Normally, my focus is not taut. My mind spins and I have to stand up and walk around, or pick up the phone, or try to remember the anatomical details of the breasts of women I've seen naked. I've read that revisiting memories helps your brain know to codify them into long-term storage, and there are some images I need to save. But with Heinrich sitting there fourteen feet away flipping pages in his book, I couldn't drift into my gauzy, favorite daydreams. He grounded me, and I lost myself in the work.

At exactly ten o'clock, he rose and went into the kitchen. A coffee grinder whirred, an earthy scent filled the apartment, the espresso machine buzzed, and he returned and placed an espresso and water on the desk beside me. He brought one for himself, sat back down, and resumed reading. I snuck glances at Heinrich as I sipped my coffee. Sitting at his desk, reading his words while surrounded by his writing, it was as though I had entered into his mind. Although the articles thus far were straightforward and factual, his voice started to emerge—confident and wry—and it narrated the life of a country rebuilding itself from war. One piece of prose stood out, detailing the moment on May 15, 1955, that Austria signed its independence treaty, sending the four occupying allied powers off its soil: "This morning at eleven a.m., Austria became free once again. After seventeen years, she is free."

Heinrich never used more than ten words if ten words were all that were needed. I continued reading, and when I left at eleven thirty, we'd only spoken eight sentences to each other. I think that's the level of interaction he wanted. I had come to Austria to escape and to explore a culture, and I had somehow stumbled into the perfect opportunity to do so. After eating half of a peculiar-tasting shaved carrot and hard-boiled egg sandwich from a bakery by the U-Bahn station, I took a train across town to meet Johanna. I don't like carrots on their own, and I can't think of a worse sandwich topping. I only bought the sandwich because I couldn't believe it existed.

On the subway, my mind slipped into its standard algorithm of scanning forward into the future and backwards into my past, searching for impending catastrophes and revisiting painful failures. I never tire of lying down and wallowing in my shortcomings. I had no idea how to index Heinrich's articles, and he would probably fire me. I had no idea who Johanna was and would certainly come on too strong. I have a bottomless well of loneliness within me, and my desire for her or anyone to fill it was infantile and doomed. As the subway approached Schwedenplatz, my hands tightened. Traveling alone had frayed my perspective into an acute hypersensitivity to my thoughts and my surroundings, and I needed time to get used to it. At Schwedenplatz, through shifting crowds of people, I saw Johanna across the square in front of an ice cream shop with a pink neon sign. She wore a dark blue coat. I walked over and we engaged once again in the cheek-to-cheek ritual. This time it went smoother. I paused at the apex to take in the scent of her familiar apricot.

"What's up?" I asked, in English.

"Should we speak in English this time? Maybe you're homesick?" she asked, arching her right eyebrow slightly.

"Let's hold off. I'm still trying to dial my German in."

"Ok, if you prefer. Shall we walk? I only have about an hour." She motioned towards a bridge and we began to walk that way. It led over the Danube canal, a narrow green waterway that lines one edge of the first district. On the bridge, we passed a bronze statue of the Virgin Mary, blackened from age and exposure to the elements.

"Beautiful, yes?" asked Johanna.

I nodded, although it was strange to see Mary so weathered. We crossed the bridge and walked along the Taborstraße, a four-lane avenue lined with shops. We had grown closer together over the phone since I'd last seen her, and the reunification of her voice and body made my heart swell and push against my ribs.

"Are you homesick?"

"Not exactly. I'm still processing where I am. When I wake up, I still think I'm in California. How's school?"

She shook her head. "There's always more to do."

We waited at an intersection although no cars passed by. She faced ahead, her eyes unfocused.

"So, what's special about the second district?"

"Well, it's different than the rest of Vienna. Calmer. The first is so busy, but once you walk over the canal, it's like another city. I started coming over here to babysit for a family friend, and when I walk home in the afternoon, I can go blocks without seeing anyone, which I like." The light changed and she stepped forward. "This was the Jewish quarter before the *Anschluß* and has started to become that again with people from the East moving in since the Soviet Union collapsed."

"Interesting."

We passed an elaborate crucifix mounted onto the exterior of a building. The city was not in want of religious imagery. The crucifix looked old enough to have been present during the forced transition of the neighborhood from Jewish to not Jewish. It had clearly failed to impart any ethical behavior.

"Could you tell me a little bit about your grandfather?"

"What would you like to know?"

"Anything, I guess. I'm just curious since I'll be spending time with him."

"He is, as you know, my father's father."

I hadn't known that.

"He was born in 1925, here in Vienna, which was not a good time for Austria. His family was very poor. His uncles and grandfather were killed in France during the First World War, and the family that survived all lived together in a small flat, so his cousins are like brothers and sisters to him."

I walked without responding, not wanting to interrupt. After a silent block, I realized she was finished speaking. Johanna motioned that we should turn left. As she turned, we bumped briefly, my side touching hers.

"And you two are close?"

Johanna stopped and turned towards me. Her face stiffened, and she scratched at her forehead.

"We are close in our own way. My mother died when I was sixteen. I couldn't handle being at home with my father and all of her things—it was too much—so I moved in with my grandfather until I began at Uni Wien. My father and I haven't—" She gathered her hair together over one shoulder and tucked it behind her ear. "It's been difficult for us without my mother. I don't actually talk that much with my grandfather. He lets me be there without asking a lot of questions, which I appreciate. We meet at least once a week and usually just sit together while he reads his newspaper and I mine." She began to walk forward. "My father doesn't care for him. When they are together for more than two hours, a pressure forms in the room and they fight."

"And he's retired?"

"He is retired, yes. Although he has told me that a journalist never fully retires."

We continued on, and after turning a corner, the street opened up into a square lined with rows of small one-story cinder block buildings arranged in a grid. Their plain, rectangular shapes resembled detached garages. They stood in drab opposition to the large ornate apartment buildings ringing the square.

"How did your mom die?"

"Breast cancer."

"I'm sorry."

She half shrugged with her right shoulder. "Yeah. I miss her."

"What's her name?"

"Elisabeth."

I wasn't sure what to say, so I didn't say anything. I wanted to hug her, but it didn't seem right.

"I like that you're working with my grandfather. I've never been able to hear a non-family perspective on him before."

We locked eyes. Her green eyes showed fatigue. She lifted her chin slightly towards a building beside us.

"We should eat lunch there one day. It's Georgian food. It's very good."

"Definitely. Maybe we could grab a coffee there now?"

Johanna looked down at her watch.

"A quick one, sure."

We walked in and sat down at a table in the center of the room. Windows on all sides let in sublime, easy light. Unwrapped from her coat and hat, Johanna's skin flushed red from the abrupt temperature change. The waitress came over and we ordered coffee, two *Oma's Häferlkaffees*, at Johanna's suggestion.

"My turn to ask a question," said Johanna.

"Sure."

She flexed her hands open and closed.

"Why are you taking a break from university?"

I sat up straight in my chair and rolled my shoulders back.

"Well—" I stopped as the waitress brought over our coffees. Johanna sat silent, lips pursed. I cradled my cup in my hands and peeked over her shoulder to check the clock in the back of the room. She couldn't have had much more time before she had to go. The Häferlkaffee was bigger than your standard, teacup-sized Viennese coffee. A solid twelve ounces of coffee and milk, it was almost American sized, and warm enough to comfort cold fingers. "I actually got kicked out of school."

"What!?" she asked, with a half grin.

"Yeah, I cheated on a paper. It was stupid. I was at Stanford but I can't go back, and I can't transfer until next fall, so I have a year to kill."

"Is that something you did regularly?"

"Cheating?"

"Yes."

"No. It was my first time cheating. Well, it was probably my second time, but, the first time I did it so emphatically. I'm sorry, it was stupid."

"You don't have to apologize to me."

"Yeah, I know. I'm just saying it anyway. I was miserable at school. I should have just dropped out instead of doing what I did."

"Why were you miserable?"

"Aren't we all miserable, all of the time?"

She laughed. "No."

"Well, it seems to be my natural state."

She looked down at her watch. "Ok, but then, why Vienna? You said the other day it 'seemed central.' I can't imagine that's a reason to come here instead of Paris, or Rome, or Berlin if you wish to speak German."

I took a sip of my coffee. The only people within earshot of us were two grey-haired women about seven feet away by a window.

"Actually, my grandfather was here for the war. His unit fought through Europe and then he was stationed in the city when it was split between the allies. He didn't say too much about it, but I used to look through his old photos, and I've always wanted to come here."

"Ahh—and you are looking for unclaimed relatives?"

"You know. I *did* think you looked familiar."

She laughed, with a wide smile and full depth of dimple. I could spend all day just trying to make her smile.

"I don't mean to bring up the war so flippantly. I'm not sure how forbidden that topic is over here."

She tilted her head to the side. "Oh, it's fine. I'm sorry, I really shouldn't have started a serious conversation now because I have to go. Before I do, I did want to mention something else."

I put down my glass.

"Yeah?"

She crossed her arms and leaned forward. Our square table wasn't large. If we had both leaned all the way forward, we might have been able to kiss.

"I was thinking, you should meet my roommate."

My blood froze. I made some expression of acknowledgement.

"Her name is Lisi. I think you two might be a match."

The room tilted five degrees off axis. I tried to look unaffected.

"Ok," I stammered.

"I don't typically set people up, ever, but I know you're new here and she's, well—available. And she's great."

Wonderful. In the span of a coffee, my dream had expired. The person with whom I shared the most natural, pure connection of my life was going to toss me over to a random woman whose chief quality was her availability. I tried to think of a way to reroute the conversation, something about asking if Lisi was Johanna's twin because then she'd be perfect for me, but Johanna stood up and said, "I'll call you. Maybe we can all meet this weekend. A friend of mine is hosting a party and Lisi will be there."

I stood to see her off, my legs unsteady.

"Are you going to stay here for a while?" she asked, pointing at the table.

"I think so." What difference did it make.

She reached her into purse, took out a bill, and laid it onto the table.

"Coffee is on me," she said and gave my elbow a light squeeze then went out the door, wrapping her scarf around her neck as she paced away. I sat back down and watched her through the window as she crossed the square. Either Johanna didn't feel what I did, which didn't seem possible, or she had another, presumably taller, love interest. Maybe the aforementioned dude she had allegedly dumped at Café Jelinek. When she turned the corner out of view, I thought about her mom, Elisabeth. She must have been kind to have a daughter like Johanna. I've always found it elucidating to meet the mother of women I like. With Johanna, that couldn't happen.

I spent the next few days working in Heinrich's apartment in the morning and wandering the city in the afternoon. The slopes and curves of his shorthand grew familiar, and my reading pace increased. I began to come up with a system for organizing his work. Although we didn't speak much, we grew comfortable with each other's presence. We maneuvered around his apartment with ease, never crowding one another, silently sharing the joy of a late-morning coffee, often with a couple slices of cake I'd purchase at the bakery up the block. On Thursday evening, I stayed up past two a.m. perfecting the first draft of a reference system. I hold my pen with my wrist bent into an arc—it's a technique I'm incapable of abandoning—and my pinky drags through the previous lines, smudging ink across the page. It took five tries and four ibuprofens for my burning tendons to hold my hand straight enough to make a flawless index page worthy of an old Austrian guy. The system was straightforward and inspired by the stockroom at Dad's hardware store. For each scrap of research, I would choose an arbitrary numeric identifier, starting with 1001. Published articles were organized chronologically with an identifier built by their year, day, and month. For example, 1952.9.7. Each article was given an info page with a list of IDs of all research used within the article and a single colored circle sticker representing one of ten different content categories. A separate index was made with prominent places or people appearing within the content, sorted alphabetically, followed by a list of matching article IDs and research IDs. It was a lot to take in, especially without a computer, but it did the job. Dewey Fucking Decimal would be proud.

I made a rough sample using fifteen articles and forty pieces of research and placed it on the coffee table in front of Heinrich on Friday morning. I took my usual post at his desk and watched as he thumbed through it, moving back and forth between indexes, files, and research. After some time, he laid it down.

"Alex, please, if you have a moment."

"Sure." I put away my pencil and walked across the room.

"I am pleased. May I buy you lunch?"

"Thank you. Yes, of course."

"There's a Gasthaus nearby, and their special on Friday is an excellent *Tafelspitz*."

"Perfect." I had no idea what Tafelspitz was.

At noon, we walked over to a dark, oak-paneled restaurant up the street. Tafelspitz turned out to be boiled roast beef with an array of dips: creamed spinach, applesauce-horseradish, and chive. The food was like Heinrich. Clean, well-presented, and familiar, yet foreign. We talked about random things as we ate. How Vienna had changed over the years, how the Alps affect the weather in the city, and how a nagging stiffness kept spreading beneath his left kneecap, despite his efforts to stretch in the way his doctor recommended. He spoke with kindness and ease and asked enough questions to keep the conversation equitable. When our plates were cleared, he leaned back in his chair and took out a gold cigarette case. He rolled his shirt sleeves up in a wrinkle-free, effortless manner that I would never be able to imitate.

"Alex, how is Johanna?"

The same question as our first meeting.

"What do you mean?"

He sat still for a moment. Then, he took out and lit a cigarette. When he took a drag, in the yellow light from the glass lamp on the wall beside him, he did look like her.

"She doesn't tell me anything. I understand why. I'm just an old man to her, but I am curious."

A conspiratorial pang pierced my chest. Should I betray her confidence in order to endear myself to him? The pang faded. I didn't have anything good to tell him, even if I was willing to sell her out.

"You know, honestly, I'm just getting to know her."

"Is she still with Lukas?"

That must be the ex. Important enough for Heinrich to be aware of him. He extended his cigarette box towards me. I deferred. He snapped it closed.

"I think they broke up, but I'm not totally sure if it stuck."

"Hmm—ok. You don't smoke?"

"I'm still learning how." I reached over, opened his case, and took and lit a cigarette. A Camel. She smokes Marlboro, he smokes Camel. I don't know if that means anything.

"So your interest in Johanna isn't romantic?"

I shrugged. "Well, is this conversation between us?"

"Of course."

"Yeah, I like her. Why else would I be hanging out with you?"

He laughed. "I am paying you."

"Oh right. Well, I don't know if it will be friendship or more between she and I, but she's great."

He nodded. "I'm worried about your courtship technique if you believe working through me is the way to her heart."

I turned my palms upwards in surrender. "I'm clueless, obviously. You're not worried about getting cancer from smoking?"

He laughed. A low, rough laugh. "Oh no. I'm already seventy-one, Alex. Life expectancy has almost been reached. Plus, smoking aids digestion."

"Yeah, ok." I thought about mentioning my grandfather's cancer but decided that would be weird. Unlike my grandfather near his end, Heinrich had a sharp, focused presence. It's reassuring to see a septuagenarian undiminished. "Johanna seems very busy with school, that I do know. I think she's really into the academics thing."

"And you're not?"

"Not right now."

"You seem very bright. What do your parents think about you traveling abroad instead of attending university?"

"Well … I will go to school. Just not right now. My mom isn't that worried, but my dad isn't happy about it. He wasn't able to go to college because he had to join the family business when his uncle died, so he pushes his career disappointments onto me."

Heinrich twisted the stub of his cigarette down into the glass ashtray at the center of the table. The thought of my parents chilled the warmth of my mood. I had to find a way to make things up to them.

"I didn't know my father well. He was very quiet."

"Was he a journalist too?"

"No, he worked in construction. I don't know how similar our interests were."

"What kind of work does your son do? Johanna's father?"

"Gerhard? He runs a bookshop that never sells any books."

We settled the check and walked back to his place in silence. I considered mentioning that Johanna did seem to carry an air of sadness, but I decided not to say anything. He paid me for the week and invited me back on Monday to continue the work. I spent the afternoon aimlessly going from one *Altwaren* shop after the next, scanning through old letters and postcards to feel the electricity of reading a stranger's intimate thoughts. My hours rooting through Heinrich's research had left me filled me with an unquenchable thirst to snoop, and Vienna revealed itself to be a stockpile of personal items available at a nominal price. Many Altwaren shops had strange hours or required ringing a bell and then waiting for minutes until their silver-haired proprietor emerged, eyes blinking back the sunlight, their expression one of indifferent annoyance.

The layouts of the shops were meaningless and expansive and I loved every aspect of them.

Johanna called with the party details for Saturday night, so I took my earnings and went shopping on Mariahilferstraße in search of a new outfit. If I was going to be discarded by her, and it appeared I was, I wanted to look my best. My goal was to not stand out quite so clearly as an American. I'd like it to take more than five seconds of idle observation to out me as a goofy fucking foreigner. There were a number of issues with my current look. I didn't have enough layers for the cold. I wore Nikes; nobody else did. Most of my shirts were Giants or Warriors related, an easy giveaway. I picked up a pair of black Adidas Sambas, black jeans, a dark denim shirt, and a grey wool jacket. Once I got home and put it all on together, I looked like Paul Reiser, who I hate. He's too earnest. Helen Hunt I like, but I don't love. It was too late to go back to the store, so I showered, dressed, mussed my hair, and walked over to Johanna's friend's place in the seventh district. Walking in the Sambas was different than my Air Pennys. Less of a sole, less of a shoe in general. My feet were nimble and weaved deftly in and out of crowds.

A black Doc Marten boot propped open the door of her friend's apartment building. I entered and followed the hum of music and voices down the hall to an open door. I descended a few steps—the apartment was semi subterranean—and took off my new shoes and laid them by a large, mixed jumble of sneakers. The air smelled of sweat and beer. I laid my jacket onto a pile inside a nearby bedroom door. Past the entrance-way, groups of people stood around in loosely formed circles, drinks in hand, chatting to one another. I walked in, trying to look at ease, and grabbed a beer from the counter. I stood there, avoiding eye contact and nodding to the music, when a hand grabbed my left wrist. Johanna.

"Alex! You made it."

"I did."

She leaned close and whispered, "Lisi is here. I'm sorry, I may have built you up too much—but there's no pressure, ok?" She smiled. She was a little sweaty, always a good look, and potentially drunk. I nodded, and she led me to a room where a group was arguing about an increase in student fees at their university. A short, thin girl, a waif really, looked towards us as we approached. Long, straight black hair, light blue eyes, and a fair complexion. Johanna was not passing me on to an ugly friend.

"Alex, this is Lisi."

"It's nice to meet you, Alex," said Lisi, in English, with a warbling accent that sounded like a precious, dying bird.

"Nice to meet you. Your English is—something."

She laughed. I liked her. I like everyone.

"Is it?"

"It is. What accent am I hearing?" Johanna gave my wrist a squeeze and backed away. I felt her eyes stay on me.

"I studied abroad in Australia and in Scotland, so I may have picked up a bit of that."

"That's, actually, exactly it. You somehow have three accents simultaneously."

She gave a slight shrug. She wore a loose sleeveless dress, and freckles dotted her pale shoulders.

"Johanna told me your German is quite good for an American."

"For an American, huh?" I turned to look at Johanna, but she was gone. I scanned the room but couldn't find her. "Why does everyone always qualify their compliments towards me as good, 'for an American?'"

"Well, your country isn't known for its foreign-language skills."

"What are we known for?"

She shifted her weight back and forth. Her eyes were very bright and her teeth a little crooked, but cute. Like actors in old movies, everyone in Austria had natural, imperfect teeth.

"Hamburgers, I guess."

"I like hamburgers."

"See?"

"Yeah."

We talked for a while, navigating the standard get-to-know-you pathways. Lisi's friendship with Johanna extended back to three years spent beside one another while sharing a double desk throughout middle school in a village outside Linz. Lisi is a lefty, so Johanna sat to her right to avoid bumping elbows as they wrote. In Austrian middle school, classes form at the beginning and then ascend as a group through each grade. Their parents became friends, and although Johanna and her family left to Vienna before high school, they stayed in touch. Lisi became Johanna's roommate when she moved to the city to study painting.

"I think Johanna's the smartest person I've ever met. She tries to hide it. She doesn't want the attention, but it came out in school."

"Really?"

"Yes. She's amazing. And it's not just academics. She's perceptive about everything. It's great for her friends, but she analyzes things so completely that she can't make any decisions. Lately, well, you know she just broke up, right? She and Lukas were going to move in together and then she dumped him on the way to signing their lease."

"She mentioned something about that. Is he here?"

"Oh yeah. That's him," she said, pointing to a tall, thin guy in the corner. He wore an untucked short-sleeve button-up with a scribbled pattern on it. His shoulders hunched forward a few degrees, and he looked relaxed, possibly high. "They were together for a long time. I think she finally made the right decision."

"Interesting. I think I need a drink, want one?"

"Yes, thank you."

I wandered around for a while looking for the bathroom, then drinks. A couple in front of me poured themselves glasses of white wine mixed with sparkling water, and I did the same. When I returned to Lisi, Johanna was standing beside her and they were talking loudly with a few guys. Johanna's face was flushed, and she waved her hands in the air as she spoke. I sidled up to them, passed a glass to Lisi, and listened in. Johanna was furious about a recent immigration case where Austria had waited eight years before electing to deny amnesty to a young Rwandan girl and her family. The legal explanation was spurious, and the girl would be forced to depart the only country she knew and move to an unsafe place. Johanna and the guys weren't in actual disagreement; they were mainly taking turns getting frothed up about the case and about Jörg Haider, an extreme-right politician gaining popularity by stoking fear of immigrants. I nodded along, and at some point, the conversation twisted in on itself and turned to global politics and the problems America makes in the world. One of the guys, Hannes, was livid about what he viewed as America's unconditional support for Israel, even after the recent invasion of Lebanon that resulted in a number of civilian casualties. I listened. Some of his points were ones I'd made before, but I didn't like hearing them from this guy. He was smart, well-spoken, and well-dressed. I waited until he was finished and then pointed out that Israel did have some right and responsibility to protect its citizens, didn't it?

"You're American?" he asked, eyes wide. I couldn't get through one sentence without being identified.

"Yeah, I am. Johanna invited me." He looked over at her, then back to me.

"Well, protecting oneself and invading another country are two different things. Israel's policies create its security issues and then they use those issues as justification for war crimes." As he spoke, he slowed his German down and emphasized the start of each word, I suppose for my benefit. A couple other people from around the room walked up, including Johanna's ex. Hannes and I were on center stage.

"I don't think you can blame Israel for groups dedicated to its extinction." I settled into the role of my Republican uncle, Steve. I knew the lines. Austria's obvious role in the history of Israel hovered in the back of my mind. Bringing up the Holocaust would be conversational napalm. I had to resist.

"They should try being peaceful. The focus on military and war only perpetuates itself and makes money for the arms dealers in *your* country." He pointed towards me. He stopped before touching my chest, but I sensed his fingertips pushing into my sternum. "Don't you know Austria is militarily neutral and we are completely fine?" His voice hardened. Maybe he liked Lisi, and I was a threat. I had no idea of the social dynamics around me. We went back and forth for a while in the classic, banal debate of America's role as world policeman. I presented my country as a reluctant, noble hero and he portrayed America as a fascist conglomerate of corporate interests. We talked past each other and interrupted one another, and I realized midway through a soliloquy about the beauty of the Gulf War that I had no idea what point I was trying to make. We kept at it though, and people from the group steadily peeled off, except for Johanna and Lisi. Hannes tilted his head forward and nodded as he spoke, and I found myself staring at his white, glistening forehead and losing the trail of his German. His hairline curved up at the edges. I doubted that his children, if he could convince a woman to procreate with him, would ever know him with hair.

"Do you speak Russian?" I asked, interrupting him.

"No."

"Do you know *why* you don't speak Russian?"

"Well, I selected French in high school."

"That's not why."

"Ok. Why then?"

"Because of the United *fucking* States of America. That's

why."

"Alex, come on," said Johanna. I glanced over at her and Lisi. They didn't look amused.

"It's the truth," I continued. "Austria isn't safe because of its neutrality. That's insane. It's safe because after losing back-to-back wars and almost all of its territory, what's left happens to be in a location where other, *much* more important countries, protect it. Israel doesn't have the benefit of living in a supportive neighborhood." Hannes's face reddened. He smelled of warm beer, and I never wanted to talk to him again.

"Just a typical American point of view. Very limited," he replied.

"I'm not sure why you think Austria is some great moral compass—did you skip history class?"

Hannes let out a loud, weary sigh. "Easy there, Alex. I'm attempting to debate you on substance, not insults."

It wasn't true, but it reminded me of something Janet might say. We continued on and the conversation drifted sideways. I looked over towards where Lisi and Johanna had been standing, but they were gone. After a long diatribe from Hannes on the upside of a common European currency, I said, "Listen, I get it. I think a lot of what you are saying makes sense, but I'm having a hard time getting my point across in German. It's hard to follow your sentences that are seventeen-minutes long, and to be honest, I really have to piss." Then, I looked into his bleary chestnut eyes, squeezed his shoulder, walked off, and did a lap of the apartment. Lisi and Johanna were gone, the party had lost some steam, and the remaining people had coalesced around an oversized brown couch in the living room. I grabbed my coat and shoes and walked out into the night air. I paced home with regret coursing through my veins. I'd been an asshole for no reason, and I hadn't even been clever while doing so. I'd probably come across as some pathetic version of Jack Nicholson from *A Few Good Men*. I do love Demi Moore with short hair though. There's nothing I want more than for her and Bruce Willis to stay married forever.

I spent Sunday lying diagonally in bed, reliving the conversation, and imagining different paths I could have taken. I should have just agreed with everyone, or tried to outflank them on the left and said some real Berkeley shit. I tried to think of arguments that were so pithy that Hannes would cower and admit defeat before me. No matter what I thought about, I couldn't suppress the realization that I had let Johanna down. She had opened her life to me, and I had embarrassed her. I decided to not call her for a while.

Over the next few weeks, I spent each morning in Heinrich's apartment, progressing deeper into his files. When the work transitioned into the 1960s, Heinrich's narrative voice deepened, and there were fewer articles of direct news coverage and more multipart investigative pieces. The stories fell within a general arc. Someone, usually a government official, took a bribe or embezzled money and was discovered through a complex investigation by Heinrich and his colleagues. Sometimes, potential targets for investigation came from anonymous tips sent into his newspaper. The tips were included in his files and varied in form: long letters, short notes, a single receipt or photograph. The shapes of each investigative arc were so similar that I began to wonder if Heinrich had massaged true stories to fit into a printable narrative, or if the plotlines were pure fabrications. The outcome of each investigation was the same: the complete ruin of the subject. Surrounding the narratives of individual lives were the central political parties in postwar Austria: the ÖVP and SPÖ. They took turns having their members lauded and disgraced in the news, with a third party, the FPÖ, a smaller but ever-present orbiting moon.

The mornings with Heinrich reminded me of time spent with my grandfather. They both have a comfort with shared silence that isn't present with members of my generation. When Heinrich did speak, it was always a fully-formed thought worthy of attention. Our backgrounds and stage of life were so different that I found him compelling. I hoped to learn something from him. After a morning emerged in his articles, my senses would numb, and my mind detached and floated somewhere within his written words and Austria's past. I would depart in a throbbing haze with nothing to do, and no one to see. I wanted to call Johanna, but if I did and she declined to see me, it would confirm that things were finished between us. I couldn't handle that. So, I spent each afternoon in the presence of strangers at a café.

Viennese cafés provided what I needed most: a place to be lonely without being alone. After a few cups of espresso in close proximity to blank, unknown faces, my mind would leave the world of Heinrich and return to the present. Back home, my main exposure to going out for coffee was with Dad at the twenty-four-hour donut place around the block, Happy Donuts. In the Happy Donuts world, there are no waiters and no pretense of fresh coffee or fresh pastries. The donut case remains in permanent stasis. The same options in the same rows, always fully in stock. Cooled to a temperature one degree above frigid, each donut tastes the same regardless of variety: a dense, singular note of sweetness delivered in dough the texture of a wet dish towel. At the table near the register, a group of old men usually sat with legs splayed, speaking Cantonese loudly. The man I took to be the leader of the group would kindly doff his hat to us, a black cap with red script, "Touchless," indicating he worked at the car wash on Divisadero. Coffee at Happy Donuts comes in one form, drip French roast, and in two sizes, small or large, both poured from an orange-lipped Bunn carafe into a thin Styrofoam cup. We'd grab a latticed red plastic tray, sit by the window, wolf our donuts down, and leave in under eight minutes. The ambiance wasn't for lingering. Our neighborhood is perpetually foggy and Happy Donuts leaves their door cracked, and the draft makes one feel colder inside the shop than outside.

By comparison, Viennese cafés are a revelation. They couldn't be more different: tuxedoed waiters, porcelain plates and saucers, full food menus, and the ability to sit comfortably for hours and hours for the price of a cup of coffee. Every café has newspapers, for reading, sure, but also as a signal that it is ok to be alone. It is state sanctioned. The absolute pinnacle of the Viennese experience is to go in the early afternoon, drink a coffee or two, see the room darken at sunset, then transition into a beer, a warm meal, and finish with a glass of heavy red wine or cognac. This progression almost certainly means staying through a shift change. When your waiter comes to you, pad clasped in hand, and apologetically asks to settle up, it brings to mind the shifting of the tides. The waiter, or waitress, is both your partner and antagonist in lonely living. They will appear promptly after you sit down, but if you aren't ready to order, they won't return for ages, and when they do, they will be curt. It's not uncommon to have one waiter cover twenty or thirty tables in a constant flash of moving limbs and silver trays. It's not a job held between jobs, it's a lifelong profession, and if you go the same time every day to the same café, you will see the same waiters.

In lieu of friends to see, the cafés became my companions. Like most of my Viennese explorations, I worked my way out from the city center, starting with spacious first district tourist havens like Café Central and Café Sacher. Whatever those cafés may have once been, they aren't anymore. Many inner-district cafés are similar—built around the fin de siècle in the final bloom of the Habsburg Empire with dark wood paneling, high arched ceilings, newspapers stacked by the entrance, and a broad glass case containing the day's cakes. When one winds into other districts, the cafés reflect their neighborhood or the decade that they first opened their doors. My favorites became Café Jelinek, where Johanna had taken me, and Café Prückel. Café Jelinek is a perfect version of a classic first district café, but it's tucked away in the sixth district so it's quieter, with locals instead of tourists. The primary waitress—a thirty-something with coarse, dirty blonde hair stretched back into a ponytail—appeared to be so incredibly unhappy at all times that I awaited her imminent suicide. The rare occasions she smiled brought me incredible relief and joy. Once, I mispronounced the daily special, *Waldviertler Mohnnudeln*, so badly that she smiled fully, revealing a missing tooth behind the canine. That smile made my week. Her colleague, a bald man with a look of permanent apology on his face, performed a soft counterpoint to her. I liked that Johanna had once worked at the café, and I liked that Jelinek only had one or two cakes at a time, humble offerings like *Marmorgugelhupf*, which can best be described as stale Bundt cake. Even when eaten directly from the oven, it tastes stale, which is something.

My other favorite, Prückel, sits on the Ring, and although it dates to 1904, it must have undergone a renovation in the 1950s because it resembles a midcentury airport departure lounge. White walls stretch up to a high, salmon-colored ceiling. Delicate wooden furniture upholstered in gold fills the room. An odd, numberless clock mounted on a plastic grate hangs above the door. Neither the food nor the coffee are remarkable, or even good, but I liked sitting there hidden within the continuous flow of people. The area to the right of the entrance gives a bustling, transitory vibe, whereas the left half offers more light, and a home for longer visits. Prückel is where I first discovered the café staple *Frankfurter mit Senf und Kren*, which is a bunless hot dog served with mustard and a small mound of grated horseradish. One dips the dog into the mustard, then the horseradish, which is an insane way to eat. To do so on a silver tray and to be served by a man in a tuxedo or a woman in a pressed white shirt and a long black skirt is an experience not possible perhaps anywhere else in the world. In Vienna, such behavior is encouraged.

Almost every single person within every single café smokes continuously when they are not eating. Some do pipes, some roll their own creations, most smoke cigarettes from white boxes of Camels or Marlboros tucked onto the table beside their coffee. To walk from the night air into a café is to be subsumed into velvet smog. At first, my virgin American eyes watered and my lungs stung but I learned to love the stench, and it helped me transition into a smoker. While exploring cafés, I worked my way through the ten or so elemental drinks present on every menu. The base of each drink is a shot or two of espresso, usually Julius Meinl, combined with different ratios of steamed and/or frothed milk. I settled on the Verlängerter as my drink of choice. It's comparatively cheap, Heinrich drinks it, and it provides more liquid to sip than a regular espresso. Often bitter and astringent, it has a tang I appreciate. When I needed the weight and comfort of milk, I went for an *Einspänner*. Named for a one-horse carriage, it's a double shot topped with thick, unsweetened whipped cream. The carriage association comes from the fact that the whipped cream on top keeps the underlying espresso warm, allowing a carriage driver the ability to slowly sip as they cruise with drink in hand. Has this ever actually happened? I'm not too sure.

The hours spent alone, and the caffeine consumed, didn't stifle my loneliness, but it pushed my roots into the earth of the city and gave me something to think about other than how I'd fucked up with Johanna, or how I'd disappointed my parents.

IV

One morning at Heinrich's apartment, I settled in and spent an hour shuffling through his research for pieces related to an article about the mysterious wealth of a farmer in Lower Austria. The farmer, Hans, owned white asparagus fields in the Marchfeld, and although the land was fertile, his personal wealth had grown to a level that suggested he was repackaging cheaply grown crops from Italy. This offended Austrian sensibilities. There was the fraud, regrettable but not uncommon among businessman, and there was the agricultural miscegenation of an Austrian delicacy, much less forgivable. While I worked, Heinrich sat at his normal spot by the window with a saffron yellow hardback copy of *Buddenbrooks*. He shifted often in his chair and periodically stood up, placed his book face down onto the windowsill, and reached one arm then the other straight up towards the ceiling in an odd, apple-picking-inspired stretch. When noon approached, he walked over to my desk.

"Lunch today? I wanted to discuss some things with you."

"Sure."

"How cold is it outside? I haven't left yet today."

"It's cold. Literally colder than I've ever been in my life during daylight."

"Let me change," he said, and walked down the hall towards his bedroom. I packed away the files strewn before me and went to use the restroom. As I passed by his room, the door was ajar, and I could partially see his reflection in the full-length mirror on his wall. As he lifted his arms to remove his shirt, a ray of sunlight illuminated his back and right side. His skin was waxen and pale. Without the cover of his well-fitting clothes, his age showed. He stepped out a minute later and I watched him walk down the hall. His body held a faint stiffness when he stepped with his right leg.

We walked to Café Schwarzenberg for lunch and sat across from one another at a table by the window to the right of the entrance. The café sits on the Ring and looks out onto the busy, dull Schwarzenbergplatz. It's more of a large intersection than a pedestrian hangout, with multiple Straßenbahn lines peeling off from the Ring and traveling through the square as they head towards Vienna's outer districts, their overhead electric wires flowing parallel to rows of tall light poles. In the square's center stood a charcoal grey statue of Field Marshal Karl atop his horse. A son of Vienna, he earned his fame by capturing Paris and overthrowing Napoleon. Heinrich and I ordered our lunch—*Schnitzel* for me, *Gemüseauflauf* for him—and we sat together quietly, each of us leafing through a newspaper pulled from a shelf nearby. When our food came, we both ate while looking out the window at the cars and people passing by. He ate with precision: a cut with his knife, barely visible chewing, and a small wipe with one of the café's red cloth napkins. My food was good. A little oversalted. When Heinrich was finished, he slid his silverware together on his plate, and I mirrored his action. We ordered coffee.

When it came, he shifted in his seat, rubbed his jaw, and said, "Did you know when I was about your age, this square was called Stalinplatz." He exhaled with amusement and raised his pointer finger into the air. "Not a name selected by this city's residents."

"Yeah?"

"Yes. This was an area controlled by the Soviets after the war. Behind Karl over there," he pointed past the statue, "is a monument the Soviets put up for themselves and their beloved army. When the fighting stopped, they left a single tank parked back there, and a few years later, they assembled a colonnade encircling a soldier perched on top of a garish red box. You must have a look sometime."

I peered out the window but couldn't see much past Karl.

"I do hope I live to see the day when it's destroyed," Heinrich added calmly, as though he was talking about fixing a broken tail light on a car. "But it wasn't just the Bolsheviks who left their mark on this square. Your countrymen have put their own precious thing over there on the right."

Beside Karl was a small, square sign emblazoned with the familiar golden arches. The scent of salt and powdered onions filled my mind.

"If the Field Marshall only knew his reward for his service was to stand watch before a Bolshevik monument and a McDonald's," Heinrich said, shaking his head with a half smile. I sensed a change between us. A lessening of distance.

"It must be crazy to see so much change during your life."

Looking back out the window, he said, "I wouldn't say crazy; however, I do encounter ghosts as I walk about. Every block has a memory, and as the memories stack up upon one another, it can be hard to keep one's mind in the present. This table—" he coughed, then cleared his throat. "This table is why I continue coming here and overpaying for lunch. I sat here with my brother when I last saw him. Before he went off and was killed by the army whose monument is back there." He rapped his knuckles onto the hammered brass table between us.

"Wow," I mumbled.

He shrugged. "That's how things are here, Alex. I understand that in America, everything is disposable, but items of substance like this can last across eras." He leaned back and scanned the room. "Much of this café has changed, but these tables have survived."

I didn't know how much concern to show for a brother killed fifty years before. Did it matter, in this moment, that Heinrich's brother had fought for the wrong side?

"What was your brother's name?" I asked.

"Erich."

"Erich," I repeated, nodding.

"Erich had a presence that cannot be replaced." He looked over and watched a group of four backpack-clad tourists, crumpled maps in hand, wander by our table. Then, he leaned forward and said, "I do need to talk to you about something else. If you are available, I could use your help with work beyond organizing my files."

"Yeah, of course."

"This work is more difficult."

"Ok."

"I have heard through contacts that an old friend of mine is potentially involved in a dangerous project. I'm concerned but I don't know the details, so I was hoping you could follow him around for a few weeks and write a report on where he goes and whom he meets. As he is a friend, I'd prefer to understand his situation fully before I contact the police."

My chest tightened.

"What do you think this guy is doing?"

"He may be planning something unpleasant at a location in Vienna. I don't want to say too much because I don't want to color your perceptions."

"Like Oklahoma City unpleasant, or like—robbing something unpleasant?"

Heinrich shook his head. "Oh no, not terrorism, I don't believe. But I do prefer to have you follow him with an open mind. It's likely he's planning nothing at all. Rumors fester swiftly in this town, especially amongst old men like myself who do not have fruitful activities to occupy their minds."

"Why me?"

"I'm impressed with your attention to detail, and, to be frank, since you are unattached here, I thought you might be capable of more discretion than a local."

I squeezed the back of my neck. It sounded interesting. Heinrich's hands were folded on the table before him. Light from the window reflected off his gold wedding ring, scuffed and pitted from years of wear.

"I would pay double your current salary, of course, as there is more risk and stress with this job. And to be clear, if you do not accept, you can stay on organizing my files. I understand if this task is not something you wish to do."

Four thousand schillings a week was a number for serious work. Roughly double what I made from Dad at the store and without any tax.

"What can you tell me about this guy?"

"His name is Emil, and he's a few years younger than me. When we were children, our families lived across the hall from one another in an apartment building in the seventh district. Because of the times, we lived almost as one family, and his mother was very kind to me. Emil and I lost touch over the years, but something remains between us. He doesn't have many living relatives, so I feel a responsibility for his welfare."

"When would I follow him? All day or certain hours, or what were you thinking?"

"I will leave that decision to you once you learn his rhythms. I will let you know if I am satisfied with your work."

I inhaled deeply through my nose, held it for a beat, then exhaled.

"I'd love to help, really, but I don't have any experience."

"I understand, Alex. But, as you have seen in my research, I have done this type of work for my entire career. It's very simple and that is why I feel comfortable asking you to do it."

He moved his coffee cup to the side, looked directly at

me, and spoke in a relaxed voice. "Follow at a distance. Wear clothes in plain colors and change often. Act natural. It's easy. People pay less attention than one would think."

"Maybe."

"Any information you can gather would be useful. I would do it myself but I have slowed in the past few years, and Emil and I—well, he would spot me quite easily."

He shrugged and smiled. He had bright, grey eyes. They were hard to look into, but I forced myself.

"Ok. I'll do it. I can't promise I'll be good at it, but I'll try. I'll play it safe and get you something. I don't want to take your money if I'm bad at it, or if I get spotted, so what if I just started at my current rate?"

He laughed. "Take the full payment. Don't get spotted."

"Will Emil be on the lookout for people spying on him?"

Heinrich smirked. "Men in pursuit of a cause that they wish to keep private develop natural suspicions." He reached into his bag and retrieved a yellow envelope sealed by a red string wrapped around a button. He placed it in the center of the table. "There you will find an advance, Emil's address, and a photo of him." I took the envelope from the table and placed it into my bag. "Thank you for your help. I appreciate it. Don't take any unnecessary risk."

"Sure. Should I still come by to organize your files?"

"The files have waited years and can wait a bit longer. Please bring me a report on Sunday evening. Let's say seven p.m. at my apartment."

We settled the bill, he paid, and we walked outside into the cool air and stood together at the corner looking over Schwarzenbergplatz.

"Which way are you headed?" he asked.

"I'm taking the D towards Franz-Josefs-Bahnhof."

"Ok, I'm walking the other direction. Thanks again, Alex," he said, and patted me on the shoulder with a gloved hand. He looked relieved. "Do you see how you stand compared to how I stand?" I looked down at my legs, then his. I didn't see any difference. "You stand with your weight on one leg, with lean. That's very American. Center your weight. You'll blend in more." I did see the difference. I tried it. "Wonderful—and no baseball hats, obviously, or things like that."

"Ok."

"And please, mention none of this to Johanna. She is very excitable and would not understand. Can you accept absolute secrecy?"

"Yes."

With a nod, he turned and walked off. I reached inside my bag and placed my fingertips onto the envelope. Best not to open it there. I walked to the Staßenbahn stop and stood beside two nuns in white cotton habits. A train arrived, and I took the last seat in the last car, well behind the other passengers. I unzipped my bag and pulled out the envelope. Inside were four salmon-colored five-hundred-Schilling bills and a folded piece of lined grid paper. While unfolding the paper, a wallet-sized photo fell into my lap. The photo was of a man who looked to be in his sixties. He stared directly into the camera with fatigued resignation; it must have been a passport photo or mugshot. Written neatly on the paper in blue pen was a name and address:

> Emil Eder
> Neulerchenfelderstrasse 75
> 1160 Wien

I put away everything and stared out the window while the Straßenbahn rolled north along the Ring. As I replayed our entire lunchtime conversation, a pressure, like the palm of a hand, pushed down into my chest. The feeling echoed the sensation from when I placed my plagiarized paper into the basket outside my professor's office at Stanford. Heinrich and Johanna had their full lives running in Vienna—a broad, coursing river flowing across generations—and somehow, I'd fallen in, swept along with their current. Back at my apartment, I lay down on my bed, fully clothed, and stared. I should return the money. The job sounded interesting, possibly incredible, but it wasn't worth the risk. This trip was supposed to be a time of reduced anxiety and an end to behavior that would disappoint my parents. When the sun set, my mind oscillated faster and faster across possible failure scenarios, and I went out for a walk.

I wandered, undirected, for miles. I kept going all the way to the edge of the outer districts where buildings start to have space between them and Vienna feels like a town. It didn't help me relax, and my calves started to burn and my Achilles tendons tightened. A mix of rain and sleet began to fall and I decided to catch the number five Straßenbahn back towards my apartment. I waited for a while at a stop, much longer than typical for Austrian transit. While I studied the posted schedule, a faint, official-sounding voice began to speak from a grey speaker atop a nearby concrete pole. I couldn't parse the voice's German over the slosh of cars driving by through the wet streets. Beside me at the stop, a tall, forty-something man appeared displeased as he pulled a pack of Camels from his jacket pocket. We were the only two people there.

"I'm sorry, what are they saying?" I asked, in German.

He motioned with his cigarettes in the direction our Straßenbahn was supposed to arrive from.

"Straßenbahn delayed because of an accident on the tracks."

He looked at me directly for five seconds. Maybe ten. To say he looked crazy would be an exaggeration: his glare wasn't off-putting, but there was an intensity within him. His face, long and weathered, widened into a grin. From his box of Camels, he tapped out a cigarette. Placing it in his lips, he carefully cradled it with his left hand, smoothly pulling and igniting a small, blue, Bic lighter with his right. He took a deep drag, tapped out another cigarette halfway from its box, and extended it to me.

"Care for a smoke?"

Perhaps I had stared too long, giving the impression I was looking for a handout. Without thinking, I walked over and took the cigarette. He smiled, held out his lighter, and lit it for me. I welcomed any distraction from myself. A flush of heat warmed my lungs. It was my first cigarette in the rain, and I liked it.

"American?" he asked.

"You figured that out after one sentence?"

He raised his left eyebrow and nodded.

"Are you Austrian?" I asked.

"Oh, god no. German."

Tucking my cigarette into the corner of my mouth, I extended my right hand.

"Alex."

He extended his. "Markus."

We both gave a hearty shake. I stared down at the wet pavement, unsure whether to continue our friendliness. As our silence extended, a voice crackled from the speaker; the Straßenbahn would not resume that evening due to issues with the electricity powering the line. It became clear, as we were both waiting on the same Straßenbahn, we would now have to walk in the same direction. The cigarette smoke tickled the back of my throat.

"Headed that way?" Markus asked, pointing south towards the city center.

"Yep." He stepped forward and I followed.

"What brings an American to this fallen imperial city?" he asked, in a clear, strong voice.

"Just some time off from university, traveling around. You?"

"I live here. Years ago, I met an Austrian girl while visiting and I stayed for her. It didn't work out, and now she lives in

Germany of all places. I'm still here."

There was a lot in that sentence.

"Is it always this cold?" I asked.

"You get a good four to six months of proper winter around here. End of March might be nice."

March was a long way away. Unimaginably far. Other than an old woman standing above her dog, plastic bag in hand, the streets were empty.

"You are here on some adventure aren't you?" he asked. My face flushed. Was this guy somehow connected to Heinrich? Maybe *he* was following me. Maybe I'd managed to fail at my new job before it even began.

"What do you mean?" I fumbled out.

"You know, American in Europe, that whole trope. Why else spend winter here looking as cold as you do?"

I guess I really hadn't figured out how to look like I belonged. He wore a heavy black coat with the collar turned up over his bushy sideburns. A few veins of silver ran through his scruffy black hair. He appeared comfortable with who he was.

"Is winter when you met the Austrian girl?"

"Yeah—Sabine. All the girls here are named Sabine."

We continued on, silently for a block, as the name Sabine hung in the air. It's a name I'd never heard before coming to Austria. The name of an ancient people from Italy. I would come to find he was right, there were a lot of girls named Sabine in Vienna. It's not a beautiful name. Sounds antiseptic.

"You don't smoke much, do you?" Markus asked.

"Is everything about me super obvious or are you perceptive?"

He grinned. "Breathe deeper when you smoke. Take your time." Take your time, in German, was *Lass dir Zeit*, which sounded nice. I found Markus's pronunciation easier to understand than the Austrians. "Why Vienna? Why not Paris or Berlin or somewhere alive?"

"Everybody keeps asking me that. It's making me start to

question my decision making."

"Vienna's kind of a forgotten city these days."

"Well—I speak German, and I like sitting around drinking coffee."

He shook his head.

"Coffee, I get, but I wouldn't say the German spoken here is any good."

We walked for a while, tracing the path of the glistening rail tracks. I tried smoking deeper and slower with a rolling rhythm. The cigarette tasted unnatural. Maybe I was licking the filter too much.

"Well, there *is* a girl here now too."

"Always is."

He stopped abruptly. In the streetlight I could see both youth and age in his face. Some grey in the black stubble on his chin, small crow's feet framing the corner of his eyes.

"Her name isn't Sabine, is it?"

"No. It's Johanna."

He bit his lip and tilted his head. "Johanna might work. That's Hannah Arendt's given name, so there's something there, but what you really want in Vienna is an ex-Yugoslav woman. You know, an Ana or Ivana or someone from that peninsula."

I had never met an Ana or Ivana, or any ex-Yugos. Tito and his fucking relay were what got me kicked out of Stanford.

"Do you have somewhere to be?" he asked.

I didn't. I knew if I returned home, I would spend the evening debating whether or not to call Heinrich and tell him I didn't feel comfortable stalking his friend.

"Not really."

"I'm on my way to share a beer with a friend, care to join?"

"Sure."

We turned into the first district, and the streets narrowed

and filled with other pedestrians, most unconcerned with the falling rain.

"Well, go on about the girl," said Markus.

The thought nagged that he could be connected to Heinrich or even Emil. Maybe this was some kind of a test. Other than Johanna, despite countless hours in cafés and many awkward attempts, I hadn't met many strangers in Vienna who were willing to open themselves to me. My intuition was to end the conversation with him, or at least not share much about myself. But, I didn't want to listen to my intuition. Continuously imagining worst-case scenarios is what I do best. It's draining.

"She's a student at Uni Wien. I don't really know her at all, and I probably already fucked things up, but I like her. We have incredible chemistry—from my side at least. I think she feels it too."

We turned the corner, and he pushed open a pale green door leading into a restaurant. Inside was a smoky room with red leather banquettes, pool tables, and lots of people sitting and standing around. We walked to a table near the front where a man sat with a beer and a tattered blue paperback book.

"Julian, this is Alex. He's American." Markus said, while pushing a chair towards me. Julian gave a warm look of acknowledgement. He didn't seem surprised that Markus had brought along a random stray from the street. Markus sat down and immediately began an impassioned, fifteen-minute-long soliloquy about an article he'd read on the fading art of Viennese bakeries. With only a barely perceptible pause to his story, he managed to flag down a waiter and order us a round of dark Polish lager and plates of goulash. Lithe with a smoothly shaved head, Julian listened intently, nodding when necessary to provide encouragement to Markus. When the bakery story ended, Markus took a long swig of beer, removed his jacket, and then embarked on a monologue about the audacity of planned increases in fees for students at the University of Vienna. The same subject discussed by Johanna and her friends at the party a few weeks before.

I sat silent and observed the interplay between Markus and Julian. Julian only spoke in brief, empathetic sentences. As Markus began to stray from whatever topic he was on, Julian would gently prod and redirect him, guiding him towards a destination, filling in details Markus withheld if the subject was something discussed for my benefit. With a full stomach and the dawn of a beer buzz, I developed the courage to speak.

"So, Markus—what about your story with the girl?"

"Sabine?" he responded.

"Sabine." Julian repeated in a reverent whisper. He reminded me of Michael Stipe and not just because of the bald head. I love R.E.M., so from me, this is a substantial compliment.

Markus leaned back in his chair. "Are you sure you want to hear about this? You are at the beginning of love and this story does not have a happy ending."

"Definitely."

"The short version or the long version?"

"The short one," interrupted Julian.

Markus nodded gravely and lifted his eyebrows.

"I was studying in Berlin, I'm originally from the East, and I came down here to Vienna to meet a friend of a friend who was renting a flat here for the winter for some reason that I cannot remember."

"Markus's dad had a *Trabbie*," Julian added.

"This is true. It's now in a field somewhere. It wasn't cool."

"They are sort of cool now," Julian retorted.

"To *you* people," Markus said. Turning to me, he continued, "Julian is from Hamburg. Do you know about the whole *Ossie, Wessi* thing?"

I shook my head. "I know a little, but only from TV. And I don't know what a Trabbie is."

"Well, a Trabbie is the worst automobile ever created, forged entirely out of plastic and Marxism. Our suffering in the East was an amusement to the West. It was, and it is, and it always shall be. Anyway, at that time, I didn't have a strong sense of the West. I mean, who does? I met her at a party, we were both wearing all black, and we walked around the city all night. When the sun rose, we went back to her apartment in the eighth district and fell asleep. For the first thirty-six-to-forty-eight-hours we were in deep, shaking bliss. For the four years after that, we argued every day. We argued a lot about who would move for the other person. I needed to return to Berlin, I was studying philosophy," he tapped a finger to his temple, "very serious, very important stuff. Europe, at that time, Berlin especially, was in grave, grave need of another philosophy student. So, we argued about me going back. She was studying language acquisition, her father is Czech, and neither of us wanted to sacrifice for the other. I surrendered first and moved to Vienna."

He scratched beneath his jaw and clenched his teeth. It was a tic he seemed to display between tonal shifts in stories.

"It wasn't easy to win an argument with her. In fact, I'm not certain I ever did. Not even a small one."

He took a long breath. His face had begun to redden. He took a sip of beer and licked his lips. Before he could continue, Julian spoke. "I should add, his telling of this story and accompanying interpretation changes with each passing season."

"True. Perspective matters. You should praise me for this evolution, Julian. Alex, are you keeping a journal during your time here?"

"No. I thought I should, but I haven't started."

"Wonderful. *Never* keep a journal. Let the mind edit and recall what it wishes. I had a journal throughout my Sabine period, and reading it afterward horrified me and paralyzed me. The best decision of my life was throwing it away. Should we get more beer? Maybe a *Helles*?"

"Yes, of course." Julian sprang up and cornered a waiter who returned shortly with three tall pint glasses containing cold, bright yellow beer with a thick, white head.

Markus pointed skyward with his right pointer finger. "One important note is that Sabine is now happily married with a child. Whenever I tell this story to Americans, they always try to put us back together, so let's just short-circuit that."

"Do you tell this story to a lot of Americans?" I asked.

"I told one American. What was his name?" he asked, turning to Julian.

"Steve."

"Yes, Steve. Julian's friend. He's a souvenir from Julian's summer spent in Florida, of all places."

"Steve was a little too optimistic for Markus."

"Got it. Don't be optimistic," I said.

Markus laughed and ran his hand through his hair.

"Optimism is ok. It's very American, but Americans are only optimistic about their own ideas, which is really just narcissism. No offense, but Americans are irredeemably insane."

"Sure. I mean, it's a big country and normally I would deny this, but you're right."

"Thank you. I do believe Julian misinterprets my feelings about Steve, but anyway, for Sabine, I moved to Vienna. I began to like the city and the university, but unfortunately, finding love freed my mind. Prior to her, I had exclusively focused on the pursuit of women. Having an actual woman to love and to hold allowed my mind to turn and focus on myself and the things I was failing to do. I made myself miserable. I became very depressed and very negative."

"And her exes were everywhere—" Julian added.

"And her exes were everywhere. Vienna is an incredibly provincial village. It would have been nice to go to a party at some point where everyone there was not either her ex-boyfriend or his brother or sister or whomever."

He stopped and rotated his pint glass so that the label, Ottakringer, faced out towards us. Julian reclined and crossed his legs, bringing one of his mustard-colored, fuzzy-suede Adidas Gazelles into view. They were beautiful shoes with the perfect amount of wear. I needed a pair.

"Eventually, I thought moving back to Germany would decrease my misery, so we did and it was worse there. We stopped having any fun together, so we broke up. No infidelity. Just one, finite breakup and we haven't seen each other since. She stayed there, claiming my country as her own, and I returned to Vienna."

I nodded.

"It was true love though."

"Yeah?"

"Yes, that's the worst part. Our love endured, but we were simply incapable of getting along."

"Did you guys consider counseling?"

"Oh, yes. She coerced me into something at Sigmund Freud University for a few sessions. They suggested Sabine didn't love me, and they only wanted to discuss my childhood in Dresden. That place should be shut down."

Julian laughed and shook his head. Markus smiled.

"Julian works there by the way. This is a source of ongoing conversation for us."

"I feel professionally required to add that Markus refuses to blame the DDR for anything."

Markus picked up and flipped over a few coasters from the table. "That's not exactly true, but I don't require the assistance of your colleague Reinhard from Salzburg to understand the shortcomings of my past. Anyway, to conclude the Sabine saga, I believe that because we were always contemplating a move or were actually moving, we couldn't build a life anywhere. I decided after it was over to never move away from Vienna. This is it. I don't even travel, if it means spending the night somewhere other than my flat."

"And it just ended with one breakup? No backslides?" I asked.

Julian shifted his weight in his chair and gave me a cautious look.

"Let's just say she left me in a complete, irreversible way."

I nodded and stared into the staggered white lines left by my beer as it worked its way down my glass.

"I feel the need to also add, since Markus neglected to mention it—Sabine was also kind of a bitch," said Julian. "Even on her best days. Beautiful, intelligent, and tragic. But a bitch most of all."

The night continued and more rounds of beer were consumed. Julian told us the story of a fishing trip with his parents on the North Sea. His father builds skiffs out of a specific variety of oak that grows in the shade outside of Köln. To complete one boat takes one year. No movement is wasted as he works, and his boats are completed without flaw. Their strength and symmetry are known throughout Hamburg, and aspiring shipbuilders often stop in to observe his process. Unfortunately, his father is terrible at sea. He has no ability to gauge the tides and currents and is so cheap that he only uses motors abandoned by friends that he's allegedly repaired. After many disastrous family trips, Julian and his mother are reluctant to ever board a boat, but last July, his father's pleading convinced them. Once they lost sight of shore after embarking from Bremerhaven, the motor rattled and slipped halfway from its mount. Julian caught it just before it went under and held on with his fingertips. He and his mother laughed so hard that he lost his grip, and it dropped, gurgling down into the dark water, leaving them stranded. Then, they laughed even harder. After three hours baking together in the sun, they were towed back by a young couple from Denmark. Julian's father didn't speak to either of them for three months.

I shared with them the time I asked my dad what the word

"beaver" meant when used in reference to a woman. It was the only conversation about sex my dad and I have ever had. We were on a trip to the dump south of the city when I asked the question. Dad pulled over immediately, somewhere in Potrero Hill. His explanation was brief. "It refers to a woman's pee-pee and I never want to hear you say it ever again." I haven't. Markus was thrilled to learn offensive American slang and planned to use the word with Steve should he ever return from Florida.

At some point in the evening, I went looking for the bathroom, lurching down a long hallway covered with posters from museum exhibitions and concerts around Vienna. Standing up and walking revealed just how drunk I had become. One pleasant byproduct of the pervasive smoking in the city is that people smoke on the toilet as well—stalls have ashtrays—so the typical flavors of American bathroom smells are blanketed over by burning cigarettes. On my return to our table, I resolved to drink water instead of beer. Some time later, as Julian and Markus spoke about a bar up the street that had recently closed forever, I remembered it had been two weeks since I had heard from Johanna, and in the morning, I would begin my new job following some old guy around. The evening would have to end and ultimately all evenings would end. The worst part of a nice evening is that they go by so fast, you almost miss them entirely. I thanked Markus and Julian for letting me join them, exchanged numbers, and headed home.

V

The next morning began with me lying on my back, mouth dry and head throbbing as dull sunlight crept around the edges of the white curtain obscuring my bedroom window. I can't imagine what it's like to wake up and feel refreshed. I'm not convinced it's physically possible for me, even when I'm not hungover. On most days, it takes a few hours and a few coffees to approach mental clarity, and if I do reach it, it doesn't last long. I checked the time: 7:12 a.m. I got up, walked to the window, and rubbed my eyes until they ached.

For breakfast, I ate day-old *Kornspitz* and *Bauchspeck* washed down with two cups of dark and oily Julius Meinl coffee brewed in a cheap French press that I had bought at the store downstairs. Though stale, the flaky bread and salty bacon combination—time-honored across the continents—revitalized me. I brushed crumbs and papers aside and unfolded my map of Vienna. Moving my fingers over the districts, working out from inside the Ring, I glided over Parliament, Schloss Belvedere, up to the north, around, and settled into my destination, Ottakring. The sixteenth district. I found Emil's street, a straight spoke extending out from the Gürtel. I made a few notes on the map to mark clear paths in and out of the neighborhood, and a few more in my notebook. I planned to stop by the national library afterward to see if I could find any books or articles about Emil.

Outside, thick and motionless grey clouds covered the sky. As I walked towards the sixteenth, I stopped intermittently to check my plexiglass compass for north. Meant to be laid flat onto a map, it worked poorly in hand. I received it my last year of Cub Scouts. I was a terrible scout, but I like the compass's bobbing bubble and yellowed chassis, and I like that nine-year-old me and twenty-three-year-old me share the same tools. Whenever I found north, I rotated until I could confirm the direction of Stephansdom and the Danube canal. A sense of place began to permeate me, and I tested myself by turning left and right down side streets, then guessing which direction I was facing. After about a half hour ping-ponging around, I made it to Emil's street, Neulerchenfelderstraße. It's a mouthful, pronounced, "noy-lair-ken-feld-er-shtra-suh." Saying long words in German requires a simultaneous holding on to and letting go of focus.

At Emil's address, number 75, stood a black gate that opened into a sparse courtyard of dead grass in front of a faceless, concrete apartment building. I inspected the call box. Emil was at number five of the twelve units contained inside. Tracing my fingers over the steel keys, a compulsion to ring his door gripped me. I resisted. The digit within each metal key was deeply etched, and their lines felt rough beneath my fingertips. I left his gate and walked in a steady, widening spiral around his neighborhood, making note of places I could stand unseen and observe a large area. Shops and empty storefronts lined his street while most of the side streets were narrower and residential with long, rectangular, four-to-eight-story-high apartment buildings in innumerable shades of beige. Many shop signs were in Turkish, some in Serbo-Croatian, and graffiti was scrawled everywhere, especially "Puber" or "1950," neither of which meant anything to me. Cigarette butts and crumpled trash lay scattered and matted against the curb, a sight unseen in the inner districts.

I wanted to get a feel for watching people before I began trailing Emil, so I selected a random woman passing by in a burgundy coat and followed her for five-and-a-half blocks until she walked into a salon, Sturmayer Coiffeur. She didn't notice me. It was about nine a.m., and as I waited outside the salon, the number of pedestrians walking around increased from a slow drip into a flowing stream. I grew bored and started to follow a man, maybe mid-thirties, wearing a faded grey denim jacket and black jeans. He carried a canvas satchel and took long, confident strides. I followed him down to the Gürtel, up the stairs and onto the platform of the Josefstädter Straße U-Bahn station. We waited for the train, I gave him about fifteen feet of distance, and I practiced balancing my weight in the center of my body like Heinrich had advised. We boarded a train heading east, he sat at the front of the car and I stood near the back while he pulled a pair of headphones on and fiddled with a Walkman. He got off two stops later, and I followed him into the eighteenth district. I approached to about seven feet when he stopped and stretched his arms out. I froze. A woman walking the opposite direction stepped into his arms and embraced him. While they held each other, I moved to a delivery van parked a few steps away, sat down on its chrome bumper, and pretended to tie my shoe. Vienna is flat and there's never a Straßenbahn too far away, so the sound of metal wheels turning over metal rails creates a persistent hum vibrating in the air. This noise prevented me from hearing much of their conversation. Something about getting together, and a friend named Risi, and the holidays. They embraced again in a full, real hug. People in Austria do the cheek-kissing thing frequently, but they don't hug front to front and genitals to genitals unless they mean it. They released their embrace, and he walked on for another three blocks with a quicker pace, then stepped into an optometrist's office. I leaned against a pole outside, and six and a half minutes later, he appeared through the window in a white lab coat, giving a child an eye exam. I had never realized how plainly people's lives were performed within public view. My breath fogged in the cold morning air, and sweat drenched my shirt and back. During the time spent following the woman and then the man, my mind had remained clear. I was ready for Emil. I returned to his street and walked to a small café two doors from his address and took a table by the window. I ordered coffee from a smiling Turkish woman with deep forehead wrinkles, then pulled out my notebook and pretended to look busy.

Time passed and I daydreamed of things to say to Janet. Though we never spoke after I received her letter, our dialog continued in my mind. The third paragraph of page two—the one about how I was irredeemably sensitive—resonated the most because it was true. A woman and child exited the gate of Emil's building and walked into a kindergarten down the block. Twenty minutes later, the woman returned alone. I recorded these things, and others, into my notebook. I tried to keep my notes abbreviated so they wouldn't be intelligible to anyone else. Over the next hour, my left shoulder began to ache, and a pain throbbed behind my eyes. The coffee I ordered turned out to be Turkish: thick, unfiltered sludge served in a brass pot with a long handle. I alternated sips of coffee with cool water in an effort to dial my mind into a working cadence.

At 10:18 a.m., a grey-haired, white male a shade below average height exited the gate. Neatly dressed in a thick, charcoal suit, hunter green scarf, and black hat, he set off southward with a brisk stride. I gathered my things, waited until the man reached the corner, and walked after him. Once I closed to within half a block, I timed my footsteps to fall within the sound of his. Feeling suspicious to bystanders, I relaxed my jaw and let my arms hang naturally.

I approached the corner where the man stood waiting to cross the street. Undoubtedly, he matched the photograph in my wallet. He turned to look up the block. Clean, even sunlight—perfect for a photograph—illuminated his face, revealing a strong jawline and a large mustache. Grey curls peeked out from underneath his hat. This was a classically drawn man. His appearance struck me. As he stepped off the curb and out of that light, he looked smaller and his age wore through. This was a classically drawn man whose lines had faded.

Giving a ten step head start, I followed him down the street past the tables of an empty farmer's market and watched him stop into a bakery. Four and a half minutes later, he exited the bakery with a brown paper bag in his hand and looped left, left, and then back home into the gate at number 75. All told, he had walked an almost perfect square. As he re-entered his gate, I waited up the block. When the gate closed, I continued to stare into the space last occupied by him. It seemed that his shadow lingered. Midway through the route, I had switched to instinct, and now my thoughts returned. My first successful operation confirmed he was an old Austrian guy who enjoys fresh bread.

I took a different post at a betting parlor from which I could faintly see his gate through heavily tinted windows. It was a poor tint job, a thick purple layer of plastic lazily smeared across the window, bubbles throughout. Time passed and Emil didn't exit. The glow of nine televisions worth of soccer games from across the continent flickering over the dour faces in the dark parlor made my head swim and my eyes strain. Not wanting to stand out, I picked up a betting card and pretended to study it and scribble on it. At two thirty p.m., hunger set in. Unsure of Emil's schedule and the hourly expectations of my new occupation, I waited longer. A pair of heavyset men with close-cropped hair two tables away kept looking in my direction. Around three p.m., the heat of their glare got to me and I left. I ate some thin, disappointing goulash at Café Schottenring just outside of the first district. It's a forgettable café, but they have an oversized, nonoperable coffee roaster named "the San Franciscan" sitting beside the dining area. It made me think of home and feel miserable, which I enjoy. The only other customer inside the café was an elderly woman drinking a glass of green tea. I asked the waiter if he had a cigarette and he sat down, rolled us both one, and we smoked together. He was from the Czech Republic, hated Austrians, and hated working in the café. Dark rings circled his eyes and a wife-beater undershirt was visible beneath his white button-up. He liked Americans, like me, because we tip well and have teeth whiter than he'd ever seen among Europeans. "Whiter than mine, when I was a baby," he said, multiple times. I considered telling him that Americans' teeth were white because we don't smoke that often, but I didn't want to ruin our moment. I puffed my cigarette until it was a nub, pleased by the heat in my fingers at the end. I promised to come back, visit him, and tip generously.

Outside, though only just after five p.m., the sky was already dark. I couldn't go back to my apartment—my body too tense and my mind too caffeinated—so I wandered into the first district, walked into a bookstore near the university, and found a couch in a back row among piles of large art books. Bright, blue-hued overhead fluorescents stung my eyes, and the smell of printed pages and plastic book jackets welled around me. As I flipped through a book about Egon Schiele featuring endless paintings of naked women in uncomfortable, spread-eagle poses, my mind shuffled through different imagined visions. Emil leaving his apartment. Emil stopping, twisting backwards, and looking into my eyes. Me being arrested by the police, pushed into the back of the cop VW I'd seen the other night, and forced to call my dad to ask for bail and explain that I had followed up school expulsion with an international felony. I turned through pictures of Schiele's later work when the light around me darkened. Looking up, I saw Johanna standing there, smiling. She wore a thick olive-green coat with the coarse texture of an old armchair. It picked up the color in her eyes. Behind her elbow, about half an aisle away looking through the new fiction section, was the guy from the other night. Her alleged ex, Lukas.

"Hey," she said, leaning over to see the book in my lap. Schiele's depiction of a woman, skirt raised, vulva and black pubic hair exposed, stared back. My pulse skipped. I didn't know what to say to not look like a creep. Before I could respond, Johanna whispered, "I love Schiele," and sat down beside me, our hips touching, and slid the book into her lap. She fanned the pages with her thumb until stopping on a painting of a man, his body craning away from the viewer while glancing back with his hand stretched out, as if shielding himself from paparazzi. He was nude, painted in multicolored splotches, and looked to be melting or fading away. Though scribbled and stylized without any attempt at photorealism, Schiele's work has an arresting clarity that's tough to look at.

"This is my favorite. That's him. A self-portrait."

I turned towards her, but we were too close. I stood up, awkwardly, took a step back, and tried to look composed.

"Yeah?"

"Yes. Have you seen his work at the Belvedere? They have a few paintings of his in their permanent gallery."

"Not yet."

"Do it."

"Ok."

She closed the book and folded her hands on top of it.

"I'm sorry about the other night. I didn't mean to be a dick, which, I guess I was—but thanks for inviting me anyway," I said.

She nodded and drummed her fingers on the book. "You were kind of aggressive. Lisi was not too impressed."

"Yeah. But I think that's best because I felt a vibe between Hannes and her."

Johanna laughed. "Did you?"

"Yeah, he seemed to be glaring at me when I talked to

her."

"Alex, Hannes is her brother."

"Fuck. I thought he was in love with her or something."

"Well—he really enjoyed arguing with you and asked me when we're all getting together again." She tilted her head to the side. "Do I receive any matchmaking credit since you hit it off with one member of their family, even if it wasn't the right sibling?"

"I don't think so."

She stood up.

"You're very American, Alex."

"That doesn't sound like a compliment."

She smiled. Running into her felt natural. Maybe Vienna was that kind of town. San Francisco is. Sunday afternoon trips to Safeway with Dad would take hours because he ran into somebody he knew down every aisle. Running your own hardware store is like low-grade politics. The business does better when Dad shakes hands and remembers everyone's name.

"How are things with Lukas?" I asked, glancing over my shoulder. He had disappeared down a different aisle.

She shrugged. "He's depressed, so we're going to dinner."

"Hmm."

"Would you like to join us?"

"Oh no. I imagine that you two are, um—having private conversations."

"We're not back together," she said, with color in her voice. She liked me. Maybe.

"Ok, but I'll pass. I need to sleep. Invite me to another thing and I'll try not to be *too* patriotic. The stuff I said isn't really how I feel. I just find myself sometimes saying whatever would be most inappropriate for the given situation."

She opened her mouth to respond but then stopped. Another customer walked towards us, a teenage boy, and we stood aside to let him pass.

"I'll consider giving you another chance. How's my grand-father?"

"He's keeping me busy." I realized I had never seen them together. "How's school?"

She shrugged. I focused on her eyes and she held my gaze. It altered the dimensions of the room. I had no idea what to say to ensure it wouldn't be another few weeks until we saw one another again. Lukas reappeared, and with an almost silent goodbye, they headed off together. His shoulders sagged and they walked with four inches of space between them. I thought of bringing her back home as my girlfriend and sitting together at Ocean Beach on an overcast morning with the wind flinging sand in our faces. I bought a copy of *Norwegian Wood*, in English, from the bookstore and went back to my place. Waiting for me in my mailbox was a letter from Hank.

> Alex,
> I ran into your dad at his store and he told me you quit Stanford and moved to Europe. That's insane! We talked for a long time, and he invited my parents and me to dinner at your house last Friday. It was cool. I don't think we've ever all been there together without you. He pulled out a world atlas and we all stared at Austria. To be honest, I had no idea where it was. Then we went around the table and mentioned the different ways you were a huge disappointment to us. Just kidding . . . kinda! Your dad is absolutely convinced you will never go back to school. Your mom asked about Janet a lot. Sorry I didn't take things well with her. I guess I dodged a bullet and Rose and I are a thing now anyway. Write me about Vienna and let's hang out when you come back if you ever do.
> —Hank

I read it four or five times in row, each time sticking on different parts, reading subtexts of aggression, or sadness, or sincerity. Seeing his handwriting—the familiar, wobbly letters tilting onto one another—brought back memories of Hank's name scrawled across the bottom of the basketball we'd play with in his parents' driveway. Our teachers from first through fifth grades tried in vain to get his letters to lean in the same direction. The thought of his family and mine together in my parents' cramped dining room made me feel half the globe away, which I guess I was. My parents inherited my grandfather's table when he passed, and even though it was a foot too wide for our space, my dad insisted we keep it. Just working a chair out far enough to sit down made you want to abandon eating altogether.

At 6:45 the next morning, I set out in the dark towards Emil's apartment. Given his age and his lack of activity during the hours I had observed the day before, I wanted to arrive before dawn in case he was an early riser. A fresh snow had fallen in the night, and I was the first to walk upon much of it. It was the first real snow I'd seen in Vienna, and the first real snow I'd seen in my life. It crunched under my sneakers, and my footprints left a meandering trail back to my apartment. The snow gave the city a clean glow, preferable to the empty grey of late fall. While I passed through long, quiet blocks of un-opened storefronts, I practiced reading the names above each door. Blumen, Top Kino, Lebensmittel. They were written in unending, subtle variations of typefaces and colors. I think the city was starting to make sense to me.

As I approached Emil's door, I saw him standing at the Straßenbahn stop across the street, his silhouette illuminated by the single headlight of a train approaching in the distance. With hurried steps, I walked down to the next stop and wait-ed. As the train pulled up with a lurch and clanging bell, I spotted Emil sitting near the front of the first car. I stepped onto the rear of the trailing car. The train took us weaving through the neighborhood, bending softly left and right through broad, angled intersections. The two cars pivoted at their coupling, and when they straightened, I could catch a glimpse of his face. At a stop somewhere in the eighth district, Emil rose and stepped off. I did the same. Though it was only my second day on the job, tracking him came easy. It was almost that the time between following him the day before and now had contracted, and my pursuit of him became one continuous moment. I followed him around the corner and down the block. The first light had begun to leak through the clouds, giving the snow a faint luminescence. Emil wore a long grey trench coat that brushed the ground on full strides, and he carried a russet leather bag over his left shoulder. Midway through the block, he checked his watch. He must have had an appointment. We continued walking for ten to fifteen minutes until we were back in the ninth district, not far from my apartment. Throughout the walk, I mapped each turn in my mind. Certainly, there were more direct routes to get wherever Emil was headed.

The street opened up into a small square as church bells clanged overhead. Stopping at the mouth of the square, I watched as Emil gingerly walked up the steps into a cream-colored cathedral with twin green spires. Compact and plain yet regal, the church resembled a homemade wedding cake. Continuing into the square, I paused at the foot of the church steps. I didn't want to go to Mass. Since talking with Johanna about the story of Isaac, I had been trying to pray more, and to pray with intention. It's almost impossible to keep my prayer from slotting into the familiar grooves of mindless repetition, but I tried. I hadn't been to Mass or picked up a Bible since my first semester at Stanford, about three years ago. I'd found the more I read and the more I listened, the less I could hold it all together. I can't reconcile the world with the book and my choices with the instructions, so I've settled into a stasis of solitary, unexamined faith. The pay from Heinrich wasn't enough to get me back in the door. But, I didn't want to lose Emil.

I scaled the steps and pushed through a heavy wooden door into the dark cathedral. Cold air hung thick and still, tinged with the scent of incense and damp earth. Emil sat midway up on the left, hat off, clasped hands, kneeling. The pews, formed from deep brown walnut, had worn patches from years of patrons standing up, sitting down, kneeling, and repeating. There were only five people in the church. Satisfied that Emil would be there a while, I left. I paced the perimeter of the square, noting the name of the church, the Servitenkirche, as well as each intersecting street. On the close of my loop, I went into a café across from the church steps. They had just opened, and a waiter was still pulling overturned chairs down from the tables. Taking a spot beside the front window, I ordered a coffee and flipped through the previous day's edition of *Die Presse*. The writing lacked Heinrich's vibrance. I took out my notebook and recorded the details of our route. Stepping inside the church had turned my thoughts to the ever-ready question of my own salvation, but I needed to remain present and an unemotional observer. At forty minutes past, three old Austrians hobbled down the church steps. None of them were Emil. Not yet alarmed, I walked to a corner where I could watch exiting parishioners from behind. Another man passed. It wasn't Emil. Not wanting to barge into the church and come face to face with him, I waited. Two more minutes, no Emil. I tried a side door to the church. It opened. Down an unlit hall, past a stone baptismal font, I stepped out into the nave before the main altar. The church was empty.

"Fuck," I whispered.

Looking up, I caught the eyes of a man perched fifty feet above me on the edge of an arch in the ceiling. It was a statue. The man stretched his arm out, elbow almost dislocated, and pointed upward. He looked as though he would fall if he shifted his weight in any direction. I jogged down through the cathedral and out into the square. The sudden transition from darkness to sunlight blinded me. In rough concentric circles I paced out from the church for the next twenty minutes. I found nothing. I had lost Emil.

I spent the rest of the day outside of his apartment. He never reappeared. The week continued without event. I arrived each day around dawn and Emil would emerge once or twice for a short, unremarkable trip. As the week passed, my focus alternated between dedicated precision and listless inattention. A job that had seemed dangerous and morally dubious shifted towards tedium. I still hadn't heard from Johanna, and my new, extended working hours prevented me from sitting in my favorite cafés and attempting awkward small talk with waiters and waitresses.

Sunday evening arrived, and I went to Heinrich's apartment at seven. He invited me in, and we sat in his living room drinking a tannic red wine. He only had two lights on, a floor lamp in the corner and a brass lamp on an end table. It was pitch-black outside, and in the large windows along the wall, I could see our reflection. I in the chair, he on the couch. The lines of our bodies echoed one another. I reached into my bag and pulled out a stack of papers clipped together. I'd stacked and restacked them until every edge lined up just right. An abstract on top summarized my findings, followed by all of my notes. I laid it onto the coffee table between us.

"There you go. All 4,000-schillings worth. My written German, is a, um—work in progress, but I think you'll figure it out."

"Tell me, briefly, what did you notice this week?"

"He rises early, eats a lot of bread, usually Bauernbrot, and goes to Mass twice a week at the Servitenkirche."

"Hardly inflammatory information," he said, smiling. He

reached over and pulled my papers towards him.

"I guess not."

Heinrich seemed to be in a warmer mood that evening than when I'd seen him at Café Schwarzenberg. Having spent a week staring at Emil Eder from a twenty-foot distance and now sitting three feet from Heinrich once again, the contrast between them was unmistakable. Both dressed well and were of the same generation, but Heinrich was taller and looked firmer. Stronger. While I had not yet heard Emil's voice, I imagined it thinner than Heinrich's baritone rasp.

"I wish I had something more interesting to tell you."

"The truth will do. Did you retain copies of your notes?"

"No, it's all there." I lied. I had made two copies over at a shop by the Schwedenplatz. One copy was left out on my desk and another tucked into the back of a kitchen cabinet beneath the manual for my fridge.

"Did Emil meet with anyone during the week?"

"Not that I saw."

"Ok. I will review your reports and call you later this evening to let you know of my satisfaction. On one hand, I am very pleased that nothing untoward was observed, but on the other, I fear something important may have been missed."

"Sure."

I took a sip of my wine and tried to savor it. Fatigue overcame me. It had been a long week. I would have liked to drink the entire bottle and then fall asleep right there in the chair.

"How did you find the assignment?"

"I liked it, but it does take a lot out of you."

"I thought you would. I always enjoyed this type of work. You will build up a capacity for it quickly. And you are certain that you were not noticed by anyone?"

"I think so, yeah."

He placed a white envelope onto the table.

"Here is the balance of your payment for the week. How

did Emil look? Did he seem well?"

"I think so. He looks lonely. Healthy, but lonely."

Heinrich blinked and scratched his chin. "Yes, his wife Anneliese died long ago. They never had children," he said, flatly. He topped off both of our glasses, and we sat in silence for a long while, each drinking our wine. The white label of the bottle peeled up at the top right corner, and Heinrich licked his thumb and smoothed it down. It was a Blaufränkisch from the Burgenland, the region of Austria pressed up against Hungary. I don't know what Heinrich saw in me, but I liked him. I went into his kitchen and poured each of us a glass of cool water. He got up to walk along one of the many bookcases lining the wall and returned with a brown book, *Winnetou*, by Karl May.

"This is a book set in the American West, by a German who I don't believe ever left Europe," he said with a chuckle. "I liked it as a boy. We all did. Since you are from out there, I thought you might enjoy it."

"Thanks," I said, and placed it and the envelope into my bag. We sat until the wine was finished and discussed what the American West is really like. It's the only place I know so I don't have much perspective, but I tried to sound intelligent. I told him the drive from Lisbon to Moscow was about the same length as San Francisco to Washington, DC. He seemed moved by this distance. I've never driven east of Sacramento, it's just a random fact I learned in school when I was twelve. Our conversation slowed and I left his apartment. Two hours later, I sat in the dark on my couch, mostly asleep. The wine had left me with a faint, thoughtless weariness. At eleven p.m., he called. His feedback was brief. He liked my approach and the way I reported things. He left me with a single directive, "Don't be seen."

Over the next week, I fell into a rhythm following Emil. Having a set time to wake each day sharpened my mind to a level that it hadn't been at for some time, if ever. I bought a few different hats and scarves from a flea market beside a church in my neighborhood and cycled through them, never wearing the same combination two days in a row. I continuously tweaked my method of trailing Emil. Sometimes, I would let him pass out of sight and then try to pick him up at a location later within his standard daily loop. Other times, I approached from behind and then brushed past him on the sidewalk. I assumed there was no way to prevent him from becoming at least subconsciously familiar with my appearance, so I wanted him to believe I was an uninteresting resident from his neighborhood. I slept in one day and staked out his apartment throughout one long, frigid evening. He never emerged. On the walk home, in the grey glow before sunrise, I stopped at a bakery and ordered a freshly baked, powdered sugar–dusted *Krapfen*, the same thing I'd eaten on my first day in the city. I asked the cashier for a coffee, "to take with me," and almost gave her an aneurysm. She'd never heard of such a thing and was offended at the concept. She made me take a ceramic cup and saucer with the agreement that I would return them. I sat on the steps outside and watched shopkeepers roll up the metal shutters protecting their storefronts. Some shutters were opaque, obscuring everything. Others were minimalist honeycombs through which windows could be seen. I didn't sleep long at home, the lack of sleep energized me, and I went back out to take my post near Emil's apartment.

I noticed patterns within his building and neighborhood. A staggering number of people moved around the same time every day, at the same speed, with the same expressions. The neighborhood was a clock turning with precision and inevitability. A family of four straggled out around nine a.m. each morning, the father holding the hand of a young son, the mother pushing a squinting daughter in a stroller. The parents' faces were weary while the son's eyes shone as he ran ahead, every day, to stand first in line at the Straßenbahn stop. At ten a.m. on Monday, Wednesday, and Friday a woman buzzed herself into Emil's building and returned twenty minutes later with an old woman dressed in black for a thirty-two-minute walk, always stopping at a pharmacy on the corner marked by a glowing green cross. It was a diverse neighborhood—Vienna's spoken tongues multiply as you sprawl out from its center—and while standing at a busy street corner just before lunch, I would hear four or five different languages in the span of a few minutes' time.

Though we hadn't spoken or made eye contact, I felt an emotional connection to Emil. I started to notice, or believe I noticed, changes in his gait and demeanor as he traveled through different moods. His loneliness was a constant. It came across in the way he avoided standing near others at intersections and how he kept his arms close to his body and his chest tight, as though he wanted to shrink within himself. He continued attending Mass at eight a.m. on Tuesdays and Thursdays. I found the rear exit he used to slip away on his initial visit, and I set up fifty yards away at a small Italian restaurant run by Turkish immigrants. They learned my name, which was dangerous, but as I was the only regular who came by at that time, it was impossible to not stand out.

Knowing almost no one and living entirely in the German language left me in a state of altered homesickness; everything was so divorced from life at Stanford that I often felt the world I had left behind had either ceased to exist or had never existed. The loss that nagged was watching basketball. I tried a few soccer games, but they were simultaneously too boring and too stimulating. There weren't any commercial breaks, so there was never a safe time to grab a drink or pee. Ultimately, almost nothing ever happens in soccer, especially when it seems like something might happen, and anxiously sitting through an entire half with an empty beer and a full bladder brought little satisfaction. I followed the NBA the best I could through copies of *USA Today* found in the lobbies of international hotel chains on the Ring. I stopped by a different hotel each day, usually in the midafternoon when a crowd of guests was waiting to check in, and read the box scores. The Bulls started the season 17–1, one win better than their first eighteen games the year before. I spoke with a few different concierges, and the Marriott agreed to put a game on for me at their "American" bar. They had a satellite feed from the UK that showed a couple games a month, the next one being Bulls at the Raptors. Due to the time difference, the game would begin at one-thirty a.m. on a Monday morning.

I wanted to invite Julian and Markus but couldn't imagine they'd be up for a game that late. It ended up being the second night of a back to back, and the Bulls had lost the first leg. I hoped for an angry, vengeful Jordan. I arrived around midnight, took a seat at the bar, and began to eat one bowl of weird bell pepper–flavored chips after another washed down by Budweisers, which, after taking into account the exchange rate, cost about seven dollars each. The bar resembled an Applebee's with less charm, if it's possible for such a thing to exist. The booths were brown, the walls were brown, the carpet a sea of purple, and the TV oddly dimensioned. It looked like about twenty-seven inches of glass, but the picture didn't fill the screen. On the far wall hung a triptych of posters from Venice Beach, each of which stirred thoughts of LA and Janet. Fuck LA. I read from the book Heinrich had given me until the game started. Reading about the Old West in German was stiff and awkward, but I was into it. I read one line at least twenty times, "Ein Greenhorn ist ein Mensch, welcher nicht von seinem Stuhle aufsteht, wenn eine Lady sich auf denselben setzen will."

In English, this would be something like, "A greenhorn is a man who doesn't give up his seat for a lady."

In German, the phrasing is insane. I tried to picture Heinrich as a boy sitting with Emil between the wars, reading this book, and dreaming about the West. The first half of the game went ok. Jordan played awful, but the Bulls were up 49–48. The halftime show came from London and featured three incredibly British sportscasters sitting in front of a superimposed, blindingly white background. They spoke at length about the city of Toronto and how "cross" Jordan appeared to be at Pippen over missing the switch on Stoudamire pick and rolls. At the start of the third quarter, a group of four guys in cheap, baggy suits arrived and sat down at a table near me. They spoke loudly in English. Clearly, two of the four were French. In the hierarchy of cultural crimes, few approach the audacity of a Frenchman trying to speak English while drunk. I had the misfortune of hearing their entire marble-mouthed, "uhh-hhh"-filled debate about which sport was superior, American football or European soccer. The Bulls pushed the lead to seven by the end of the third when a tall member of their group with wisps of white, straw-like hair floating about the top of his head walked over and placed his hand onto my shoulder. He spoke to me with the warm vanilla-and-corn odor of Jack Daniels on his breath.

"Hey, are you Austrian?" he asked, with a Chicago-tinged nasalness to his vowels.

"I'm American."

"Oh, wonderful. Me too. Are you visiting or do you live here?"

I could tell that our black-vested bartender was listening in as he refilled the tiny straw section of the mid-bar plastic contraption that contains cocktail supplies. I doubt that thing is ever really cleaned.

"I live here I guess."

"Oh great, do you know your way around?"

"Sort of."

"Excellent. We're looking for an, um—a gentleman's club. Do you know a good one?"

One of the other men, a shorter guy, ambled over and stood beside us.

"I do not."

"I've heard that Austrian women are very beautiful," said the shorter one, obviously French.

I shrugged. I'd never heard that, and I wasn't convinced that he had either. Marie Antoinette was from Vienna and the French had cut her head off.

"We're here on business. Industrial generator sales, multimillion-dollar type of deals, and I'm trying to show these two Frenchmen a good time. They are incredible clients, so it would be a *big* help. Supposedly there are some high-class clubs on a street called "the gertel," but we don't speak German. Do you?"

"I do, yeah."

"Do you wanna join us? My company is going to cover everything."

"I actually want to watch this game, if you don't mind."

The short guy beside him screwed his face together and spread his arms wide, palms up.

"Basketball over women? Americans!"

I considered a number of French military–related responses, but I couldn't think straight, as the Bulls had started to turn the ball over and Popeye Jones was scooping up every fucking rebound. I shrugged and the salesmen retreated and continued to talk loudly about Austrian women, French women, American women, and everything but the game. I'm not sure women are that different across borders, but I haven't had the opportunity to research the subject as much as I'd like. Rodman got a late tech and was ejected. Jordan didn't score at all in the second half, which was essentially unprecedented. The Bulls lost 97–89, it was four a.m., and I felt completely empty. Of all the games to stay up for, I got this one. The salesmen left, sufficiently drunk enough to overcome their shyness about asking a taxi driver to take them to see naked women. Part of me wanted to tag along to push my bad mood further and experience complete self-disgust.

I finished my beer. Most of the bar's lights were off, and I needed to leave. I had walked down a narrow hallway in search of the bathroom when I came across a fuchsia pay phone mounted on the wall beside a stack of phone books. Other than the brief call with Mom to let her know I was alive, I hadn't spoken to my parents since I'd landed in Vienna. I pulled out a phone card I had bought from Safeway, laid it on top of the phonebooks, and scratched away at the back with my apartment key until the pin code appeared. The smell of the shit that rubs off, a sweet metal tang, brought memories of lottery tickets and failure. I jogged in place and jumped up and down a few times to wake myself up so I'd sound sober, then picked up the phone and dialed. I really wanted my parents to appreciate that my trip meant more than an escape from school, even if it didn't. A curt female voice with an English accent informed me that I had seventeen minutes of talk time left. I could "top up" now or continue on. I continued. After a series of clicks, pulses, and buzzes, my mom picked up.

"Vogel residence."

I took a deep breath and rubbed my eyes. "Hey, it's Alex."

"Alex? Where are you?"

"I'm in Vienna, Mom."

"I know that, I mean—how are you?"

"I'm good."

"Ok, Alex. Are you sure?"

"Yeah."

"I know this call must be expensive. Your dad wanted to talk to you about something—here he is."

"Alex?"

"Hey, Dad."

"How is it in—Vienna, right? Austria?"

"It's good, Dad. I like it. The public transit is great, much better than home, so it's easy to get around and there's a lot to see. I also get to speak German everywhere, which is cool."

"That's great, Alex. That's great. Hey—I wanted to ask

you something. I can't get the VCR to record *60 Minutes* correctly. It keeps recording *Touched by an Angel* instead. I'm using the VCR-number thing on our new VCR that's supposed to just work."

"VCR Plus."

"Yeah, *exactly*. VCR Plus. You helped us pick this one out at Christmas, remember? I tried to use the code from the *TV Guide* but I don't know what I'm doing wrong."

I placed my forehead against the rough, thick, ivory-colored wallpaper of the hotel hallway.

"Are you there, Alex?"

"Dad, I can't—I can't troubleshoot from here. Try unplugging it and plugging it back in. Maybe have Mom read the number out to you while you type it."

"Ok, ok great. Got it. Let me write this down. Ok . . . um . . . plug it back in and then have your mother read it out to me and that's it. Ok, is this costing this you a lot of money? I should let you go."

"It's ok, Dad. I have a phone card. But yeah, I should go. It's late."

"What time is it there anyway?"

"I'm nine hours ahead. I'll call again in a few weeks."

"Ok, bye Alex. Did you see the Niners lost? Do you get the games over there?"

"Not really, but I did watch some basketball today. I didn't know about the Niners, they're still in first though?"

"Yeah, they are, but Young gets hurt every game. It's not our year. I'll let you go. You are going to come back, right?"

"Yes, I'll come back."

We hung up, and I stood there in the hallway as the remaining lights of the bar were flipped off. I found my way out of the hotel and took the late-night bus home. It took a long time to fall asleep that evening.

VI

It was now December, and with each passing day, the sunlight compressed into a few hours of pale yellow and grey bookended by darkness. My phone rang often and each time I'd freeze, lift the receiver, and hope for Johanna's voice. Unfortunately, the caller would be either a government employee asking if I watched public television, or a woman with an Italian accent looking for someone named Paolo. Emil didn't leave his apartment at all for two days. I sat at a nearby café and read, finishing *Winnetou* and *Norwegian Wood*, which did little to decrease my growing loneliness. I don't believe in Watanabe as an authentic character. Every single woman in the novel eagerly pursues sex with him even though he possesses no apparent charm or appeal. Murakami must have written it to live out unfulfilled fantasies.

After another long morning of no visible activity at Emil's, I went home to nap when Markus called and invited me to a concert that evening near the Danube canal. He told me if I arrived early and helped the band set up, I could have all the cheap red wine I could drink. I accepted the offer. In the afternoon, I didn't have any more books to read, so I sat on a stone staircase a block from Emil's door and smoked one Marlboro after another. The cold in my fingertips made it hard to light each cigarette. At about two p.m., the door to his building opened and he walked out. He wore a brown hat and a trim-fitting hunter green sweater and carried his usual messenger bag. He passed me. I waited a few beats, then followed. Once we crossed over the busy Gürtel, he turned right, and we continued through quiet, rolling streets. About fifteen minutes later, we turned left onto Westbahnstraße. It's a short street, only five blocks, that I'd never walked down before. The first two blocks featured a stunning lineup of camera shops, each with a broad plate-glass window containing rows and rows of evenly spaced, pristine cameras. The zenith of these shops, the Leica Vintage Shop, had the most expansive display, with a progression of modern to classic models stretching back into the 1930s. Prices were propped beside each camera, scrawled in silver pen onto wedges of folded black paper. Separating me from over five hundred thousand dollars' worth of chromed beauty was only two millimeters of glass.

I needed a camera. My uncle shot for the *Chronicle* in the '80s, and sometimes he would let me paw through his box of semi-working bodies and spare lenses. On the job, he mainly used Nikon gear, but he had an assortment of things he'd picked up, my favorite of which was a Hasselblad 500C/M from 1978. It's a descendant of the models used in the Apollo missions, and my uncle loved to tell me how over the course of the program they'd left twelve Hasselblad bodies behind on the lunar surface to reduce cargo weight. The cameras are still right up there, lying in the dust, and if we could just get to the moon, we could have them.

I love the way the whole 500C/M comes apart, like a weapon. Its chrome dark slide is a perfect miniature of the cleavers that magicians use to slice their assistants in half. Lining it up and sliding it in is satisfying. I always experience a lightness when I look down into the camera's waist-level viewfinder. People appear flipped horizontally and seem to float, like ethereal ghosts. The camera is medium format so it's expensive to shoot, but we could use my uncle's bathroom as a darkroom and we would make prints down at a communal lab in the Castro. Most of my photos were of street signs and doorways near the beach, and my friends. A Hasselblad is heavy—it's not meant for street photography—but I liked lugging it around and waiting for puffy, late afternoon clouds to blanket the sun, letting soft light bleed through onto the city. I only shot at $f/2.8$, the widest the 80mm Planar could go. Whenever I gave a portrait to someone and saw it end up on display in their home, an unmatched pride filled me. Any credit I received was misplaced—photography is a technical skill, not an art—but I accepted it anyway.

Emil stopped beside a few storefronts and then stepped into a narrow shop and spoke with a clerk behind the counter. He opened his leather bag, took out a silver camera—some kind of 35mm—and handed it over. I walked a block and a half away and stood against the wall. I had been following too close. The days without action had warped my perception, and I wanted to grant him a wide berth. Standing there, I witnessed the incredible charm of Westbahnstraße as a public theater of window shopping. A steady trickle of shoppers turned onto the street and paced slowly, staring and motioning into each window, faces stern and focused, lips parted. They leaned back and forward, hands flat along their brow to shield the sun. They spoke in hushed tones to their companions. One old man in a khaki coat remained in one spot, unmoving and bewildered, for at least eight minutes. He didn't look like a tourist. He must have seen many of these cameras on sale for decades, and yet, the wonder remained. Only about one in six customers actually went into a shop, and I'm not certain anyone bought anything in the twenty minutes I waited outside.

Emil came out and walked directly towards me. I turned away and ducked into a stationary store. Through its front window, I saw a Straßenbahn pull up and Emil board the second car. Once he took a seat, facing forward, I sprinted out and stepped onto the last car as the doors closed. He disembarked near the Rathaus but nobody else did. It was a quiet afternoon without much foot traffic. I wanted to maintain distance, so I waited another stop, jumped off, and hurried back. I caught a glimpse of his hat as he entered a slate-grey building. A sign at the entrance in round, sans-serif font read *Wiener Stadt und Landesarchiv*. Vienna City and State Archives. It was the most substantial action I'd seen in over two weeks of following him. I circled the building. Most of the windows had their shades drawn. The few that didn't only revealed pale government employees slouched over their desks.

About an hour after going in, he walked out with great haste, headed due west. He checked his watch a few times without stopping and moved faster than I would have imagined possible. We reached Josefstädter Straße U-Bahn station, the station closest to his apartment, and climbed up to the northbound platform. During this portion, the U6 line sits on elevated, open-air tracks. I'd never see him take the U-Bahn before. We rode one stop to Alser Straße, and he stepped off the train and onto the platform as passengers surged in both directions around him. I did the same, two cars away. When the doors started to close, he stepped backwards onto the train. I did as well, but the doors of my car slammed hard into my collarbone, jolting me with enough pain to buckle my knees. The doors retreated an inch with a lurch, allowing me to stumble on board. A man standing by the door glared at me, his hand gripping an orange loop hanging from the ceiling. He made no effort to help. The train accelerated, and I shuffled to an empty seat facing the rear of the train, reached into my bag, and changed my jacket and hat. I rubbed at my collarbone. It wasn't broken but it ached, and the lines of the door were visible in purple on my skin. We rode to the end of the line, and Emil got off at Floridsdorf: a shining, sprawling new station in the middle of nowhere.

He ascended four flights of stairs then sat down at a table with metal chairs by a bakery kiosk. From his position, he could see freely in any direction. I crouched a few steps beneath his level with a partial view of his face. Someone sat down across from him, and they began to talk. Emil appeared to be listening intently. I'd already taken things too far. This was the longest I'd been close to Emil on any single day. I crept up a half step, craning to glimpse the other person—a man, black hair, maybe in his fifties—when a firm "Entschuldigung" came from beside me. It was spoken by a man in a suit as he passed by on the stairs, brushing against my shoulder. I instinctively retreated down a flight, heart thumping. I couldn't push things any further. I descended into the subway and took the first train that arrived.

The look on Emil's face had been unlike any I'd seen from him yet. Stiff around the eyes, lips tensed. It was fear. I worked my way back across town and walked into the archives building. A white hallway with a low drop ceiling reminiscent of my mom's surgical ward led to a woman at a reception desk. She directed me down a stairway into the public access room. It was an expansive, subterranean space with long tables down the center and binder-filled metal shelves along the wall. In the corner, facing the room, sat a clerk behind a desk. He wore a blue shirt and square glasses and was leaning back with a book in hand. His long legs stretched out beyond the desk, pant legs riding up to reveal white, hairy ankles. I pulled a random orange binder from a shelf and sat down. It contained a record of property sales from the last ninety days in Vienna. Apartments were much cheaper than in SF, although I didn't have any real feel for how large a square meter was. At one of the central tables, a man in a navy button-up shirt and jeans looked over a blueprint. After five minutes of running his hands over it and making various grunts, he rolled it up and carried it over to the clerk. Without closing his book, the clerk reached to his side, picked up a wooden clipboard and extended it towards the man. The man scribbled something on it, laid the blueprint on the desk, and left. A minute later, the clerk placed his book face down and carried the blueprint down a hallway behind him. When he returned, I took a breath, released it, and walked over. The clerk looked up with tired eyes. The only natural light in the room seeped in from small slit-like windows just below the ceiling. Metal hexagons were embedded into their glass for an extra layer of security. It couldn't have been a nice place to sit all day.

"Hi, I'm a student at the University of Vienna. I'm sorry, it's my first time in here. I'm doing a research paper on the construction of the Parliament building. You know, the one on the Ringstraße. I was told that I can check out relevant files here?"

"Yes, we have things like that. For which course is this?"

An odd question, but there was no way this guy knew every course at the university.

"It's a class for exchange students. We each have to do a report on a building from the Ring. I wanted the Rathaus but somebody else took it first, so they're making me do Parliament. I don't like the way it looks, honestly."

The clerk closed his book, a green hardback copy of *Siddhartha*. He blinked a few times, then opened his eyes wide. The lenses of his glasses made his pupils appear to levitate in front of his face.

"May I see your student ID?"

"I actually don't have it yet. I just got here from California."

He bit his lip and stared through me.

"Ok, then you cannot take anything with you, but you may view things here. One moment."

He turned and went down the hallway. On the clipboard beside his chair, I could see Emil's name written in pen alongside a reference number, HB400148275. I repeated it over and over in my head until the clerk returned with a weathered, ten-inch-thick leather book. He laid it down onto the desk and turned the clipboard towards me.

"And your name?"

"Mike."

"Please sign here, Mike."

I wrote the name, "Mike Mercker" in clean print. It was the name of the kid I hated most from our middle school baseball team. Mike never missed an opportunity to flick me in my ears or gleek on me during bus rides to our games. Beside the name, the clerk wrote the reference number of the book, then "Fritz K".

"Fritz K?"

"That is me."

"Thanks for your help."

He smiled and bowed with a flourish. I nodded back and carried the leather book to a table far from him. I would have to come back another day to ask for Emil's item. My right shoulder stiffened where the U-bahn door had closed on it, so I used my left hand to flip the book's pages. They turned smoothly and smelled of rubber cement and raisins. The book contained a list of files related to the Parliament building. I understood almost none of the abbreviations, and I'm certain the book hadn't been opened in at least fifty, maybe a hundred years. I scribbled down the reference number of what I took to be a plan of some part of the staircase leading into the building. I went back to Fritz and asked for the file, and he disappeared again. I quickly took out my pad and jotted down the reference number Emil had requested. Fritz returned after some time with a four-foot-long black leather tube. I accepted it, walked over to a table, uncapped it, and pulled out a thin, semitranslucent piece of paper containing an intricate and beautiful outline of the Parliament's front steps, hand sketched in blue ink. In the upper left corner was a golden double-headed eagle with *Kaiser und Koenig* beneath it: the official mark of the Kaiser of the Austro-Hungarian empire. In the bottom right, it was signed *Hansen 1872*. To be able to walk in without any ID and access 124-year-old pieces of paper was phenomenal. In the rooms through the door behind Fritz must have been thousands upon thousands of items like that. Looking over the sketch of the staircase, I couldn't believe someone could be so skilled with their hands. I can barely address a letter successfully. It's almost suffocating to imagine how much past there is out there, stacking up, filling rooms and rooms with personal and official detritus, especially in Europe. I requested a few more things from Fritz for the hell of it. I asked him what his favorite building was in Vienna. He said the Hundertwasserhaus, which I pretended to be aware of and adore as well. I left with the plan to return in three days and request the same file as Emil.

I still had a few hours before I needed to meet Markus, so I went back to Westbahnstraße in search of a camera. If I'd had one, I could have photographed Emil's meeting at Floridsdorf. I'd wanted to ask my uncle to borrow one before the trip, but he's my father's brother and I wasn't ready for the lecture on academic dishonesty required for a chance at an old Nikon. I did a steady loop down the street and back, peering into each shop's window, before walking into the Leica Vintage Shop. It is unquestionably the best shop I've ever seen or could even imagine. Inside, glass cases with mirrored backs lined every wall, and cameras filled every inch of every case. The store had multiple rooms, each a different shape, each a slightly different height, so you had to take awkward little steps up or down as you went from one room to the next. They have Leicas, obviously—in fact, I believe they have every Leica ever made—but they also have every camera of note from any manufacturer going back to the advent of photography. Multiple employees milled about, one standing behind the counter by the entrance, one half visible in a stock room, and another sitting in the rear at a desk, overlooking an opened ledger. I crouched down and scanned through cases for so long that my thighs began to burn. I lost track of time staring into a case that held the progression of Leica from the II's and III's into the M series, and on to the most recent model, the M6. The transition from the chrome bodies and lenses of the '60s to the black cameras of the '80s was a sartorial misstep. I asked to look at the most expensive thing I could find, an f/1 Noctilux, the fastest production lens ever made by Leica. With it, you can take a photo at the edge of darkness. The employee, a short, tanned man named Karl, handed it over without pause. Its weight substantial in my hand, I worked the aperture blades opened and closed. They wound smoothly together, all ten of them, and at each stop formed a close-to-perfect circle. I put it down and wiped my sweating hands on my jeans. This was an early prototype version, listed for the equivalent of $25,000.

"This is a very special lens, you see," said Karl.

"It's incredible."

Karl reached into the case, pulled out a mint-condition, used black M6 body, and placed it onto the glass countertop. With a click, I mounted the lens and mimed taking a photo across the room.

"Do you do a lot of night photography?" Karl asked.

"I would like to." Aiming and twisting the Noctilux felt like maneuvering the cannon of a tank. At wide open with someone the minimum distance away, your focus area would be half the length of a person's eyelashes. I couldn't afford the lens, or any of the Leica stuff. I unmounted it and handed it back to Karl.

"I definitely want to go Leica, but I can't today. What bodies do you have for 35mm with a couple prime lenses for around 3,000 schillings?"

"Rangefinder?"

"Doesn't have to be."

He returned the M6 and Noctilux to their homes, came out from behind the counter, and led me to a far corner of the room.

"We have a Minolta that is fairly priced. It utilizes an M39 mount, so it is quite versatile. It comes with a 50mm Rokkor, which was the standard kit lens. But, with 3,500 schillings, you could also add an 85mm Super Takumar, which is astounding."

He pulled the camera and lenses from the case and put them onto a nearby counter. I mounted the 50mm and actuated the shutter a few times. Compared to the quiet shutter of the M6, the clang of the Minolta mirror sounded like a metal chair falling over.

"It's not quite the M6."

Karl smiled. The camera smelled like a wet cigar and the vinyl backseat of an Oldsmobile parked in the sun. I liked it. The 85mm Super Takumar lens was coated and gave off a rainbow sheen in the light. I bought it all and a few rolls of 400 Tri-X.

At eight p.m., I met Markus and helped his friends lug their equipment out of their brown VW van, down a staircase so narrow my shoulders brushed against the walls, and into a compact, windowless cinder block room that served as a music venue. It had started to rain, and water flowed down the staircase's edge and pooled at the bottom in a black puddle. The strain loosened my aching shoulder and cleared my mind. Markus apparently runs a small record label and manages the band for free. According to him it was "nonprofit, although, not intentionally so." After setting up, while the band tuned their instruments and warmed up, Markus and I sat together in a side room that had a toilet in the corner, so I guess technically a bathroom. There wasn't a sink, though. We drank boozy red wine from plastic cups, as promised. The acid in the wine pulled out chemical scents from the cup, but I didn't mind. Buzzing and fuzz from the band's bass player thumped through the wall, and Markus tapped along with his foot. I showed him my camera while I loaded a roll of film and we made small talk, but thoughts of Emil and Heinrich swelled inside me. I'd managed to stay composed and forward moving by trying not to reflect beyond the previous fifteen minutes of my life. Not having friends in Vienna made this easier. Drinking with someone who might become my friend threatened my stoicism.

"How's it going with the Austrian bird, Johanna? Any updates?"

I shrugged. "I can't remember when you and I last talked, but I think I fucked it up with her, but maybe not completely."

Markus nodded vigorously. His green T-shirt was damp with sweat from lifting equipment.

"What did you do?"

"Said some stupid American shit."

"Hmm. Perhaps forgivable, given your background."

"Thanks. I ran into her after the incident, and I apologized. I think I'll see her again. I hope so at least. How about you?"

"I have not been out offending women with my American sensibilities."

"Really? The American thing can be charming."

"That is certain. I'm being charmed by it right now."

"Thanks. Are you seeing anyone at all? You mentioned the other night that I should pursue a Balkan girl instead of Johanna. That was very specific advice."

He rubbed his hand along his jawline. His stubble was longer, approaching a beard, and the extra length made the silver strands stand out.

"Are you listening to what I say? That's unadvised."

"I'm listening."

"I did consider coming out of retirement for an Ana—*the* Ana—but it's not looking too promising."

"Why not?"

He pressed his palms together and squeezed his fingers closed.

"I used to believe, when I was young like you, that the

myriad of life experiences, especially the difficult ones, would aggregate within me and help me develop into a strong, capable person. I believed that's what aging was. Unfortunately, I've come to find out that as the years and memories pile up, it's harder to remember the details of anything, and that the painful experiences have only diminished me. Ana deserves better."

"I don't really follow."

"I would be a shitty partner. Too much baggage. Too needy."

"Shouldn't you let her decide that?"

"There's no responsibility on the seller to adequately represent his goods?"

"No. Dating is all about delaying the reveal of your limitations." Markus smiled. We each drank wine from our cups, and I stared at the toilet in the corner. There is something about being in a room without windows. The air hangs motionless and thick, making it easier to get drunk and easier to be open. "But I know your real problem," I added.

"Do you?"

"You are too articulate."

"Never been told that before."

I laughed. "You are smart so you can put a story together that sounds convincing, but you're overthinking it. You're just scared." He lifted his eyebrows and tilted his head to the side. "I'm just making this up, though. What's Ana like?"

"Ana is insane. She's from the countryside, so she's the sort of girl who relishes eating plain bread and butter and things like that. A delicacy for her is strawberry jam. We're the same age, forty-one, and her first husband was an abusive man. He died, so she brings no living baggage. She's sweet."

"Ok."

"She told me something I keep thinking about."

"Yeah?"

"She was at my apartment. We were going to dinner, so I

took a shower and got dressed. Once I was ready and waiting by the door, she came up and hugged me and smiled and said she loved that even after showering I still smelled a bit, like a real man."

"Amazing."

"I know. I'm uncertain how I'm supposed to respond to this information."

"Marry her."

Markus nodded and ran his hand through his hair. We continued dissecting the merits of Ana's rural childhood, but the expression on Emil's face at the station kept nudging me out of the conversation. I tried to focus on Markus's eyes, or the taste of our wine, but I couldn't bring myself back into the room. Different phrasings of different sentences flashed through my mind. I blurted out, barely audible, "Hey, can I tell you about something?"

Markus leaned forward. "Of course."

"I'm doing some work for Johanna's grandfather and it's illegal."

"What kind of illegal?"

"I, well I don't know if it's illegal, actually. He's having me follow around some old guy for him."

"Follow him around and do what?"

"Just report what's he doing. Her grandfather told me that this guy might be planning something bad."

"You know not to trust anyone in this country born before 1935, right?"

"I've wondered about that."

Markus stared blankly for a few moments while the riff from "Interstate Love Song" came through the wall. I hate STP, but I love that song.

"What's her grandfather's name?"

"Heinrich."

"Heinrich," he repeated. Markus seemed to put a lot of stock into names. "Does your girl know?"

"Johanna? No. She's really not my girl though. Not yet."

He picked up the wine bottle and put it down again.

"Do you have any idea what it's really about? Why Heinrich has you doing this?"

"No."

"I suppose it might be regular old man shit. Or, it might be old man Nazi shit."

The word spoken in German, *Nationalsozialistische*, rung out. It stuck in the mind, all nine syllables of it. I didn't want to be the American that assumed every grey-haired Austrian strolling through Vienna was a former commandant at Auschwitz, but hearing Markus, a German, broach the concept, released some tension. I needed to consider all possibilities. I had to.

"Yeah. I don't know. The guy I'm following, Emil Eder, is researching something at the city archives, but I'm not sure what. I know that he and Heinrich go back to childhood and I know that Heinrich's brother died in the war, but that's about all I know."

I finished my wine and refilled our cups. The wine came in a one-and-a-half liter magnum bottle. Five more, unopened, sat in the corner of the room, a little too close to the toilet.

"Pardon my question, but is Johanna worth this? Or did you just fall in love with the first girl you met once you stepped off the plane?"

I laughed. "I mean, she wasn't the *first* girl I met. It was day *two* in Vienna, so—but, I like her. There's actually not a lot of strain with her. There is around the details, but the vibe between us isn't one I think I can just pass up. It might be pretty rare. Maybe singular."

Marcus nodded reverently. "Is there anything else Heinrich has asked you to do?"

"No. Well, I was doing some file organization stuff before following this guy, but nothing interesting."

"Do you trust him?"

"Prior to our conversation right now, I did, yeah. I like him, but I'm biased because I'm lonely as fuck and he's been the only person I talk to on a regular basis. Obviously, because he's Johanna's family, I desperately want him to like me. What makes you suspect the Nazi angle?"

Markus leaned back and looked up at the plaster ceiling.

"A negative intuition, I suppose. I grew up beneath the Stasi with everyone spying on their neighbors all of the time. I don't have patience for that way of life anymore. I don't understand why he would select you for this."

"He said it's because I don't know anyone in Vienna, so I was more likely to keep it secret. He used to be a reporter, and I think this type of snooping is normal for him."

"Perhaps. Or perhaps you are disposable and he's grooming you for something worse. Wrap it up and focus on the girl. Whatever is between these old bastards, you want to stay out of it."

"Ok."

Speaking about it, admitting to someone what was happening, weighed my body down. I knew I wouldn't be able to quit. I liked Heinrich, and I enjoyed the work.

"He did tell me he wanted to see the Russian monument by Schwarzenbergplatz destroyed."

"Well, the man has taste at least. "

We talked a while longer and then people began to filter in, and the concert started. I dug the band. They didn't have a PA and the acoustics were abysmal, but they played loud with a scratchy, natural distortion and it worked. Around thirty people showed up, and they all seemed to either know the band and each other. The lead singer, Sophie, had a shaved head and played an aquamarine Fender Jaguar. She sang in English in a mellow growl without any accent, which was surprising because we'd spoken beforehand and her conversational English had been thickly Austrian. Their songs sounded like something halfway between Pulp and Oasis. After about forty-five minutes of playing, the drummer stood up and extended his sticks towards Markus. Markus sat down, and they ran through the last four songs of the *Abbey Road* medley. The wrinkles around Markus's eyes revealed that he was fifteen to twenty years older than the rest of the band, but he kept a strong, driving beat and killed the solo at the start of the "The End." When the medley was finished, he got up, everyone clapped, and the original drummer returned for the band to close with a cover of "Common People," which is a fantastic song. Sophie looked directly at me through most of it. We helped them load their stuff into their van, and then she and I shared a long hug. She was sweaty and beautiful. They were headed to Graz to play a concert the following night.

The next day, Johanna called and invited me to meet her and her friends on Sunday afternoon at a restaurant run by a winemaker on the outskirts of the city. Her friend's mom was close to the owner, and due to a mix-up while bottling their harvest, they had an excess of white wine. We were commanded to drink as much as we could. I made plans to meet with Heinrich beforehand and deliver my report. For the rest of the week, Emil only left his apartment to buy bread and go to church. When I wrote my report, I left out the fact that I had visited the archives and figured out the reference number to the file that Emil had requested. Speaking with Markus had shifted my position. I wanted to evaluate the situation independently of Heinrich's influence, and I wanted leverage. If I learned something meaningful, I could test his truthfulness. I decided to wait a few more days to request the file so I wouldn't alert the clerk, in case it was a memorable artifact. When I delivered the report, I gave a brief summary to Heinrich over coffee in his apartment. As I spoke, his face turned ashen.

"I see. And you don't know whom he met at the station?"

"No. I actually bought a camera later that day so I could take a picture if they met again, but they haven't."

"What did the other person look like?"

"A regular guy. Mid-fifties. Black hair."

"And you don't know what Emil did inside the archives?"

"No. He was in there for about an hour. I stayed outside." My face warmed, but I kept a blank look. Heinrich looked down into his coffee.

"This is not good, Alex. Thank you for your help. Please, do not follow him anymore until I give further instructions. I will need some time to think about what's next."

"Sure. Did you want me to come organize files, or—?"

"No, no, that's ok. I will be in touch soon."

I left and headed to the restaurant to meet Johanna. It was far away. I had to take a Straßenbahn, the subway, and then a bus, which left me to endure expanses of time staring at strangers and floating in thought. The number of fragile old women in brown fur coats wobbling around on Vienna's public transit is beyond calculation. Their coats look like squirrel tails crudely sewn together into a cloak that extends down to the ankle. Without exception, every woman in fur drags along a small dog. Perhaps the coats are made from the dog's ancestors. The women were short with boxy shoulders and hips, and I imagine they were on the way to or from their husband's long-cold graves. I had not yet visited a cemetery in Austria, but gauging by the quantity of the red mourning candles available within each grocery store, graves must be well attended.

Eventually, I made it to the restaurant. Johanna and her friends stood inside the entrance. She was in the middle of a conversation when I entered, so I orbited on the periphery of their circle, nodding to nothing in particular. When the group moved to sit down, I ended up thrust into the back corner of a wooden booth next to another stray foreigner her friends had picked up, a curly-haired girl named Zeinab. Everyone else seemed to know one another, so Zeinab and I paired off and discussed our lives. She made continuous eye contact with me as we spoke, and said my name a lot: "Listen, Alex" and

"Alex. You are kidding me." We shared stories about the pain of attempted Austrian integration over wooden cutting boards piled with cold slices of meat and cheese. She was an Erasmus student from Stuttgart living in Vienna for a semester. Her background was Lebanese, and she was tired of everyone in the city, Austrians and otherwise, assuming she was Turkish. She spoke German with an amusing dialect; every word had a "le" added to the end of it. I liked it. She didn't eat pork, so I ate hers, and mine, and impressed myself with the amount of food I was able to put down. Johanna sat at the next table over, and I snuck glances at her throughout the evening. I looked so often that Zeinab said, "Johanna huh? She's very pretty."

"Oh, what?"

"Oh, come on, Alex. You are staring at her."

"Sorry."

"It's ok, I was with her earlier at her flat. I'm friends with one of her roommates. We were all chatting, and Johanna mentioned you were coming. *The American.*"

"Oh yeah? Did she say anything else?"

"No, but I can tell that she cares about you. I think she is a very smart and serious girl. I don't know that she's like an American girl."

There was a lot to unpack in that statement. We both watched Johanna for a while. She was an active listener, prodding her friends with sincere questions during discussions and frictionlessly steering them towards her position. She may have looked our direction a few times, but I'm not certain.

"When did you move to Germany?" I asked Zeinab.

"I was born there."

"Oh, so you're a German."

"No. It's not like America. You can't be German unless you are *German.* No matter how long you've been there. Not to most people, at least."

"Do you feel German?"

"In Germany, I feel Lebanese. In Lebanon, I feel German."

Johanna smiled widely at something the girl across from her said.

"See, she's very pretty, I told you," said Zeinab.

"Yeah, I'm aware. You said Johanna's not like an American girl. What does that mean?"

"Oh, haha. American girls are just—you know."

"Do I?"

"Maybe you don't know."

She refilled our wine glasses from a large carafe in the center of the table. The wine was dark, almost golden, and thickly sweet.

"Can things work between foreigners?" I asked.

"Maybe."

"I don't think I understand the Austrians yet."

"What's to understand? Have you made any friends here?"

"I know one East German and one Austrian, but the Austrian is seventy-something years old."

"What?"

"Yeah, he's Johanna's grandfather. I needed a job, and she connected us."

"Oh, brother. It's hard for foreigners to be together in a real relationship. Hooking up is very easy with foreigners, but not love. My boyfriend is American."

"Uh-oh."

Zeinab leaned her head back and laughed, a wrinkled-nose, hearty laugh. She wiped her eyes, then said, "The thing about foreigners is that the things you assume are the same for all people, the foundations, all turn out to be wrong. Your relationship will be built on sand. *But* you speak her language somewhat, so that's good. My boyfriend doesn't know any German and he absolutely refuses to learn."

"Somewhat? Everyone tells me my German is great."

She laughed again, louder than last time, and put her hand onto my knee.

"Alex, nobody expects anything from Americans. Your pronunciation could be much better."

I stared forward. "Damn. What do I say wrong?"

"The Ö."

In German, the name of Austria is *Österreich*. The Ö is the hardest of the extra letters in their alphabet and is pronounced something like "oeh." It's a terrible language.

"You mean I can't even say Österreich right? I live here."

She shook her head. "No, you cannot. But who cares. Österreich is such a backwards country anyway. You say Deutschland very well, come live there. I have friends who love Americans."

We continued for a couple hours, observing Johanna and drinking wine. Zeinab was impossibly open and told me literally every piece of information she knew about everyone else at the restaurant. I didn't doubt that whatever I shared with her would be shortly broadcast to all of western Europe. I stood up, slightly unsteady, and went in search of the bathroom. It was at the end of a tiled hallway, and there was a line. Standing in back wearing faded, snug-fitting black jeans and a loose white T-shirt was Johanna. I walked up and pushed her gently in the shoulder. She turned and smiled, her cheeks flushed red from drinking.

"Hey, Alex! Thank you for coming."

"Thanks for inviting me."

"You met Zeinab?"

"Yeah, she's great. We're taking turns talking bad about Austrians."

Johanna grinned and rolled her eyes.

"How's school?" I asked.

She shrugged. "It's bad."

"Just quit. I did, look at me."

"Hmmm—I like what I'm studying, though. I think I'm the problem, not the school."

"That's harder to fix."

"How is it spending so much time with my grandfather?"

The bathroom door opened, a guy walked out, a short woman went in, and the entire line took a step forward.

"He's keeping me busy, but it's interesting. You and he are similar, I think. He's just much older and male."

She smiled, and I saw her dimple again. The only light in the hallway came from an exposed bulb dangling high in the corner above the bathroom door. I would have loved to grab my camera and take her picture. Her face would be in shadow, but her silhouette would be crisp. I didn't really know if Heinrich and she were similar, I just wanted to sound clever.

"What are he and I like?"

I shrugged. "I'm not sure my German fluency is enough to describe the intricacies of the Trost family."

Her eyes narrowed. "Try in English."

"Well, your English isn't that good."

"You have no idea how good my English is! I've offered, but you always want to speak German."

"Serious question. Do I pronounce the Ö right? Do I say Österreich well?"

Her eyes shone. Someone came up behind me to get in line, so I moved an inch closer to her. My pulse quickened.

"I like the way you say it."

"But is it right?"

"Of course not. But I don't want you to learn to say it the right way."

"Come on, teach me."

"It's *Österreich*. You say it more like *Österreich*."

"You just said the same word the exact same way twice in a row." She placed her hand around the back of my neck and shook her head. "Fuck. Ok, next time we'll speak in English, and I'll make you feel bad. I've been dreaming in German— bad German, obviously—and when I can't figure out how to say something I wake up, and my calves feel tight and I can't sleep, so I'm overdue for English."

The bathroom door opened once again, the woman walked out, and another one in front of us entered. Johanna pulled her hand away and we stepped forward. Now, she was first in line. I didn't have much more time with her. I was drunk. I'm not sure she was. She opened her mouth to say something but stopped. Before I could speak, the bathroom door opened, and the woman walked out, looking down as she slipped past us. She was so quick, there was no way she had time to do anything in there. Johanna and I stood by the open doorway, a vague hint of lavender in the air.

"Let's hang out. Just us, sometime soon," I said.

"Like a date? I don't really go on dates."

"A date? No way. *Definitely* not that."

She took a step backwards into the light of the bathroom and leaned her head to the side.

"Ok. I'll give you a call next week if I have time," she said, and closed the door. The door's paint was fern green with a glossy shine that revealed each brushstroke. Pits and valleys hinted at underlying layers of different colors. It must have been repainted a thousand times. A few minutes later, the door opened. I backed up, and as she passed me, she smiled, her eyes darting up to look into my mine. She gave my side a small squeeze and continued on. After peeing, I went back to the table and Zeinab.

"I saw Johanna in the hallway. I asked her on a date."

"And?"

"She said she'd call me if she has time."

Zeinab lifted her glass into the air.

"She will have time, Alex."

I raised my glass, and we tapped them together. A plate of cold fried chicken appeared from somewhere, and I ate almost all of it. Another half carafe of wine later, I departed. I exchanged numbers and cheek kisses with Zeinab—we'd formed a bond—and gave a nod towards Johanna. On the long, multi-transit ride back, my body hummed with alcohol and anticipation. Things might actually work out. The night was black and starless, and by the time I reached my apartment, it was after nine p.m. I changed out of my clothes, downed a few glasses of cold water, and lay on my bed. I was so overcome with joy that my thoughts receded, and I fell into real sleep. Sometime later, the phone rang. I sat up in the darkness, eyes heavy. It took a moment to realize where and when it was. I grabbed the receiver.

"Alex, are you there?" It was Heinrich.

"Yeah, hey, yeah. It's me."

"Your report this week was excellent. Exceptionally thorough and very well organized."

"Ok."

"Can we meet? There is something for us to discuss." His tone was dry and calm.

"Sure, when? Tomorrow?"

"Now is preferable. I can come to your apartment if that's easier."

I stumbled over to the window and looked out onto the square below. It was cold outside, and I wanted to lay back down and sleep until whenever.

"Can't we just talk on the phone?"

"It must be in person, Alex. I'm sorry for the inconvenience."

"Yeah. Ok. How about meeting outside the Bank Austria at the corner of Porzellangasse and Fürstengasse? I'm not really set up to host here."

"Ok. Twenty minutes?"

"Let's do thirty."

I stared for a while and watched Straßenbahn after Straßenbahn careen from around the corner into the square, stop in front of Franz-Josefs-Bahnhof, and then continue into the city. From this height, their movements appeared organic yet unsettling, like centipedes. Occasionally, one of the stiff metal arms that extend from their first car to draw power from the overhead lines would slip and spark an arc of electricity, casting blue on the faces of waiting passengers. I put on my shoes and clothes and rushed down the stairs and towards the bank. The freezing air outside grabbed me immediately. It assaulted every piece of exposed skin; my cheeks and ears and ankles stung. The brief sleep had transformed my wine buzz into a pressure headache that pushed out from behind my eyes. As I approached the bank, I saw Heinrich standing there, at ease in a black coat, black hat, and long grey scarf neatly tied. He smiled when I reached the steps.

"Alex, thank you for meeting me. I do realize it's late."

"It's ok. What's up?"

He extended an envelope in his gloved hand. The guy certainly had a lot of envelopes and an aversion to exchanging loose items. I took it and looked inside. It contained many hundred schilling bills. More than I'd seen at once before.

"I would like to pay you double this week. I have a special request. There are two keys there."

I squeezed the envelope with my cold, exposed fingers. Something hard ran alongside the bills.

"The keys are for Emil's apartment. Outer and inner doors. Your news about him at the archives accelerates things. Although helpful, the only thing we really learned is that we might be running out of time. I need you to go into his apartment, document all that you see, and take anything that looks suspicious."

"What?"

"We don't have much time. I fear another week without more information might be untenable."

I stared at Heinrich. "I'm not going to break into someone's apartment."

"That is why I'm giving you a key."

"I could get thrown into jail or deported." I looked at a clock across the street. Its white face glowed brightly. Thick black lines marked the minutes. "Sorry, but I don't think I can do this." I extended the envelope back towards him. His hands remained thrust into his pockets. The cold didn't seem to affect him.

"I can guarantee that Emil will not be home from seven until nine tomorrow evening. There is no risk." A silver Mercedes station wagon passed by, washing the bank behind us in yellow light. "For your protection, I cannot tell you more, but it is important that you do this. You'll have to trust me."

I lowered my hand with the envelope to my side. The escalation that Markus warned me about had arrived.

"What am I looking for?"

"Things indicating an obsession with a person or a place. Maps, photography, research that contains a single focus."

"You should just call the police. I mean, I'm just some random guy. I'll probably fuck it up, and if I get arrested, I'll be honest, I'm going to tell them you put me up to this."

His face remained calm.

"I understand your fear, but it is not yet a matter for the police. This still requires delicacy. As I said before, Emil is my friend. I wish him no harm. If you are caught, please do give my name, and I will see to it that you are released. You would likely have to leave the country, but I could ensure that you would avoid prosecution."

I took a step back and flexed my hands. I should have put on my gloves and hat before coming outside. The cold wind increased the volume of my headache, and my vision blurred. I thought of Markus and his advice to focus on the girl. But I trusted Heinrich. I wanted to help.

"If you're so close with the police, why can't you just ask them to be discreet?"

"Vienna is a village, Alex. Especially amongst people as old as Emil and me. If I speak with the police, everyone will know before day's end. The fact that you appeared when you did—an intelligent, unconnected person—is remarkable."

He looked over to the clock and then back to me. "Although I have disconnected from Emil, I remained friends with his mother until she passed a number of years ago. She was the last living person who really knew my own mother, and I feel I owe her. I'm sorry to put all of this on you."

I took the keys from the envelope and slid them into my back pocket.

"It's ok. I'll consider going into his apartment, but I can't promise it. I might change my mind at the last minute. I'll keep the keys but leave the money for now." I folded the envelope and pushed it down into Heinrich's pocket.

He reached out and gripped my left shoulder, not unlike how Johanna had held my neck hours before.

"Thank you."

"How long is it going to take me to get used to this weather?"

"You do look miserable."

"I am."

"Buy a good hat made from wool felt. Try Nagy Hüte in the first."

"Ok."

"I do appreciate this, Alex. Let me know how it goes, either way. Like I said, he will be away tomorrow from seven until nine in the evening."

With a shake of my shoulder, he turned and walked away. Though my face and hands were freezing, my back was sweating, so I opened my coat on the walk home. I pushed open the door to my apartment building and entered the tall stone hallway that leads to my elevator. After taking a few steps into complete darkness, I turned back and groped along the wall until I found the light switch. In theory, I was impressed by the Austrians' effort to conserve electricity by having lights automatically turn off. In practice, I hated it. The elevator, obviously retrofitted into the building, clicked and whirred as it descended through the center of the stairwell. Across from me was a bronze sign mounted high on the wall inscribed with a message: "This building was destroyed in 1945. It was rebuilt in 1948–1950 by the City of Vienna under the mayor Dr. HC Theodor Körner."

Such an odd, direct summation of tragedy. Vienna overflowed with small signs and memorials, easily overlooked. Stepping into the elevator, I took out one of Emil's keys. It was thick, with crisp ridges and dimples, and weighed twice as much as my parents' house key. It smelled of pungent oil and must have been freshly cut. I realized I hadn't asked Heinrich where he'd gotten it. Returning to my apartment, I twisted the deadbolt behind me, listening closely for the thunk of sliding steel. I have a fixation with ensuring doors are locked. I have to stare at the lock, feel the bolt move, and say to myself, "I locked the door." If I don't, an irrepressible urge grows in my chest to return and check the lock. Over time, this remembrance ritual becomes routine, like prayer, requiring me to vary it in some way to have it effectively imprint the door's locked state into my short-term memory. If this trend continues unabated, by my thirtieth birthday, it will take me over an hour to lock a door.

I placed the keys onto my white bedside table. I couldn't believe this was the same night that I'd been at the restaurant with Johanna and Zeinab. I stripped down, went into the bathroom, and tried to mentally prepare for a shower. My water heater, which had taken weeks to comprehend, only held the capacity for a third of a warm shower and was wired to reheat only once per day. The moment the hot water depleted, the water temperature would drop to the level of Alpine snowmelt. I had developed a depressing system of getting barely wet, soaping up with the shower off, and then frantically rinsing as fast as possible. After completing my hectic routine, I went into the kitchen and peeled the cellophane from a fresh box of Marlboros. I lit one on the gas stove, then gathered all of the unspent money I had earned from Heinrich and laid it out in a grid on my kitchen table, a wrinkled, faded array of coral, brown, and blue rectangles featuring various mustached individuals. While it was the most purchasing power I had ever possessed, the emotional weight of foreign currency doesn't measure up to American cash. The musty essence of the thousands of Austrian hands that had held and sweat into the bills unmoored me. I stacked up the money, wrapped it in a piece of paper, and taped it into the tangle of silver pipes beneath my kitchen sink. If I was allowed enough time with Johanna before everything fell apart, we might be able to grow our connection into something strong enough to endure. My hunch was that wouldn't be the case.

VII

Early the next afternoon, I went to the city archives to request Emil's file. I left on foot, and as I walked, I sensed the presence of someone else. I lingered at a stoop and took stock of everyone nearby. An elderly woman walking a dog, a teenager standing at the corner, and a man about my age walking in my direction. While I waited, they all continued on their way without looking towards me. I walked further, taking a right at the next three intersections. No one followed, but the sensation of being watched pressed into my shoulders. The question of where Heinrich had obtained Emil's keys stuck in my mind. When I reached the archives, the same clerk as last time, Fritz, was sitting behind the desk. The room was otherwise empty.

"Ah, the American. You have returned. How is your report?" So much for anonymity. Fritz had a small, half-empty ceramic cup of coffee next to him.

"You guys have coffee here?"

"We do have a machine in the employee breakroom."

"Hmm. Must be nice." I said, looking down at his cup. A coffee would cut right through the smell of books and stale air stifling the room.

"Would you care for one?"

"Absolutely."

"I must warn you, this coffee is not good. It is only very slightly better than having no coffee at all."

"I'll take anything."

He disappeared and returned with a ridged plastic cup, similar to what you might use to provide a urine sample at the doctor. I smiled and took a sip. Not good. Somewhat reminiscent of an actual urine sample, but not undrinkable.

"Thank you, how much?" He shook his head and flicked his hand away.

"It is a gift from the city of Vienna."

"Thanks. How do you like working down here?"

"I quite enjoy it. I can read all that I wish and it is peaceful." Fritz had a warm, pinkish glow to his skin. He looked happy. I noticed a silver wedding band around his finger. "And do you need some files today, or did you just come for the complimentary coffee?"

"I do have a few requests." I had practiced this dialog on the walk over. I pulled out a piece of paper with Emil's reference number in the middle of a list with similar numbers in sequence, as well as a few completely random numbers. He took the list from me and studied it.

"Where did you get these from?"

"My professor—he gave them to me over the phone, so it's possible I have a digit or two wrong here or there. I'm sorry if that's super annoying."

He lowered the note and looked into my eyes. I held his gaze.

"And which professor is this for again?"

"Professor Körner." It was the first name that came into my mind. Körner was the former mayor of Vienna inscribed into the sign in my apartment's stairwell.

"And do you have your ID yet?"

"Still waiting, sorry."

Fritz nodded, apparently satisfied, and disappeared down the hall. I had planned for our exchange to be nonchalant and unmemorable, but without a doubt, he would be able to recall every detail of this interaction. I took out some paper and pens and sat down at a table across the room. Fritz was gone for at least twenty minutes before he returned, rolling a metal cart containing a number of books and documents.

"I'm sorry, but some of those reference numbers did not exist. You will need to check with Professor Körner."

"Ah ok, sure. Sorry about that."

Onto each item on the cart, Fritz had attached a Post-it note with their respective reference number. Emil's number was there, pasted to a long metal tube. I busied myself with the other things first: a book containing all property taxes paid in the sixteenth district in 1962, a binder with death certificates from February 1893. Finally, I pulled Emil's document from its holder and unrolled it onto the table, using the other books to pin it down. In the upper left-hand corner, where the blueprint of Parliament had displayed the symbol of the Habsburg Empire, a different bird waited, wings outstretched, neck sharply turned. A black eagle clutching a wreath encircling a swastika. The map was of a portion of the Augarten, a park in Vienna, that had been converted into a military base. It outlined the placement of buildings, roads, forests, and an antiaircraft tower. The date of the map was October 1, 1944. Grandpa Charlie would have been in northeastern France by then. I pulled out my Minolta, anchored it against my chest, held my breath, and photographed the map. Then, I went over each square of the map's grid in detail and compared it to my own modern map of Vienna. The broad outlines of the park were the same and the antiaircraft tower remained, but most of the other military structures in the 1944 version no longer existed. Emil must have been looking for something in the differential between then and now. I spent another hour pretending to busy myself with the rest of the items, then stacked everything on the cart and wheeled it over to Fritz.

I walked out of the room, up the stairs, and out of the

building. Leaving the airless, fluorescent-lit archives and stepping into the cold afternoon made my mind return to the moment. I was fucked. I only had a few hours left to decide if I was going to break into Emil's apartment, and although his interest in Third Reich–era blueprints didn't prove he and Heinrich were Nazis, it certainly supported the theory. I walked home and considered calling Markus, or my dad, or Hank, or anyone, but all I did was sit on the edge of my bed and think about Janet.

The night when I finished my plagiarized paper was the last good night that we'd had together. We sat cross-legged on my bed and shared a supreme pizza from Round Table. She tried to tell me some story about her Japanese lab partner, Yuki, and a Bunsen burner, but whenever she approached the punchline, she laughed so hard she couldn't keep going. She had a nice laugh that could truly overtake her. If she fought hard enough and covered her mouth, she could reduce it to a slow, rolling convulsion, but then her eyes would water and when she wiped them, the laugh would erupt again. The first few times she laughed like that I assumed it was an act, but it wasn't. She abandoned the lab partner story, and I pushed the pizza box aside and laid my head in her lap. She stroked my hair while I bitched about school and the paper and other boring things. She always took my side when I told stories. Every cell within me wanted to not cheat on the paper, but it was too late and I didn't want to fail the class so I yielded to my plan. I went to the shared kitchen at the end of the hall to make a pot of Folgers so I could stay up and write, and when I came back, Janet was asleep. Like a cat or a child, she could fall asleep anywhere, anytime. After I finished my paper around four a.m., I printed it out, nudged her over, and laid next to her on the bed. Still asleep, she gave me a single, soft kiss on my cheek. Although I've considered every possible permutation, I haven't quite pieced together the timeline of when she met Charles and started cheating on me, but I'm sure it was before that night. I suppose both of us sensed something missing between us, but she could have just broken up with me before looking elsewhere. The way things ended sullied all of our memories, but I was still forced to carry them along with me, even thousands of miles away in a foreign country. I was in a trance, replaying the opening lines of her letter, when the phone rang.

"Hello?"

"Hi, Alex?" It was Johanna.

"Hey, what's up?"

"Not much. I had lunch with my grandfather today. He mentioned you."

"Uh-oh."

She laughed. "No, he said you're a great help to him." I wondered if Heinrich knew she was leverage over me. He must.

"That's good. Anything he thought I did well in particular? Perhaps how well I pronounce Österreich?"

She laughed again. "He didn't mention that. He did say he was surprised that someone so messy looking could be reliable."

"Come on."

"No, really. It was a compliment. That's how he does it. It's always wrapped in an insult."

"He's probably the cleanest, best-smelling man I've ever met. He must shower and shave immediately before I see him."

"He is clean."

Outside on the square, a police car drove past with its siren on, throwing red and blue light across my bedroom.

Johanna cleared her throat and said, "I was wondering if you are free tomorrow afternoon?"

"Not for a date, I hope. I don't go on dates. We discussed this."

She laughed once more, completing the triptych. A real laugh.

"Of course not. Me either."

"I thought you were always busy? You don't have a test Wednesday morning or something?"

"I do. But it's ok. It's an easy one."

"Awesome."

"Come by my place, 5 Dietrichsteingasse, apartment 6, around three p.m."

"5 Dietrichsteingasse, apartment 6."

"Yep. Near Bauernfeldplatz."

"Ok. And I promise, I will shower right before I meet your grandfather from now on."

"Perfect. See you tomorrow, Alex."

I took out the keys to Emil's apartment and rubbed them between my fingers. One was long, with only a few notches but many dimples, the other short, with no dimples. I needed to leave in the next twenty minutes to reach his place by seven. If I could have had a few days to withdraw and consider everything, I could have probably made sound decisions. I should have gone straight to Johanna, handed her the keys, and told her everything Heinrich had asked me to do. He was her family, and I wasn't responsible for his behavior. I liked him, though.

I rushed across town and waited up the block from Emil's in the shadows beneath a watch repair shop's awning. At three minutes past the hour, his gate opened. Dressed in a grey suit and overcoat, he stepped out and took a right, heading north. The precision of Heinrich's prediction was unsettling. Was there any possibility that he and Emil might be working together to set me up and fuck me over? I waited a period of time long enough to prevent any observer from seeing a reflection of Emil's movements in my own. Then, feet unsteady, I stepped off the curb, crossed the street, and walked to his doorway. The first key, damp from my palm, slid neatly into the keyhole. With the slightest of jiggles, the lock released, the key turned, and I walked into the building. I had guessed correctly that the shorter key was for the outside door.

I paused for a moment by the mailboxes in the hallway, mumbling a line about having checked mine earlier in the day. I focused on the tapping of my shoes on the floor, forcing each step to fall even and controlled. As I walked deeper into the building, the flush of guilt and indecision that had tormented me the entire afternoon faded, and I reached the door of his apartment with a clear mind. I pushed the second key into the keyhole, wrapped the white, hooked doorknob with a small washcloth, and turned it up and in.

The apartment, a humble one bedroom, was tastefully decorated. A brown leather couch, a round glass coffee table, and an old Bosch metal refrigerator dominated the living room. The refrigerator hummed and knocked, amplifying the surrounding silence. I scanned for an alternate exit should Emil return. A long window ran the length of the wall, looking out into the courtyard of the building. I could slip out and jump down if needed. I pulled a pair of purple latex gloves onto my hands. Then, I lifted up the glass top of the coffee table, placed it onto the couch, and slid its heavy concrete base over to the entrance door. It wouldn't stop a determined visitor, but it would, perhaps, suffice to slow a quizzical old man unsuspecting that a young, misguided American was fucking around in his apartment.

The bedroom contained a thin mattress lying on the floor in the corner of the room with a reading lamp beside it. Opposite the bed sat a simple wooden desk with a few pieces of mail, a folded newspaper, and a weathered, chrome Leica M3. It had been used extensively. Its black vulcanite was almost completely chipped off, and brass showed through the silver at every edge. I pulled off my gloves and dried my hands on my jeans. Then, I picked up the Leica and removed its lens cap. Mounted was a 50mm Summilux with a dented barrel and stunning, flawless glass. The film counter on the camera read thirty-three. I opened the top desk drawer and found various photographic equipment, including unshot rolls of Kodak 400 Tri-X, the same black-and-white film I had in my Minolta. I opened one canister and held it briefly to my nose, taking in the familiar, sweet, inky smell. I rewound the Leica and pulled out its film. It was Kodak 100 TMax, a low-grain black-and-white film, better for outdoors than the Tri-X. I loaded the un-shot Tri-X, and with the camera back open and film exposed, advanced through until three shots remained. It was an early double-stroke M3, so each advance took two pulls, which felt right. I set the dial on the back of the camera to 400 ASA and rubbed everything down with my shirt to remove any finger-prints. Hopefully, Emil wouldn't remember which film he had loaded.

With an eye on the time, I broke each room down into four sets of quadrants and then worked through them. Un-der furniture, behind the toilet, beneath the sink, I inspected everything. The apartment smelled of dandruff shampoo, like my dad, and contained no alcohol or tobacco. It was empty of personal effects save for a small amount of clothing and a col-lection of books grouped into five stacks by his bed. I stooped down by the books. Some novels by Thomas Mann, a few by Goethe, and a bunch of authors I didn't recognize. I thumbed through half of them but didn't find anything hidden inside. A brown Bible with a water-stained cover sat midway in the stack nearest his bed. Inside the front cover was a dedication, dated 1933, from his parents, Otto and Susi. Wedged through-out the Old and New Testament were small slips of paper, handwritten notes, and photos. They were from throughout his life, most decades old. I looked at a few things, then closed the book and put it back. I was intruding into a man's most personal sphere. I picked up the Bible once more and held it, spine down in my hand. With a gentle rock I checked where it opened: the Book of James, first page. A green train ticket from Wels to Vienna from November 2, 1946, marked the place. Age had dried the ticket to the texture of a dead leaf, and its ink had faded, leaving only the impressions of letters. Emil must be a real Catholic to be coming back to the Book of James. Chapter 2, verse 20, is one that sticks with you: "Do you want to be shown, you shallow man, that faith apart from works is barren?"

I replaced the Bible and dragged the coffee table base back into the middle of his living room. While I strained to center the top over the base, two drops of blood dripped from the corner of my mouth down onto the glass. Reflexively, I released it with a thud, and tried to smear the blood away. Somehow, the glass didn't break. I held my wound closed with my tongue and wiped the table with the washcloth I had brought to open the door. The glass squeaked clean, and I rushed out of the apartment with the roll of undeveloped film in my pocket. I stepped out his front gate into the winter air, drenched with sweat, and removed my coat. A few blocks away, I threw my gloves and washcloth into a trashcan. My head throbbed with disgust for myself for becoming a criminal, and disappointment in myself for not being thorough enough. I should have stolen his Bible and gone through every item within it.

The next morning, after a breakfast of scrambled eggs, dark bread, butter, and apricot jam, I leafed through the phone book in search of a one-hour photo shop on the outskirts of the city. I wasn't sure what was in Emil's photos, and I didn't want to accidentally hand them over to someone that knew him. Heinrich had warned me many times that Vienna was a village. He would be expecting an update on the break-in, but I had to see the photos before speaking with him. I needed to know if they changed whom I could trust. I found a shop out by the Danube towards the end of the U1 line and headed out.

I took a seat in the next-to-last subway car and held the roll of film in my right coat pocket. In the car behind me, visible through a heavily scratched window, a dark-haired man in a burgundy jacket stared in my direction. He was tall and wiry and had wide green eyes with puffy lower lids. At a stop earlier than planned, I remained seated until right before the doors closed, then got up and stepped off onto the platform. We made eye contact as the train pulled away, and I saw the faint lines of a smirk spread across his face. Probably nothing, but maybe not. When dropping the film off, I ordered two sets of prints, one for Heinrich, and one for myself. While I waited, I walked along the Danube. It wasn't beautiful or blue like the Strauss song had claimed. It was grey and forgettable. It's strange to think that the river connects Vienna and Budapest directly to Belgrade, linking the poles of the Austro-Hungarian Empire permanently to Serbia, its World War I–stumbling block. Losing almost everything to try and hold the Balkans was a miscalculation exceeding even that of the Blazers taking Bowie over Jordan. After an hour passed, I retrieved my prints and took them into a sad-looking restaurant overlooking the river. With ample outside seating and a vague nautical theme, it might have been a lively place in summer, but in winter beneath an overcast sky, it was drab. Other than one man drinking coffee and reading his newspaper at the bar, I was the only customer. I sat with my back to the wall in the rear of the restaurant and ordered grilled *Zanderfilet* and a glass of *Grüner Veltliner*.

Once the waiter departed, I took out the photos and removed them from their white paper sleeve. They were still warm and smelled like gin. The shots, confidently focused and evenly exposed, were primarily of buildings in Vienna. There wasn't a single face in the roll. Most were taken the same way; Emil must have stood directly in front of each building, stepped backwards into the middle of the street, and captured the image. All angles were right angles; the photographer's shoulders parallel to each building, the camera parallel to the ground. A series of photos were from four-way intersections with a picture taken in each direction. Once again, these photos were perfectly square; the photographer stood at the exact center of the intersection, ignored traffic, and took a clean shot. In one picture, I recognized a street sign, Große Sperlgasse, from my walk through the second district with Johanna. I unfolded my map and laid the photo onto the street. I did the same with other photos with visible street signs. The edges of buildings lined up across some photos, and by working together these sequences with other pictures with street signs and intersections, I was able to roughly place twenty-three of the thirty-three photos onto my map. Taken altogether, they formed a broadening spiral that covered the northwest tip of the second district, stretching out towards the edge of the Augarten, the large park on the northern periphery that Emil had been researching in the archives. Three of the remaining ten photographs contained a nondescript apartment building captured at morning, midday, and dusk. The photos were black and white, which accentuates texture, and the ruts and lines within the apartment's coarse exterior resembled a dry riverbed.

I slid the photos under my notebook when the waiter approached with my food. The Zanderfilet was cooked perfectly with a crisp, buttery crust on the outside, and it paired well with the cool sweetness of the wine. The photos lined up with Heinrich's original suggestion that Emil had a preoccupation with a specific area, but Emil wouldn't need a map from 1944 to plan something in the present day. Johanna had mentioned that the second district was the Jewish quarter before the Nazi era, so any history that he was trying to document or remember from the 1940s might not be innocent. Still, it didn't mean Heinrich was involved, or really prove anything at all. I finished my meal, settled up, and went straight to Heinrich's apartment without a plan. On the subway, I zipped the photos into an inner pocket of my bag and decided not to mention them. The sense that I shouldn't trust Heinrich burned in my mind. Just before my stop, I took the photos back out. I needed to be done with this.

Heinrich buzzed me in, and I walked up to his floor. I

paused outside of his apartment and said a quick prayer. Then, I filled my lungs with one deep, alveoli-straining breath, released it, and entered. Heinrich sat in a chair by the window wearing brown slacks and a white button-up shirt with the sleeves rolled to his elbows.

"So, Alex. How did it go?"

"He left at seven, just like you said." I walked over, placed the white sleeve of photos onto the window sill in front of him, and took a seat on the couch. "The keys worked. I looked through everything in his apartment. Nothing stood out, but he doesn't have much stuff. I took one partially shot roll of film out of his camera and had it developed." I gestured towards the prints. "It's a bunch of pictures of the second district leading out to the Augarten. I think that's the area of interest you were looking for."

Heinrich didn't reach for the photos. His face stayed smooth and expressionless. If anything, he appeared relieved.

"Great work, Alex."

"Do you know why he's interested in that part of the city?"

He sat up straight and leaned his elbow onto the window sill.

"Oh, I'm not sure, but it's good news. It is clarifying. I cannot thank you enough. If you would, let me take it from here. Do not follow him anymore. I'm sure his anxieties are alerted, and I don't want to put you at risk."

"What are you going to do?"

"I prefer not to say."

He must have already suspected Emil's interest in the second district.

"Could I grab a glass of water?"

"Oh, certainly."

He walked to the kitchen, filled a glass, and brought it to me. He sat back down but still didn't touch the photos. I drank it completely. My heart pounded, and I looked down into the bottom of the glass as I flatly asked the question, "Do you know what Emil did during the war?"

"Emil? Why do you ask?"

"Well, I thought it might be important, given the history of the area in his photos."

He sat, unmoving, his face still.

"Ah, well, Emil is young. November 5, 1928, I believe. In the war, he was just a *Flakhelfer*. You know, shoveling bricks about with the other children under the auspices of antiaircraft defense."

I walked over towards him and stood at the far edge of the window.

"And you?"

"Me?" he asked, and looked up at me with tired, grey eyes. "Military service," he said, in a low rasp. The air left the room, and I knew that the question had ended our friendship. I took a half step backwards and looked around.

"Do you need any more help with your files or anything?"

"Oh, not right now, no. I will be in touch if I do. Thank you again for your work, it has been excellent. Please don't mention any of this to anyone, especially my granddaughter."

We stood there without speaking. He rose and gave me an expectant look.

"Ok, I'll head out, I have to meet some friends."

"Thank you, Alex. Goodbye."

I walked out, pulling the door closed behind me. I'd spent most of my time in Vienna in that apartment. However likely it was that he and Emil had spent the war murdering the residents of the second district, it was more likely that they hadn't and this entire thing was some stupid personal vendetta between them. There certainly wouldn't be any more calls from Heinrich to Johanna about my good behavior. I was supposed to meet her in thirty minutes, so I headed towards her apartment. I stopped at a pay phone on the way to call Markus. I wanted to get a second opinion on everything, but he didn't pick up. He never picks up.

Once I turned onto her street, her gravity pulled at me. For the last twenty-four hours, I had been lost in the fog of Emil and Heinrich. Throughout my life, everything that isn't immediately in front of me has been hard to keep track of. I pushed the small, grey button for her door.

"Hullo," Johanna's voice crackled through the speaker.

"It's me."

"Hi. We're on the first floor."

The door buzzed open. A dimly lit concrete stairway wound through the center of the building. The door to the right of the first landing stood ajar, and I lightly rapped it as I stepped inside. It opened into a small kitchen, barely larger than the square table pushed up against one wall. The room smelled of clean towels and cigarettes. Johanna stood at the sink washing a bowl, her hair gathered into a loose braid over her shoulder. Grey light filtered in from the hallway, softly framing her green eyes as she turned to me.

"Hey."

"Hi."

A burst of warmth entered the kitchen as Lisi exited an adjoining bathroom in shorts and a T-shirt, hair wrapped up in a white towel. She gave me a wide grin.

"Have you come to recruit us for the American military?" she asked.

"Ha, well—"

"I heard you think you think I should date my brother."

"Oh, my. Not exactly. I'm sorry about the other night, it's just that I have a terrible personality. There's no known cure."

She leaned in and kissed me on each cheek, lips barely brushing skin. Stepping back, she made firm eye contact. She looked and smelled clean. Her cheeks were flushed.

"No problem, Alex. What are you guys up to?" she asked.

I looked over to Johanna, who was bent down above a large, mixed pile of shoes.

"Can I borrow your black boots?" Johanna asked Lisi.

"Of course."

Borrowing someone else's shoes offends my germ-conscious sensibilities. I don't think I've ever done it. Sitting down to pull on the boots, Johanna said, "I was thinking we could get a sandwich from Spar and walk around. It's supposed to be sunny for another hour or so."

"Sounds fun," answered Lisi. Then, she turned and walked down the hall.

I leaned against the door and ran my fingers through my hair. I probably should have washed it in the morning. Finishing her lacing, Johanna looked up at me.

"Ready to go?"

"Sure."

"Tschüß, Lisi," Johanna called back towards the hallway.

We stepped out into the afternoon and headed east. The streets were quiet, and the low-hanging sun made the patches of snow on the ground glow, giving the city a stunning clarity. The snow was coming often enough that it thickened in certain spots each day, never fully melting off. We walked without speaking and at first the silence fit well, but I began to sense something wrong with Johanna. As we waited at a crosswalk for the light to change, I gave her a light push on the shoulder.

"You've got a melancholy vibe today—everything ok?"

She gave me an intent look. The signal changed and she stepped off the curb.

"I dunno."

"Anything you want to talk about?"

She stopped once we'd crossed the street. I leaned back against a burgundy marble wall behind me and let the sun warm my face.

"It's just—it's lame."

"Let's hear it."

"I'm tired."

"Physically tired or mentally tired?"

She shook her head. "Both. I wake up exhausted. I'm

tired throughout the day. I go to bed tired." As she spoke, she moved her hands slowly through the air. "My anxiety builds up so I put pressure on myself to get everything done but I don't, so I add more pressure the next day but that doesn't work either." She blinked back a tear. "Do you ever feel like that?"

"Sure. Pretty much every day of my life until I quit school. I'm sorry for putting pressure on you to hang out—I didn't realize you were so busy. I mean, I knew you were busy, but not *that* busy."

She laughed, and a gathering tear welled over and slid down her face, leaving a glistening trail. She stepped forward, without hesitation, and kissed me. I'll always remember her lips at that moment. They were slightly chapped, a perfect rough texture with warm softness beneath. She stepped back.

"I'm not trying to give you a guilt trip. It's not just about being busy—it's … I think that my entire perception of time and work and everything is wrong, so unless I change, there won't be any relief for me."

"Sure," I said. We turned to walk up the block. Our kiss had felt like two magnets coming together. I sensed it moments before it should have been possible to sense such a thing.

"Which responsibility is stressing you out the most?"

She raised her hands up to waist level and rubbed them together.

"Nothing interesting, school, future, present, and so on …"

There seemed to be an item missing from the list.

"And Lukas?"

She nodded. "He's stressing me out too, yes, but not, like you might think, or, I think you're getting at. We were together for such a long time and everyone assumed we would stay that way, but it didn't work anymore between us—for me. I love him still, like family, so I wish for him to be happy, but I can't be the one to make him happy."

"Why didn't it work?"

Her shoulders slumped. "I don't know. That's the question he's asked me, maybe ten thousand times? He asked me it again, in a different phrasing, at the bookstore just before I saw you, and at the party the other night, and so many times in between. I don't even want to be in a relationship ever again because I feel terrible that I'm not in love with him anymore. I'm just not. I haven't been for a while. Maybe it was never the right kind of love or maybe I'm flawed, but I haven't found the words to describe my feelings, which sounds banal, I know, and is infuriating to Lukas." She rubbed her eyes, then gathered her hair together, pulling it behind her left ear. "Everything I say about it sounds clinical—and I don't know how good your German is for things like this. Somehow when I'm talking to you I feel like I'm speaking infant German or insane, schizophrenic German, even though your German is quite good. I'm only very aware of the fact you aren't a native speaker."

I laughed. She did too, then wiped another tear from the corner of her eye with her wrist.

"So, what I'm hearing is that even in your sad stories, you don't miss out on opportunities to insult my German."

She smiled and rubbed her eyes some more. "Let's walk, I'm hungry," she said, and we continued up the street.

"Ok. We don't have to talk about Lukas. I just brought it up because he's been following us for like three blocks," I said, gesturing backwards. She froze and turned back. "I'm kidding," I added.

"Fuck you, that's awful," she said, and shoved me.

"Sorry. I am awful. German *is* clinical. I don't know what I'm missing when people tell me things, but you're overthinking it with Lukas. If it didn't work, that's enough explanation. When I was dumped, my ex gave me four pages of reasons, and it didn't help at all."

She smirked. "Four pages?"

"Yeah. Front and back, so technically eight."

"What was her biggest complaint?"

"Penis size. Too large."

"That took eight pages?"

"It was more of a drawing really."

She stopped and rolled her eyes. "Oh, my. I agree, rationally, that I don't have to justify things to him, but because I don't know why it happened, I'm terrified it might happen again. I'm anxious about it ruining my future relationships, and no matter how tired I am, I seem to wake up around four in the morning with inane thoughts."

"Such as?"

"Well—" She paused and looked over at me. "Don't think I'm some crazy woman."

"Could be too late for that, but go on."

Her eyes narrowed. "Last night I was worried about being pregnant."

"Ok," I said, stopping. My body suddenly leaden. "That's good to know."

"No no, I'm not pregnant or anything. I haven't, well, you know, I'm not pregnant. Trust me." She coughed and cleared her throat. "Even though we only finally broke up a month or so ago, it was over in some ways for much longer." We looked at each other. I liked that she couldn't seem to regulate the things she said. Despite the delivery, I was glad to hear that she might actually be something close to single and not stuck in a critically ill relationship.

"Ok," I said.

"Right, well, what I mean is, last night when I woke up, I was worried about *ever* being pregnant. Would I ever want that? Would I ever find someone I'd want to share that with, and if I did, what guidance would I be able to tell my child about any meaningful questions, seeing as how I'm struggling through every day?"

"That sounds like a lot for four a.m."

"I know, right? Here's Spar." She entered a doorway leading into an overly lit grocery store, and I followed. My earlier response to her troubles had somehow earned a kiss. It had come instinctively. This felt like another pivotal moment, but unfortunately, my mind locked up when considering potential responses.

"Those are all valid questions, but maybe they aren't ones you have to answer anytime soon?" I said, stiffly.

"Oh, I know that. Should we get a couple sandwiches made?"

"Sure? I have no idea how this works. I thought this was just a grocery store."

She led me to the rear of the store. Two women in white lab coats stood behind a large glass case containing rows and rows of meat and cheese. When confronted with so many possibilities of food, I always wonder how old the oldest things are.

"Why don't you order for both of us?"

"Ok. Do you eat Leberkäse?"

"What's that?"

"It's a loaf of liver sausage. See here." She tapped, thunk-thunk, onto the glass. Beneath her finger sat a pink loaf of meat. It was easily the least appetizing item in the entire case.

"Well—"

She laughed. "Ok, so you aren't Austrian yet. I eat Leberkäse when I'm in a bad mood."

"Are we in a bad mood?"

"Well, no." She smiled. "I eat it when I'm full of emotion. We could choose two different sandwiches and share halves."

"Sure." That sounded beautiful. We were already a couple. She ordered two *Semmels*, one with *Bauchspeck* and one with *Kümmelbraten*, and we headed out. "Do you think we could go to the Augarten?" I asked.

"We could. Why there?"

"Oh, it's sunny today, and I've never been. I read about it

somewhere."

"Let's do it."

We walked with idle chatter and ate our sandwiches, switching halfway. The Lukas topic seemed behind us, and she moved with a relaxed, joyful step. Dense, building-lined streets gave way to space and trees as we ambled towards the second district. In front of a shuttered grey building, Johanna stopped abruptly.

"I guess since you know my situation—more than you wanted to know, probably—you should tell me if you are in love with anyone in America or anything like that."

I, of course, had no one. The only possible obstacle between us was Heinrich. The last few rays of sun bending over the horizon shone on her face. I didn't like winter, but it did help me appreciate sunlight.

"Do I sound cooler if I say I have someone?"

"I don't think so."

"I'm single."

She blinked, smiled, and we continued walking forward. An inevitability enveloped us, and the distance between us grew wafer thin, translucent. Minutes later, we stepped into the Augarten. Originally a large hunting preserve for the Kaiser, the park is composed of fields, forests, and tree-lined pathways. It carries a look of order run ragged at the edges, not dissimilar to a neatly formed haircut left to nature for longer than planned. When we turned from a small trail onto the main thoroughfare, the antiaircraft tower from the map in the archives slid into view. Grey and tired yet resilient, at eighteen stories high, it loomed over the surrounding trees and fields. Its dark color vivid against the empty whiteness of the park, it served as a stark reminder of the past.

"Wow," I mumbled.

"What, oh, the Flakturm?"

"Yeah, that looks incredible."

"Think so?"

"Absolutely. Could we walk around it?"

"Ok."

Save for a mother and her child in an adjacent, barren field, we had the expansive Augarten to ourselves. Approaching from the south, the severe, concrete wonder of the tower increased as we walked. Faded pink and yellow graffiti covered portions of its base, and mangled, thick, reinforced grating held some of the upper pieces together. When we reached the tower, I removed my glove and placed my hand on its cold, rough face.

"You know, I've never really noticed it before," Johanna said, softly. The tower seemed to quiet her. I hit the palm of my hand against it, creating a dull slap that echoed out over the field behind us.

"Really? It's the only thing I can see in this park."

She brushed her hair away from her face with her gloved fingertips.

"Yes, I have seen it, of course. There is a second one in this park to the east, but I don't look too closely at them." I stepped back and tried to take in the complete tower. Ringing the top, one hundred and eighty feet up, were round circles, presumably where the guns had been mounted. Rusted, savage rebar poked out here and there.

"The design screams Third Reich," I said.

"It does," she responded. I stretched my woolen glove back onto my hand. The snow crunched lightly under Johanna's feet as she backed up a few steps. "Do you mind if we go? I'm not—I guess I'm feeling strange standing here by this thing."

"Sure, of course, I didn't mean—"

"No, I know. I just don't want anyone to think we are some kind of neo-Nazis."

We turned and walked towards the nearest exit of the park. Emil and Heinrich must have seen the tower in full operation. I wonder what it looked like new, and when seen in a positive light. As protection. When we exited the park, I glanced at Johanna. She looked tense, her jaw closed tight.

"Do you know the Heldenplatz?" she asked.

"The big square in front of the Hofburg?"

"Yes, exactly. It's also the name of a play by Thomas Bernhard that came out a few years ago. The play was a massive controversy here. Do you know it?"

"No."

"Ok. Well, the story takes place in an apartment on the Heldenplatz and is about how Austria hasn't truly changed since people filled the square to see Hitler. My professor adored the play, so we studied it in school. Some people's parents complained and kept them home during the lesson."

She looked over at me for a moment and then continued.

"I was fifteen, and we had been taught about the war, of course, and National Socialism, constantly, but it was always placed at a distance, as if it wasn't only something done by Austria, but something done *to* Austria. Just before we read the play, my professor showed us a recording of Hitler's speech at the Heldenplatz. Halfway through, the camera cuts to the crowd, and it looked like all of Vienna was there. People had even climbed up onto the statue of Prince Eugen for a better view. The ecstasy on their faces—"

She paused and scratched over at her left elbow with her right hand.

"I don't have a conception of it, how that time happened, what people felt, anything. When I was younger, I believed I did, but not anymore."

Sometime between the field and the last tree cover of the park, the day had faded into a heavy slate grey. We continued through the park's exit and down a broad, four-lane road with steady traffic.

"Once a year, a woman comes by our apartment at Dietrichsteingaße and leaves white roses for a Jewish family that was taken from our flat and killed at Treblinka."

As we walked, the grey dimmed, and cars began to turn their lights on, throwing yellow and white light over the road.

"But I guess it's not like that in America? It's a good story for you guys?"

"Yeah—we are raised on a lot of John Wayne movies and the idea that the Americans in the war were our 'greatest generation.'"

She let out a weak sigh. "Greatest generation?"

I nodded.

"Not the way we look at it here." We stopped at a corner. She had been leading the way and looked unsure where to turn next. "My mother's father was unquestionably a Nazi. She hated him. He killed himself by walking in front of a train when she was in her last year of high school."

I sat down on a nearby bench, and she sat beside me. The wind picked up, blowing dust and sand from the street onto us. She turned sideways on the bench, pulling her knees up to her chest.

"Under my bed growing up was an officer's saber my grandfather took off of a dead German somewhere in France. I found it in the back of his attic," I said.

Johanna's eyes opened wide. "Americans are fucking crazy," she replied.

"It's true."

She shook her head.

"This was from the grandfather that was in Vienna?"

"Yes. He drove a tank in Patton's Third Army. I wanted to know more about the saber and his time in Vienna, but I was always too afraid to bring it up. Once, when our family was at his house on Christmas, I prodded my uncle to ask him how it was in Europe. My grandfather squinted and said, 'What do you want to hear about that for?' Then, he talked about baseball for fifteen minutes, before he mentioned that on the way to Germany, through France, they drove through a lot of pine forests. He didn't mention anything else."

"That was it?"

"That was it."

"He's dead?"

"Yeah, he died about eight years ago."

"I'm sorry."

I shrugged. She looked out over the intersection.

"I hope that Grandpa Heinrich wasn't a Nazi. He seems too dignified, which I know is naive but feels true. I know his older brother died in the East late in the war. I've visited his grave in the Zentralfriedhof with my father." A police van drove by, sirens blaring, numbingly loud. After it passed, the siren dropped in pitch and reverberated around us. Johanna turned back towards me. "I did go into Grandpa Heinrich's desk once when I was living with him. I was trying to find some tape. In the back of a drawer, I found an envelope with a Mother's Cross, I assume from his mother. It's a medal they gave Aryan mothers who bore children during the Reich. It was white and blue with a large swastika in the middle. I put it back without saying anything."

I took a slow, measured breath. Johanna looked drained. The color washed from her face, and her eyes tired. Her voice remained strong.

"He told me about the brother that died in the war, Erich."

"What?"

"Yeah. We were drinking coffee together at a café on Schwarzenbergplatz, and he mentioned that the table we were sitting at was where he last saw him."

"Unbelievable! He's never mentioned Erich to me. I only know about him from my father."

"I was surprised when he brought it up. It kind of came out of nowhere. I just nodded and let him talk."

"Maybe you've become his friend?"

"Maybe." The thought cut through me. If we had become friends, we weren't anymore. The weight of my situation returned, and I realized how cold it was outside.

"Random question, has he ever mentioned Emil Eder to you?" I asked.

"No, why?"

"I've seen the name in his papers a few times. It seems like he might have been an important person in his life."

She shook her head. "Could be, but I don't know."

I considered telling her everything, but it would ruin the day. I wanted to preserve her hope for Heinrich's goodness until I knew definitively otherwise. She studied me for a moment. I think she was withholding something as well. At the edge of my vision glowed the lights of a Würstelstand.

"I think I'm getting hungry—you?"

"Of course."

"I think that's a Würstelstand up there," I said, motioning up the road.

"Let's do it."

We walked over. Behind a wide, sizzling grill stood the sausage vendor, one hand resting on his hip, the other holding metal tongs that flashed in the air as he rotated the many plump sausages of various colors and shapes glistening before him. The soft warmness of burning fat and salt filled my nose while accordion-heavy Slavic music blared from a rectangular green radio on the counter. The accordion is an underrated instrument. I turned expectantly to Johanna.

"What do you recommend?"

She looked over the options that lay before us.

"I would say—either a Kaiserkrainer or a Bosna."

"What's a Bosna?"

"Bratwurst in a bun with onions, mustard, and curry powder."

"Sounds amazing. Two Bosnas, please," I said to the vendor. With a slight nod, he turned and began assembling our order.

"Is it too cold for beer?" I asked Johanna.

"Yes, but with your first Bosna, I believe it's necessary."

"And two Ottakringers, please."

While we waited, the air outside cooled, fully entering into night. Johanna sidled closer, slid her hand into mine, and guided our fingers, now intertwined, into my jacket pocket. I realized that life, with its madness and furor and quiet and rhythm would never surpass this moment. The vendor passed over two bright yellow cans. I withdrew my hand from Johanna's, reluctantly, removed my gloves, and took the cans. Cold and wet, they stuck to my bare fingers. I opened one and passed it over to her. The cold had blushed her cheeks and nose. I opened my beer and extended it. She tapped hers to mine. We each took a swig. Sweet and effervescent, the simplicity of an Austrian Helles matched the moment. We gathered our Bosnas, and, as if on cue, a Straßenbahn arrived behind us. We entered the last car and walked to the back where it was possible to stand. The car had heaters beneath a few seats and was very warm. Johanna leaned back against a rail and wordlessly passed me her beer and sausage so she could unravel her scarf and coat. I did the same, removing my jacket, and as the train traveled up the road, we ate. The warm sting of the raw onions blended well with the salt of the sausage and tart of the curry. Johanna stood so that her right foot brushed against the inside of mine as the car continued into the night, bouncing left and right, smoothly across the rails, taking us deeper into the city. We stepped off near her building and walked up into her apartment and then her room. She switched the overhead light off, leaving the room bathed in yellow from a lamp on her desk. She removed her clothes, but not her underwear, and I followed suit, and we laid together on her bed and talked. Taped to the wall near her head was a single photo: a younger Johanna grinning while being embraced by a woman whose face echoed hers.

"Is that your mom?"

"Yep. That was my fifteenth birthday."

"You guys look a lot alike."

"People always say that, but she was much more beautiful. I have too much of my father's nose." She turned in profile and ran her finger along the bridge of her nose. It was a great nose. It was hers, and I couldn't imagine one better.

"Have you had anyone in your life die?" she asked.

"Yes, but just grandparents, and I didn't know them all that well."

She nodded.

"My mother's death I have accepted. I understand that she won't be here for parts of my life like marriage, and children, and things like that. What has surprised me is how hard it is to remember the details of when she was here. How she really was. Her voice. The way memory decays doesn't feel fair, so I keep her photo here. Sorry if that seems odd."

"It makes perfect sense."

"When I think about the afterlife—if there is one—I wonder if we will regain our memories, fully. If we will be able to go back and inhabit them."

I had no idea, so I closed my eyes and held her hand. We shared stories of our families for hours until the pauses between comments extended, and I fell asleep. Being alone with her relaxed me, months of tension released, and my body just shut off. Sometime later, she woke me with a kiss. The only light in the room shone in from the courtyard around her half-pulled cotton curtain. We kissed awhile in a dreamlike state. She removed her underwear, and I mine, and we made love. It was blinding and true. Then, we drifted into a heavy sleep.

Some time before dawn, I stirred, my calves tight and legs restless. Johanna slept, her chest gently rising and falling. Her unmistakable scent of apricot mixed with a lingering of sweat from earlier in the evening. I got out of bed, stepped over to the window, and looked out onto the empty courtyard. I nudged the window open, letting in a rush of cool air. The immediateness of the day spent in step with her had faded, and my anxieties returned. I didn't understand the fragility or dimensions of Johanna's and my connection but I wanted to protect it, and I was certain it wasn't possible to feel this way with any other person. I'd have to come clean about the work I'd done for Heinrich and what it might mean about his past. Returning to bed, I reached over and pushed her arm. She moved but didn't wake. I pushed again, softly, but held it longer. She turned and opened her eyes and smiled. Then, she sat up and reached over to hug me.

"You're crying! Why?"

I shuddered, overcome with tears.

"Alex, hey, Alex," She cradled my head, turning it towards her.

"Alex, what's wrong? Tell me."

"Sorry . . ." I mumbled, warm tears flowing.

"No, it's ok," she responded, her eyes starting to water.

"I just have a lot on my mind." My heart thumped. Returning to the warmth of closeness with her, I knew I couldn't talk about Heinrich yet. If things between us could run a little longer, they might be able to weather the shock.

"Like what?"

"I have to tell you something." I did, in fact, now have to tell her something since I had woken her up—anything other than what was actually on my mind.

She sat up very straight.

"Is it about us?"

"No."

"Are you sure?"

"Definitely."

"I'm just, I have no idea where I'm headed in life."

"Ok?"

"I wish I had some purpose or mission, and I'm afraid I'm just going to end up having to go back to the USA and—"

"Hey," she interrupted.

"Yeah?"

"We might have something here, between us?"

"Maybe so."

A tear slipped down her face.

"So, you're better off than you were a month ago, or a day ago?"

I nodded.

With a smile, she leaned forward, gave me a kiss, paused, lightly pressed her lips against mine once more, and then laid back down, facing me.

"That's something?" she asked, confident in my answer.

"Sure."

I laid down next to her and she put her arm over my chest. Her breath slowed and she looked to be falling asleep.

"So, crisis averted for now, delicate flower?" she asked, with a half grin.

"Yeah, sorry."

"No problem."

We lay for another moment, her hand rubbing my neck, my anxiety fading.

"So, one of us has an exam tomorrow, and one of us does not. I won't say who is who, ok?"

I nodded, smiling. "You can go to sleep," I said.

"You sure?"

"Goodnight, Johanna."

She gave my shoulder a soft kiss before turning away towards the wall. I studied the lines of her shoulders and a small, brown mole at the base of her neck. I closed my eyes and imagined myself once again shooting three pointers for the Bulls, toes just behind the arc, ball gliding to the basket.

VIII

The next morning, I awoke alone in Johanna's room. A rolling, metal shutter outside the window had been lowered almost completely, and the only light that came in filtered through small perforations in the connective frame between shutter slats, casting a grid of sunlight over the bed. I sat up and checked my watch. It was 12:34 p.m., the latest I'd slept since I'd been in Europe. Beside me, instead of Johanna, sat a folded note written in flawless cursive.

> Hey,
> I had to go to class and you seemed very asleep,
> so I didn't want to wake you. Thank you for a
> nice evening and see you soon.
> —Johanna

On the large off-white pillow where our heads had laid together was an oblong crimson spot. My mouth had bled onto the pillow. I rubbed the spot with spit, then flipped the pillow over. This was the second Austrian bedroom I'd been in, alone, in the past forty-eight hours. The room was compact with just enough room for a twin bed, a plain birch desk, and a dresser. It had high, *Altbau* ceilings and white walls adorned with a few postcards and the single photo of her mother. A number of books were stacked along the wall in a large pile that abutted the desk. A pale cream bra hung from the desk chair. I put on my clothes and lingered. A temptation within me to rummage and snoop pushed up against a stronger temptation to lay in bed and remain in the afterglow of our evening. While having sex brought us closer together, her leaving me alone in her room was the next level of intimacy. I took a quick peek into the adjoining bedrooms, no one was home. In the kitchen, I sliced some day-old, heavy, dark bread and slathered it in butter and strawberry jelly from the fridge. Their refrigerator was a nightmare. The size of a large shoe box, it contained more food than appropriate for a refrigerator twice as big, and absolutely none of it was sufficiently wrapped. No Tupperware, no Ziploc bags—just loose items stacked on top of one another. The bottom edges of cheeses were hardened, a small pack of prosciutto dried to the texture of a magnolia leaf. I poured a glass of milk and carried it and my bread into her room and sat down at her desk. I cracked the window that looked onto the courtyard, and the white hum of the city filled the room. It was peaceful. I wasn't ready to leave, so I decided to finally write a postcard to Hank.

After choosing a card from my bag and taking a pen from her desk, I wrote his address and considered possible openings, trying to find the right layering of sincerity and wit. We hadn't spoken in so long, I wasn't sure our friendship was salvageable. It was a good sign that he had written me first and had done so in a kind way. In a single, continuous burst, I put pen to paper and wrote:

> Hank,
> I'm in Vienna. It's colder here than you can
> imagine. There's no ocean, everybody smokes,
> and you can ride on the subway drinking a beer.
> I think I'm in love with a local named Johan-

na, but her family might be fucked up so I don't know what's going to happen. I'm writing you this from her apartment. If I don't make it back, you'll have to visit. Your apology about the Janet situation is accepted with the stipulation that you'll accept mine as well.
—Alex

I wanted to say something different—this wasn't enough, it was too dry—but it's what came out. I licked and stuck on a bunch of stamps. I had no idea how many were necessary. The postcard was a photo of the Riesenrad, a sad Ferris wheel out in the Prater I had visited alone one rainy morning. Instead of chairs or pods, its long iron spokes rotated dusty, barnlike passenger compartments. I put the postcard away, stretched, and got dressed. The detailed apology I couldn't give to Hank was that my initial attraction to Janet was based upon observing his interest in her. Although I'd feigned giving him space to pursue her when he requested it, I undermined him at every chance and put my charm on maximum blast whenever I had the opportunity. I accentuated aspects of myself I could tell she liked—my intelligence, my likelihood of conventional success—and hid the core of my personality. Even though Hank feels guilt for how he cut off our friendship, he must know that I had fucked him over. If I admitted it to him how deliberate it was, I'm not sure he'd want to remain friends. All I could do is hope that the residue of the episode would fade away.

I cleaned up my dishes, threw a few decaying items out of their refrigerator, and left their apartment, pulling the door shut. Apartment doors in Austria are curious. They exist in a naturally locked state; one only needs to close them. Fastening a deadbolt requires a key, but not the basic door lock. Most doors don't have exterior knobs; to open them, you turn your key and press forward. Maybe these are meaningless design decisions or a byproduct of old mansions being sliced up into modern apartments, but I don't think so. I saw the opaque, intrinsic security within each door paralleled in the faces of people on the street.

Outside of Johanna's apartment, I wasn't sure where to go. I dropped Hank's card into a mailbox and tried calling Markus again, but he didn't pick up. I walked over towards Emil's apartment and took a table at the café near his gate where I'd sat on my first day. Heinrich had asked me not to follow Emil anymore, but I had to. I needed a resolution that I could bring to Johanna. About thirty minutes later, Emil came out, moving faster than normal, and I followed. He walked down towards the Gürtel once again, took a right onto Kaiser-straße, and proceeded through the seventh district. A woman walking the opposite direction stepped suddenly around a bus stop and their shoulders smashed into one another, knocking her down onto the ground. He stood over her, glaring, then continued without lending a hand. He turned onto Westbahn-straße and went directly into the Leica shop. I stood across the street and smoked a cigarette beside an apron-clad cashier from Spar on her smoke break. A faint, cold rain fell upon us, and the sensation of being watched grabbed at me. The face of the man on the subway—puffy eyelids and sallow skin—came to mind. People in Vienna don't look one another in the eye unless they have to, but he had looked into mine. I let my cig-arette burn down and singe my thumb before I pressed it into the wall and twisted. I still had Johanna's smell on my body, and her warmth radiated in me. Without a plan, I stepped for-ward, crossed the street, and walked into the store. My heart buzzed while I pushed the door open, clanging the bell that hung from the ceiling. No one looked my way. A young couple in the far room peered into a case of Canons. Emil crouched down across the front counter from Karl, the salesman I'd met last time. Squinting, he examined a row of Leica IIIs. Pointing to one, he asked Karl, "Could I see that one? The IIIb?"

His voice sounded different than I'd imagined. Softer.

Apologetic.

Karl bent down, opened the cabinet from the back, and held his hand, fingers askew, hovering over a beaten-up IIIf.

"Uh—to the right," Emil corrected.

Karl placed his pointer finger on the knurled rewind knob of the next camera over.

"Exactly."

As Karl pulled the camera up, Emil removed his grey jacket, folded it, and placed it onto the glass countertop. Then, he laid his hat atop his jacket. In one continuous movement, he took the camera into his broad hands, removed the lens cap, set the shutter speed, rewound the camera, and actuated the shutter. He moved quickly through each exposure time, craning his ear towards the camera body, especially so at the slower end of the scale.

"Not bad for a sixty-year-old camera?" asked Karl.

Emil nodded. "Yes, not bad." He held the camera to his eye and looked up at the light fixture hanging above him. "Sixty is not as old to me as it may be to you. I remember when this camera was released," he said, mumbling somewhat.

I took a few steps forward, into their orbit, and Karl turned towards me.

"Ah, the American."

"Hey, how's it going?"

"Very well. How is the Minolta?"

"It's great. I got my first roll back. I underexposed a few, but the ones that came out well, came out really well."

I wondered if Karl remembered every camera sale. Emil turned towards me and gave a small nod. Up close, he was shorter than I expected. Shorter than me. His hair and mustache were thin, and liver spots dotted his forehead. His eyes were pale blue. Maybe he knew someone had broken into his apartment. He held the camera to his face once more and focused on something on the far wall. His hands wavered slightly.

"It is strange to go back to a separate viewfinder and rangefinder," he whispered.

"You are used to the M then?" asked Karl.

"Yes, I am." He pivoted, turning towards me and then the edge of the counter. "Unfortunately, mine needs adjustment." He held the camera at arm's length and looked at it from different angles. "I have a box of screw mount lenses from my brother, so this may tie me over. How do I adjust the diopter of the viewfinder?"

Karl moved his glasses from their resting perch on his forehead down onto his nose.

"It's been awhile since I've used this model," Karl answered.

Stepping closer to them, I reached halfway to the camera. "Mind if I?"

Emil turned to let me by. His eyes scanned me as I took the camera. I don't think he recognized me in full, but I believe he sensed a familiarity with my presence. I reached for the diopter control, tucked beneath the film rewind knob. I fiddled the control back and forth and showed Emil. We made eye contact and I forced a confident half smile.

"Here you go."

"Wonderful. This is some knowledge for a young man. Especially an American."

I shrugged as I handed the camera back to him. "My uncle is a photographer, so I grew up around cameras."

"And you speak wonderful German," Emil said, with a soft chuckle. I knew, in that moment, that I couldn't go on following him. I think I knew it when I entered the store. As he looked through the viewfinder and adjusted the diopter, emptiness spread within me. I was fucking things up. He placed the camera down, unscrewed the lens, held it aloft, and worked the aperture blades open and shut.

"And do you sell just the body or only the two together?"

"This one is sold on consignment only as a matched set. It

comes with the original box and manual."

"Quite right," said Emil, while screwing the lens back onto the camera. It was a Summaron, 5cm, f2.8. Not the fastest or the sharpest lens, but acceptable.

I scratched the scruff on my chin, then said, "If you don't mind me asking since you are a contemporary of this camera—sometimes I think about getting a Leica III and other times I think about a Contax II. I've heard that the Contax had a better reputation back then, is that true?"

Emil put the camera down and rested his elbow on the counter. Karl bent behind the counter and retrieved a Contax II and placed it alongside the Leica.

"That was a long time ago," Emil said, pausing to look at both cameras. "My brother had the Leica III. He had a friend from Wetzlar where they were fabricated, so it was never a question for him. Do you know why the standard roll of 35mm film is thirty-six exposures?"

I shook my head.

"Oskar Barnack, the father of Leica, took a roll of uncut film—" Emil extended his arms forward, hands together, then spread them vertically, as if unrolling an invisible spool of film until he couldn't stretch further. Then, he mimed letting the film hang from one hand as he reached up with the other and cut the dangling strip loose. "He measured like this, and it just happened to be thirty-six exposures. It became the standard."

Karl nodded approvingly.

"So, Leica is Leica," he shrugged. "But it is a camera to be put to use, not left as a fetish for the shelf. A Contax is fine as well." He raised his pointer finger and held it aloft, "But only from before the war. They were from Dresden and were never the same after, obviously." I reached between them and picked up the Contax. Broadly rectangular with its name written in a silly sans-serif font across the front, it looked like a workman's tool next to the edgeless series of circles composing the artist's Leica III. My interest in the Contax began when I read *Slight-*

ly out of Focus, Robert Capa's autobiography. When Capa waded through the chilled waters of Utah Beach at dawn on June 6, 1944, he carried two Contaxes strapped around his neck. That was enough of a recommendation for me. While I removed the back of the Contax and ran my fingers over its heavy rolling metal shutter, Emil purchased the Leica. I clenched my jaw a few times while Karl searched beneath the counter for the correct lens cap. This encounter had taught me nothing while erasing my anonymity. I placed my palm onto the thick, beveled glass of the counter. I had to create some context for future interaction between Emil and me.

"It might be nice to take photographs together sometime," I blurted out.

Emil turned towards me as he placed the Leica into his well-oiled leather satchel.

"No thanks," he said, with a perfunctory nod and left the store, leaving Karl and me alone. My face flushed warm with shame. After a few parting words to Karl, I left. Emil was nowhere in sight, and even if he had been, I couldn't risk following. That era was now over. I trudged home and lay down on my couch. I flipped the channels on my TV and fell into a hazy remembrance of the night with Johanna. The rawness of her presence was impossible to retrieve from memory. Being apart from her made me doubt that the previous night had happened, or that she even existed. I picked up the phone and called her.

"Hey, Johanna?"

"Hallo, how's it going?"

"Good, good. Did you maybe want to hang out again tonight?" I asked. My body tensed. It was a clumsy, direct approach.

"Of course. Some friends and I are cooking dinner together this evening. Maybe you could come over afterwards, around 9:30?"

"That's perfect. How'd the test go?"

"Let us never speak of that test."

"Oh shit, sorry."

She laughed. "Our time was worth the sacrifice. I have to run now to buy groceries—see you tonight?"

"Sure, see ya."

We hung up. To speak with her, even for a moment, gave the feeling of being understood. It's second to none. I pulled out all of my notes and sketches detailing Emil's walks and laid them across my bed. Then, I unfolded my map and placed his photos with clear signs of origin onto the spots they were taken. There had to be more information to extract from the raw materials at my disposal. I couldn't understand why Emil had shown so much interest in the second district and the Augarten yet hadn't walked there in all the days that I had followed him. Maybe he'd already done whatever he needed to do. Seeing him up close at the Leica shop, he didn't look capable of something dangerous. He looked washed up. I decided to try and find the apartment building that he had photographed at three different times of day. Based on the placement of other photos, the apartment was likely in a twenty-square block area below the Augarten's southern tip. Before I left, I knelt down beside my bed, prayed, and tried to stifle the stress pushing up from inside of me.

Although only five p.m., the sun had slipped below the rooftops, its last light casting a grey pallor over the streets. I headed east over the Danube Canal by way of the Friedensbrücke Bridge. Just over the water, outside an U-Bahn station, a disinterested vendor hunched over a rusted, makeshift grill roasting chestnuts. The smell stuck in my nose, even blocks away, a lingering tinge of burning wetness and earth. I knew the chestnut roasting song, but I'd never seen the real thing before. Into the twentieth district I walked upon the broad, colorless Wallensteinstraße. I stopped to look into the window of an Altwaren shop when I noticed, about thirty feet away, the dark-haired man from the subway a few days earlier. He wore the same burgundy jacket and stared in my direction with his hands thrust into his pockets. I didn't make eye contact and stepped forward at an even pace. He did the same. I stopped again after about a block and looked into the reflection of a bike shop window. He remained, now about twenty feet away. Without haste I walked further, turned the next corner, and ducked into the first door I came across, a betting parlor. Overwhelming cigarette smoke and near total darkness enveloped me. The room was filled with emotionless men staring up blankly at television screens. I was being followed, unquestionably, but what was most alarming was that the man didn't seem to care that I noticed. He wanted me to notice.

Inside, I considered all possible options. The cashier wouldn't let me use their phone and there wasn't a back exit, so I didn't have any good ones. There weren't any windows facing the street either, so I couldn't be sure the man was waiting, but I sensed it. I stood near the exit with a betting slip, and when a group of men walked out together, I followed close behind. Outside, leaning back against a tree was the man in the jacket. He had patchy black stubble and was two or three inches taller than me with a bored, languid expression. I walked straight towards him, looking into his eyes, and brushed hard against his shoulder as I passed. A few steps later, I glanced back. He was in the same spot with a wry, amused grin. Casually, he leaned forward, and stepped towards me. Images flashed through my mind. I could run, I could turn back and fight, or I could find a place to call for help. I walked quickly with my hand in my pocket down the next block, took a left, and then a right, slowly working a five hundred schilling bill from my wallet. I altered my speed to hear the sound of his steps falling behind me. I worked the bill loose and just as I turned the next corner, I let it flutter to the ground. Then, I waited. When I saw the top of the man's head dropping to retrieve the bill I stepped forward and swung my fist into his temple. It was a clumsy, half-connected shot, but he fell sideways. Standing over him, unsure what to do next, I picked up the bill and took a few steps away. Then, I turned back and slammed my heel directly into his nose, breaking it, spilling dark, thick blood all over the sidewalk. I'd never hit anyone before in my life. Feeling the crunch beneath my foot sent bile from my stomach up into the back of my mouth, and I gagged. Down the block and across the street, a couple looked our way and then turned and ran. Without thought, I spit on the man as he struggled to get to his feet.

"What the fuck do you want?" I asked, in English and then again, more politely, in German. Now halfway up, he looked at me and swayed his head slightly back and forth, smiling incredulously. Hunched over, he turned to walk away. After a few steps, I came up behind him and rifled through his coat pockets where his hands had been. His fingers flailed over mine to stop me, but they were too slow. Finding something in his right pocket, I pulled it out. With my right forearm in the small of his back and my left hand clasped around his neck, I shoved him up against a wall, scraping his face onto the bricks. Then, I took his wallet from his back right pocket and sprinted away. Over my shoulder, I heard him yell profanities at me in accented German. A few blocks away, I unfolded what I had taken from his pocket. It was a photo of me, sitting in the café near Emil's, taken from up the street. On the back, in Heinrich's unmistakable clean, looping script, was my name, address, and passport number, which I had never given to Heinrich. I suppose one side effect of writing well is to have your hand be immediately recognizable. The cold air stung my lungs as heavy, flat pain pulsed from my fingers to my wrist and up into my elbow. My rightmost two knuckles were compressed and akilter. The man's wallet had no ID, just a few schillings and a single-ride Straßenbahn ticket. I ducked into a dark, windowless alley, went to the far corner, and threw up. Then, I sat down on a cinder block, chest heaving and mind blurred. Fuck this country.

If Heinrich was sending men to stop me, I must be close to something. I had to keep going. Checking my map under a streetlight, I continued forward to my original target, a trapezoid of blocks south of the Augarten. As I walked, my right wrist stiffened and began to feel wooden. I shook and flexed it, but it didn't help. I reached the angled intersection of Leopoldsgasse and Kleine Pfargasse, pulled out the corresponding photo from my bag, and held it up until the lines from the streets ran straight into the lines of the picture. I could see quite a ways down each intersecting road. I took a left down the smaller, narrower street. I weaved my way through the blocks of the neighborhood, a series of two-lane roads intermixed with quiet, one-way residential alleys. When possible, I matched locations to photographs and marked off streets on my map after clearing them. Halfway down the short alley Rotenkreuzgaße, I realized I had walked with Johanna down the block a day before. Without her, the street felt narrower and the buildings stark. At the corner, I could see my destination: the apartment building Emil had photographed at three different times of day. It was located at the exact center of his other photographs.

Five floors high and about a third of a block long, its exterior didn't stand out from the neighboring buildings. In person, it was pale yellow, a mild surprise given that it was grey in Emil's black-and-white picture. On the top floor, a woman leaned out of her window, chin in hand, smoking. As I lifted a photo into position to confirm the building, a street light reflected off of something in the sidewalk. I walked over to get a closer look. A perfect square had been cut out from the pavement, and a clean, brass plate placed into the hole. Rough black grout, about two fingers thick, held the plate in place. Carved into the brass were four names: Lana, Leo, Felix, and Rosa Hirsch. Beneath each name was a birthdate followed by "Am 15-10-1941 Nach Theresienstadt Deportiert Im Holocaust Ermordet," which means: "On October 15, 1941, deported to Theresienstadt, murdered in the Holocaust."

The youngest, Leo, was four when he was taken. Lana, presumably his sister, seven. The light reflecting from the plate revealed no scratches and little dust. It must have been freshly lain. I rubbed the black grout and held my fingers to my nose; it smelled earthy and sulfurous. I only had 100-speed film in my camera, too slow for dusk, so I ripped out a piece of paper from my notebook and placed it over the plate. I shook a piece of lead out from my mechanical pencil, held it in my fingertips, and attempted to make a rubbing. It didn't work well—the lead broke a few times and my fingers felt incredibly cold—but it was something. As I rubbed, careful to gather the grooves and channels that formed the names without piercing the paper, I began to cry. It's hard to feel anything, especially over unknown dead from the past, but I did.

After finishing the rubbing, unsatisfied with its clarity, I wrote the details of the Hirsch family into my notebook. Holding a pencil in the three good fingers of my right hand made my pulse throb heavy in my ears and inflamed the dull ache coming from my knuckles. The outside of my forearm became fully numb. Behind me, the horse-hooved clop of a pair of women in boots approached. They passed me, they were about my age, and continued on, oblivious or uninterested in the small brass memorial. My thighs began to burn from crouching, so I sat down onto the cold pavement with my back against the building. I tried to imagine that within the walls behind me, people had been dragged out, sent off, and clinically murdered. Emil and Heinrich must have been involved. It wouldn't be easy to tell Johanna. I wanted to know if the Hirsch family had been pulled from their home in daylight or evening. Had their neighbors watched, cigarette in hand, from open windows? Did Leo and Lana understand what was happening, or did their parents keep it a secret for as long as possible? By 1941, it would have been difficult to fool the children. When a life ends in murder, does the finish eclipse all the years before it?

Looking over my map, I annotated the building, stood up, and headed east when a long, black Audi sedan turned onto the street, its bright headlights blinding me for a moment. It slowed when it passed by, freezing me in terror, but it kept going. I couldn't make out the driver. Halfway down the block, I came across another brass plate. Though the names and dates were different, the meaning was the same. People from the green building beside it had been killed in the Holocaust, or, as this plate called it, the Shoah. The catastrophe. I walked around the district in an expanding circle for two hours, locating all of Emil's photos, and counting eight similar memorials. Though I'd walked the neighborhood with Johanna, I'd somehow missed them. The plates were compact, tucked close to walls, and easy to overlook. I also came across a number of rectangular, black metal signs mounted above doorways, each inscribed with wartime remembrances. Similar to the one from the lobby of my apartment, they explained that the building had been damaged or destroyed during the war and later rebuilt by the city. There were other signs without text that I didn't understand. An extruded beehive on a building's corner. A mosaic of a coiled serpent high on a wall.

I returned to the original brass plate. Throughout Emil's thirty-three photos was a portion of sixty-two different buildings in the district. It was clear that if one took pictures of that many buildings in Vienna, it would be easy to find a place with bodies attached. The frequency of the memorials made it less definitive that Emil and Heinrich were involved in any one incident, or any incident at all. The years didn't line up either. The Hirsch family was taken in 1941. Heinrich would have only been sixteen, Emil thirteen. If I ignored that detail, the fact remained that much of what happened there was documented well enough to be commemorated. What was known was already unimaginable. The only ones who could be shocked by further revelations would be the friends and families of the perpetrators. People like Johanna. I needed to be at her apartment in about twenty minutes. I checked my map and headed west.

Under the streetlight across from her place, I examined my fist. Swollen and purple, there was no hiding it. I could barely move my last two fingers. I crossed the street and buzzed her apartment. With a click, the door opened. Halfway up the stairs, a surge of emotion hit me. I shouldn't have been there. I should have been booking a flight home or talking to the police. I continued on. I couldn't miss an opportunity to see her. I rapped on her cracked door with my working knuckles, pushed it open, and stepped inside. The kitchen was warm, the sink was full of dishes, and the scent of hot cooking oil and baked pork wafted about. Lisi and Johanna sat across from one another at their small kitchen table. They looked over and smiled. Johanna's hair was pulled up into a ponytail, and she wore a loose white T-shirt and swimming-pool-blue Adidas track pants with navy stripes. Lisi wore a tight-fitting black unitard-type top and jeans. Down the hall, I could see the moving shadows of another roommate in one of the bedrooms.

"Hey. I, uh—this is weird, but I actually just got in a fight on the way over here," I said, pulling my injured arm forward. Under their fluorescent kitchen light it looked grey and green and far worse than outside.

"Oida!" exclaimed Lisi, backing up in her chair with a loud squeak. Johanna came over and placed one hand at my elbow and the other at my wrist.

"What happened?"

"I'm not sure. I was coming down the street up there," I said, pointing towards the far wall, "on Thurngasse—and a guy shoved me into the wall and tried to grab my wallet. I swung at him and then ran."

"I'm so sorry," said Johanna. She guided my arm straight

and ran her fingers over my knuckles, gripping each briefly. "You should get this checked out."

"Yeah?" I asked, turning it over, trying to flex it.

"Definitely, but the wait at the hospital would be terrible now." She paused, turned sideways, and walked to the cabinet and took out a bottle. "Let's do ibuprofen and ice it, and I can take you to my doctor in the morning. There won't be a line, and he won't give you a hard time about not having a medical card."

I nodded. I guess I was spending the night again. Lisi looked intently into my eyes with concern and with something else. Maybe distrust. I noticed a few spots of blood on my right pant leg. I turned so the stain was in the shadows. My legs weakened, and I grabbed the counter with my good hand. "Do you mind if I sit down?"

"Oh no, of course not," said Johanna, positioning her chair for me. Seated, I bent my elbow and straightened my arm a few times. "Are you hungry? We have leftovers."

"It smells like a feast in here. Food would be great. Do you have any shorts that might fit me or anything? Coming in from the cold, I feel a little stuffy and dizzy." I glanced at my shoe beneath the table. Streaks of half-dry blood smeared its back. Johanna and Lisi looked at each other for a moment.

"I might have something," replied Lisi. She ducked away and returned a moment later with wide grey cotton gym shorts.

"They're from an ex. You can keep them."

"Thanks."

Johanna pulled a plate from the cabinet and began opening pots and pans on the stove. The smell of warm sauerkraut and roasted pork filled the air.

"Johanna, could I change in your room?"

"Yes, of course."

I walked to her room. Getting my coat unbuttoned and my jeans off with only my left hand was not easy. I stumbled against the door and knocked some of Johanna's books onto the ground. I stripped down to my white undershirt and Lisi's ex's shorts. Although the stains on my shoes and jeans were small, a blood stain is hard to miss. With spit, I managed to rub the smooth black leather of my Sambas clean. Having a mix of my spit and some random guy's blood on my fingers made my mouth dry, and I started to gag. Frantically, I dried my fingers on my jeans, rolled the jeans into a ball, and stuffed them in the corner. Without touching anything else, I went to the kitchen, quickly ducked into the adjoining bathroom, and washed my hands with a tired, yellow bar of soap that sat on the remains of its predecessors. The water flowed frigid and clear. I bent down and gulped mouthfuls of it, splashing it into my face, tracing my eyes with my fingers.

The other day, I had overheard two Viennese talking about their tap water. It flows directly from the Lower Austrian Alps in thirty-six hours motivated only by gravity. As it ran coolly over my injured knuckles, I sensed it might be the last time I would see Johanna. I drank some more water and stepped out into the kitchen. At the table waited an overflowing plate, Johanna, and Lisi. The heat and steam from the stove gave the room a cozy warm haze. I sat down and studied the food and Johanna in astonishment. Her green eyes shone brilliantly, almost luminescent. She reached out and hovered her finger above my plate.

"Schweinsbradl, Semmelknödel, Rotkraut, Vogerlsalat," she said, pausing after announcing each item. Translated into English, some mystique is lost. Roast pork, a bread dumpling, red sauerkraut, and a leafy green salad.

"This looks wonderful, thank you."

"Have you had Semmelknödel before?"

"Can't say I have."

"Lisi worked on it for over an hour. That ball is made from one million pieces of torn bread pushed together."

I poked it with a fork. It didn't give. Orb-like and textured, it resembled the moon. I sliced a piece off, dabbed it in the juices from the pork, and took a bite, chewing slowly. It was warm and savory. I cut off more, added a piece of pork, and ate it. It was difficult to imagine a heavier, more satisfying bite. I shook my head and said, "Incredible."

"Yeah?" Lisi asked.

"Definitely." I chewed and swallowed. I reached into my mouth and pantomimed searching for something. "Is it supposed to have a fingernail in it?" Lisi rolled her eyes. "Just kidding. This is great, thanks."

"Would you like something to drink?" asked Lisi.

I reached for the ibuprofen bottle and popped it open with my left hand.

"Probably one beer with this won't kill me, right?"

"Nah." Lisi leaned back, opened the fridge, and pulled out a dark blue can of Wieselburger. Turning to Johanna she asked, "Weisser Spritzer?" Johanna nodded in assent. Lisi pulled out a three-quarters full bottle of Grüner Veltliner and a green glass bottle of sparkling water from the fridge. Then, she took out two wine glasses, one larger than the other, and placed them in front of Johanna and herself. She filled each a third of the way up with wine and then added another third of water. Raising her glass to me, she smiled and said, "Mahlzeit." We all took a drink.

"You just missed Zeinab, she wanted to see you. She's your biggest fan, I think, outside of Johanna," said Lisi, with a wry grin.

"Ah, where'd she go?"

"She had to call her American boyfriend when he gets off work. They talk on the phone all night, every night."

"That's beautiful."

I worked my way through the meal methodically, layer by layer, consuming an astonishing amount. The salty, rich flavors settled my nerves. As I ate, Lisi spoke in detail about her studies at art school and her relationship with the original owner of the shorts I was wearing—"Don't worry, they've been washed"—and her current romantic situation. Although Johanna had told me that Lisi was available, she was actually in love with some Dutch guy who may or may not have been moving to Vienna to be near her. While he seemed romantically interested, in every conversation with Lisi he made it clear that she was *not* the only reason he was coming to Vienna.

Johanna talked about a paper she was writing for school. She'd spent four months observing Bosnian kids in a refugee house in the neighborhood and had to analyze how their German language acquisition mapped to their socioeconomic status. She had to write the paper in English, and, for that practical reason alone, she was interested in maintaining, "some level of relationship," with me. When I asked if she had any other native English–speaking suitors, she demurely lifted her shoulders and informed me that, "America isn't that small of a country." I propped my arm up on a stack of boxes and periodically placed frozen peas beneath my wrist, twenty minutes on, twenty minutes off. The ibuprofen and beer helped, and the pain dulled to a slow, even pulse. After a second helping of food, and then some time spent over the pot with my fork, randomly eating bits of Knödel, I collapsed down into my chair, completely full.

"Hannes has been asking about you. He wants me to give you his number," said Lisi.

"Oh yeah?"

"Yeah. He believes he has a few ideas that will change your mind about everything. He's essentially continued your conversation in his mind for weeks. That's what he likes to do. Arguments with him don't end. They're just paused until he gathers more ammunition."

"Who wins when you two fight?"

She blinked and looked off to the side. She was so thin, it was impossible to look at her and not worry a little. The other night we had only spoken English. In German, her voice was a register lower and huskier.

"He's older, so it used to be him, but in the last few years I've won a few."

"Interesting. Sure, give him my number, I'll keep fighting with him. I have to say, this was probably the second-best meal I've ever had in my life. Honestly."

"Why not the best?" Lisi asked.

"Oh, well my best is sort of unapproachable, so to be my second-best meal is really like being anyone else's best ever."

"Is that so?"

"Yeah."

"What's number one?"

I lifted my wrist and flipped the frozen peas to their colder side.

"I broke into In-N-Out one time with my friend, Hank, and we made our own burgers. It was the best meal anyone could possibly have."

"What's In-N-Out?"

"You don't know In-N-Out!?"

"Never heard of it."

"It's a burger place in California."

"Your best meal is a burger? You are so American," said Johanna, shaking her head.

"Yeah. Stereotypes are all true. That's why you aren't allowed to use them."

She shrugged. "What's the story?"

"Well, my friend Hank has a cousin, Ray, who managed an In-N-Out. Ray slept at Hank's house all the time because their entire family is close and Ray has issues with his parents. One night, we were playing Super Nintendo in Hank's living room when Ray came home after the restaurant closed. He reeked so badly of grease and fries that Hank's mom made him strip naked outside and put his clothes directly into their washer, so his keys, including *the* key to In-N-Out, were left on top of the dryer. When Ray fell asleep, we grabbed them and drove there around four a.m. It's in Mountain View, which is a nothing town forty-five minutes south of the city, but it's an easy drive and we took Ray's new Honda—a Prelude, which I haven't seen around here, but is pretty cool. It's a two door and he never let us drive it, so we had to take the opportunity. When we got there, we made our own burgers. The first two fell apart on the grill, and our fries were not good at all—they tasted like fish for some reason—but the third burger I made was the best thing I've ever eaten. I think it was luck, and that I cooked it medium-rare, which they won't do at the restaurant. Plus, we had a six-pack of High Life, which—you can't normally drink beer at fast food places in America."

"Why can't you drink beer?"

"I dunno. I think maybe because everyone knows if In-N-Out starts serving beer, every other restaurant will go out of business. Anyway, I used raw onions, because I don't know how to grill an onion, and it gave the burger this great bite. I also toasted the bun in the grease leftover from the first two failed burger attempts then smashed everything down with the spatula, like a panini."

"Did you get in trouble?" asked Johanna.

"Oh no, we cleaned up when we left. I'm not sure anyone ever knew. We never told Ray. We drove back up 280—a more scenic highway than the one we took down—and watched the sunrise come over the fog on the mountains."

"I want to do that."

"Ray doesn't work there anymore, unfortunately."

"Tell Ray to get his job back."

"I could, but Hank isn't talking to me right now, so Ray probably isn't either."

"Why's that?"

"Ah—it's too late to go into. But it's my fault."

Our conversation flowed for a while, I bored them with more details of home, and at some point, cigarettes emerged and we entered into a relaxed, disassociated comfort and quiet. Johanna broke the silence with a question.

"Have you seen my grandfather lately?"

"We met on Sunday briefly, you?"

"We are going to have lunch tomorrow. He mentioned he wasn't feeling well, so I'm worried about him. Thursday is the anniversary of my grandmother's death."

My legs grew heavy and stiff, and the balance of everything within me tilted. I didn't know what to say to her. Even if I decided to tell her everything, I wouldn't know how to say it. From a shelf high on the wall beside us, a black, plastic clock radio began to crackle. A man's voice came into the room.

"Would you mind turning that up?" asked Lisi. With my good arm, I stretched and twisted the volume knob clockwise.

"Tonight, I'm going to do something different. I'm going to play an entire album from start to finish," said the voice from the radio. Baritone and weary, it was hard to place, but I'd heard it before.

"What is this?" I asked.

"Radio Seven. You don't know it?" asked Johanna. I shook my head. "It's a famous radio station in Vienna. It's from a man in his apartment with a transmitter. A pirate station. You can only receive it in the inner districts, and he broadcasts at random times. Nobody knows when."

"Seriously?"

"Yes."

"He just plays music?"

"Yes, and he rambles. About his day, the weather, anything. He has a dark sense of humor. People love it. At first, the police and the radio commission tried to find him and shut him down, but now everyone listens, even the chancellor. We bought this radio just for him, and we leave it tuned into his station. Once, Lisi missed an exam when he broadcast in the middle of the day because she couldn't make herself leave to go to class."

I stared at up the thick red digits of the time on the radio.

They appeared to vibrate slightly. At that point, most of the German spoken to me in Vienna went down smoothly, but the word Johanna used for broadcasting stood out: *Rundfunk*. It's a great word. I wasn't sure how to explain its charm to them, so I kept it to myself.

"He always plays the best music. It's always the right song for the moment. It's eerie," said Lisi.

From the radio the voice continued, "Recorded at 8:43 p.m. on January 12 in 1963 at the Harlem Square Club in Miami."

"I think I've met this guy," I said.

Lisi and Johanna looked at one another and grinned.

"Nobody knows this guy, Alex," said Lisi.

"What do you mean?"

They shook their heads in unison.

"He's anonymous. He doesn't even have a fake name. He's just a voice," answered Johanna.

"Cool."

I'd like to be a DJ. The record was a concert by Sam Cooke. Loose, raw, and pure, it was great. I'd heard Sam's hits a million times before, but never in a live performance. We listened through the first two songs in reverent silence.

"This album is great," I said and stood up to stretch. They remained quiet as Sam performed the song "Cupid." I began to fade out of the moment and into sadness. We'd go to bed soon, we'd wake up, and I'd have to do something. Somewhere across town, a guy was tending to his broken nose and probably planning how to hurt me back. As Sam began to cajole the crowd, partly singing, partly preaching, Johanna stared blankly forward. She wasn't as warm as the night before. The longer I waited to tell her everything, the more risk I took with our bond. Time spent at less-than-full honesty could rot our roots. I took the wine bottle and hovered it over her glass, she nodded, and I poured a splash. I turned towards Lisi, she nodded as well, and I topped her off.

"Could I grab another beer?"

"Yeah, of course, we have to stay up for the music," answered Lisi. I took a beer from the fridge, opened it, and gathered some plates together.

"Mind if I?" I asked, motioning towards the dishes.

"Go for it," answered Johanna.

I scraped the remains of Knödel into their tiny, toy-sized garbage can. There was no way all of the trash would fit. My hand made it difficult, but I managed to work through a third of the plates while they listened to the music and drank wine.

"I have a depressing question for you guys, if that's ok," I said, breaking their trance. Lisi turned towards me and pulled her legs up into her chair and held them. "It's Second World War related," I added. The sound of the needle gliding into dead wax came over the radio. A light click blipped when the DJ flipped the record, followed by an inaudible needle drop and Sam Cooke's voice, rough and ragged as he sang "Somebody Have Mercy." The cymbals crashed loudly, overshadowing the vocals at times. Johanna looked at me, her face stiff. She had her feet stretched into my empty seat and her left arm hanging over the back of her chair.

"Go ahead with your question," she said.

"Remember how you were telling me about the flowers left at your door for Holocaust victims?"

She nodded and pointed towards the window behind me. The kitchen window, frosted over, faced out into the dark stairwell. Along its sill, dry and fragile, were four, once-white roses bundled by a piece of grey wire. A sadness filtered into the room. "Sorry to bring the mood down," I said.

Johanna looked concerned, Lisi curious. I shook my right wrist. The pain was increasing.

"No problem. It's that time of night," answered Lisi.

"Ok, so—on the note of memorials, have either of you seen the brass plates in the sidewalk beside buildings where

Holocaust victims lived?"

"Yes. They are new, but I've seen them," said Lisi.

"Me too," added Johanna.

"What do people think about them?"

Johanna bit her lower lip, then answered, "It depends on the person, of course. Day to day, most won't notice them, but if they do, I hope they appreciate their presence." Lisi nodded. Johanna shifted in her seat and then continued, "Austria has not done well with wartime guilt. There's always some new type of denial happening. Either people refuse to rename streets named for anti-Semites, or someone won't give stolen art back, or some politician lies about if they were in the Wehrmacht or the Schutzstaffel. Objects like those plates can be good because they are persistent and resist misinterpretation."

"Interesting."

"Do you know what they're called?"

"No."

"*Stolpersteine*. Something like, 'stumbling blocks' in English."

Lisi put her legs down, sat up straight, and spoke, "Even some who do wish to remember don't like the plates. The act of stepping on them is—it can feel disrespectful. Like walking over a grave. Do you know the monument against fascism in the first, near the Albertina?"

"I've seen it, yeah."

Lisi used a word I'd never heard before, *Mahnmal*. The deeper we got into subjects, the more my foreignness with their language emerged, forcing me to only partially understand things, or to be unaware when I completely misunderstood them.

"It's become a symbol of Austria's confusion. The intention, I think, was good, but it has a figure of a Jewish man forced to scrub the street after the Anschluss. If you look at it a certain way, it's humiliating. It's not the right way to honor the victims."

"I'm sorry, what does Mahnmal mean?"

"It's a monument to something awful, so people won't forget. How do you say that in English?"

"We don't really have a word just for that. Memorial I guess, but memorials could be for something good or bad."

"Strange."

I was still working towards my actual question. I'd already managed to deplete our joyful spirit, so I had to press on. From the radio, Sam Cooke continued to sing. Each song slowed in the middle and settled into raspy spoken word sections, almost like prayer. His voice held such grace, but too much of it made me sad. I couldn't help but think about how his life had ended with a gunshot to the chest at a motel in LA. I put down the dish I was working on, looked towards the table, and asked, "Do you think that people that actually murdered those mentioned in the Stolpersteine ever come across them? The perpetrators can't all be dead or in prison, right?"

Lisi looked at me and rubbed her eyes. Everyone seemed tired. The kitchen light reflected off her black hair.

"It must have happened, sure," said Johanna, calmly.

"That's fucked up, right? Like, oh yeah, Viktor *did* used to live here. I remember when we killed him."

"Yes. It's fucked up."

"What do those people do all day long? Are they just regular members of society?"

Johanna looked down and ran her fingers along the deep grooves in their kitchen table. Maybe she knew I was hinting at Heinrich. Lisi cleared her throat and said, "Well they're old now. The truth is, most continued their lives in the same jobs or whatever they were doing before the war." She paused and rubbed the back of her neck. "My father told me about a book in the sixties that came out that listed the West German politicians who used to be high-ranking National Socialists. The government denied most of it and nothing changed. For our generation, it's less about worrying about our grandparents and more about the FPÖ."

"What's that?"

"Basically the new Brown party. You don't know Jorg Haider?"

"I don't think so."

She gave me a surprised, disappointed look.

"He's the head of the FPÖ. They're modernized, mainstream neo-Nazis. A very anti-immigrant, anti-EU, 'Austria for the Austrians' type of party. They are gaining power, even in Vienna."

I took a drink of my beer. They were both silent, Johanna staring down at the table, Lisi at the door.

"So, you don't like Austria very much, do you?" asked Lisi.

"No, I do actually. Sorry, I didn't mean to be negative."

She glared at me, and I went back to cleaning, moving on to the pots they had cooked with. The sharp, biting scent of lemon suds floated about. While I washed, Lisi and Johanna talked about an upcoming weekend they'd planned at the Wachau, a wine region near the city. My right shoulder cramped from the awkward mechanics necessary to grip a sponge with only my thumb and pointer finger. On the radio, the last notes of the record faded out, followed by ten seconds of a low, faint hum. With a cough, the DJ returned, whispering, "Just one more for you all tonight. From their 1988 seven-inch Sarah Records debut, this is the Field Mice with 'Emma's House.'" Jangly guitar chords filled the kitchen. Through the door to the hallway, I could hear the song coming from the neighbors. Johanna stood and cranked the volume. I leaned back against the counter and filled a freshly washed glass with water from the tap. Johanna and Lisi sat in a meditative state while the song played. Mellow and foggy, the song did fit the mood. When it ended, the DJ whispered, "Goodnight, Vienna." Johanna and Lisi both rose silently, looked at one another, and Lisi left the room.

"Bedtime? Do you need more ibuprofen?" asked Johanna.

"I think I'm ok."

We went down the hall to her room. A procession without the joy of the night before. She changed into a large T-shirt, took off her pants, and climbed into bed. I laid down next to her. Looking into her eyes, we shared our first genuine connection of the evening.

"Are you ok?" I asked.

"Yeah, I'm tired though. You?" She placed her hand onto my injured wrist.

"Sure."

"Alex, was your story about how you hurt your wrist the truth?"

"Yeah, why?"

"It felt like a lie."

I took a slow breath and stretched my injured hand towards the ceiling.

"It's not the complete truth, no."

She turned onto her back and faced the ceiling.

"I don't think you should stay here if you are going to lie to me."

"Listen—Johanna." She turned towards me. "I'm sorry for lying, but I really can't tell you more right now. Hopefully soon."

"Why can't you tell me now?"

I couldn't mention Heinrich until I confronted him. The possibility was slim that he was well intentioned, but it remained. I also didn't know how she'd react. Her running to him in anger might interfere with my pursuit of the truth.

"Telling you why I can't tell you would pretty much be the same thing as telling you."

"Then, you should go. I'm sorry."

I rolled out of bed and began to look for my clothes.

"Does it involve my grandfather?" she asked.

"No, no."

She sat up in bed.

I pulled on my pants, awkwardly.

"Would you help me? I don't think I can get my shirt on."

She rose, pulled my shirt around me, and buttoned it up. She kissed me softly on my cheek.

"I promise you I'm not a bad guy, or at least, worse than average."

She laughed. "All you can promise is average?"

I shrugged. "Last night was more fun than this, huh?"

She nodded.

"I'll call you and explain everything soon." I said.

"I hope so."

I left her apartment and jogged in the direction of mine. I took well-lit streets and checked behind me every half block. Part of me was relieved to have her prepared for an impending revelation, but the rest of me felt hollow. As I turned onto my square, I realized that the voice of the DJ was Markus. Once upstairs, I cracked a beer, downed four more ibuprofens and dialed his number. I had no plan. As it rang, I tuned my living room's radio to his station's frequency. It wasn't broadcasting, so I increased the volume until the static was overwhelming, then backed off a hair. The phone rang five times, and Markus picked up.

"Hello."

"Hey! It's Alex."

"Hello Alex. Are you ok? It's a little late—" He sounded awake. Hearing his voice rattling through the tinny phone handset confirmed he was the DJ.

"Yeah, I'm ok. Is it too late? Do you have a minute?"

"Sure, hold on." I heard him mumble something in the background.

"You have a lady over there Markus? Ana?"

"I wish. It's my cat, Paula."

"Listen, I have a stupid question for you. You're this guy on the radio, right?"

"Which guy?"

"This Radio Seven pirate station guy."

"Ah, no—but I have gotten that before." If I focused, I could hear the smirk on his face.

"Come on."

"Seriously. I know the station, but it's not me. I wish it were."

Now, he sounded sincere. Maybe it wasn't him.

"Ok, well, Johanna is a big fan of Radio Seven."

"Good to know, Alex. Was that why you called? You sound haggard."

"I may be in some trouble."

"With the grandfather? Heinrich?"

"Yeah. It's gotten worse. He had me break into the house of the guy I was following, and it's possible they are both war criminals. I still don't know for sure. At the very least, Heinrich sent someone to follow me, and I beat the shit out of them. I didn't really have a choice. It just kind of happened."

Markus let out a heavy sigh. "You beat up an old guy?"

I laughed. "Nah, the guy was young. But I know he was working for Heinrich."

"Does Johanna know about all this yet?"

"No. I didn't know how to tell her since I don't have any proof or anything—"

"Ok, well, don't blame her. Everyone's family here is fucked up."

It hadn't occurred to me to blame her.

"Ok, I'm not."

"Can I help you?"

"Maybe, but I don't know how. I don't know what I'm doing."

"How about drinks tomorrow evening? We can talk it out. Let's meet at Delfina at nine in the seventh district. It's a pizza place with a great bar."

"Ok."

"Alex. Hang in there."

"Sure thing."

We hung up, and I lay on the bed for a while, hoping the right song for my mood would come from Radio Seven. It didn't. I took out my Discman and played the Pearl Jam album *Vitalogy*. Twenty-four hours before, I had been lying next to Johanna. Now, I was very alone. I tried to replay each event of the day to find some connection I'd missed, but I got stuck on a loop remembering the way the cartilage in the guy's nose folded beneath my heel. *Vitalogy* is a great album, but even with the volume twisted to the max, I couldn't force myself to pay attention. Eventually, a plan coalesced in my mind. Heinrich was increasing the pressure on me, and I would have to respond in a significant, determined manner. I knew where he lived, and I knew he would be meeting Johanna for lunch at noon. I'd already broken into one old man's apartment, it was time to move on to the next.

IX

The next morning, I woke at dawn with pain gnawing into my right wrist and a stiff, fitful tension twisting my back and shoulders. I filled my bathtub with ice and cold water, sat down on the tile floor next to it, and submerged my arm. I needed to see a doctor, but I didn't have time. At eleven a.m., I walked towards Heinrich's place. It was on a small street near the Volkstheater, and when leaving to meet with Johanna, he would most likely head south towards Burggasse and then east until he could catch the D Straßenbahn. I went north of his apartment and stood as far off as I could and still glimpse his entryway. At eleven-forty-five a.m., the tall wooden doors opened, and Heinrich stepped out. I waited until he turned the far corner and then walked to his entrance. With a gloved hand, I swiped over every apartment's doorbell, sending a ring to all thirty-two units. The lock whirred as someone buzzed me in, and I stepped inside. I went to his door, #3, on the first floor. Imposing and heavy with ornate carvings, there would be no kicking or prying to enter. I walked into the building's inner courtyard, a drab, paved square that held cans for garbage and five different types of recycling: paper, plastic, metal, clear glass, and colored glass. Each wall of the courtyard was lined with a four-by-four grid of windows, each window spaced ten feet from the ones neighboring it. On the wall with the entrance to the courtyard was the window above Heinrich's kitchen sink. Looking up and scanning the other units, I noticed something that I had learned was a constant in Vienna. If there were ever more than three windows in a row, a disinterested person was staring out of at least one of them, usually smoking. Two levels up from Heinrich's window, a middle-aged woman with grey, tousled hair gazed out blankly. She wore a pink spaghetti-strap blouse and had her coffee cup balanced on her window's edge. She smoked with vigor, shaking her head often, and repeatedly lifted and placed her cup. A level below her, the next wall over, a man tended to a small hanging herb garden that looked completely dead. If I tried, I could probably drag the garbage cans over, stand on them, and break into Heinrich's window. Unfortunately, it would draw their attention.

I had no real plan, and being there was a mistake. I checked my watch and considered my options. I decided to walk over to the library to search for newspaper articles on the *Stolpersteine*. Whoever laid the stones must have worked from a database of victims. Maybe I could access it and find out which military units were involved. I stepped out the door to the street, turned, and came face to face with Heinrich. He wore a black hat and a navy scarf. He smiled at me with a look of sadness or pity. I'm not sure which.

"Alex. Can I help you?"

"Yeah. Can we talk?"

"Of course."

He walked into the building and up to his apartment. I followed. We went in and stood about eight feet from one another in the middle of the room. I raised my right hand and turned my purpled knuckles towards him.

"I broke my fucking hand fighting the guy you sent after me. What's going on?"

"Yes. You also broke Marko's nose. He was not happy.

Why did you do that, by the way?"

"Why did you have him follow me?"

He sighed, removed his coat and hat, hung them on a hook, and sat down in the chair by his coffee table.

"I needed to make sure that you were being honest with me in your reporting. I had reasons to believe otherwise."

"What reasons?"

"After you mentioned the archives, I went by and inquired with the clerk about files recently accessed by Emil. I've spent quite a lot of time down in that basement over the years and have a relationship with Fritz. He mentioned an American had come in requesting the same files. Why didn't you tell me?"

"I wasn't sure I could trust you."

"Well, then our lack of faith is mutual. Marko is the son of a former colleague. He's obviously not very good at trailing people, but my intention was never for violence."

I sat down on the couch across from him. "Tell me what's actually going on with Emil."

"Alex, it's time for you to leave Vienna."

"No."

"For your own safety. I'm sorry that I pulled you into this. It was a mistake."

"I'm not leaving. Whatever this is, it must be important."

"Please, Alex."

"I located the building that Emil photographed three times. It's at the center of his other photos, and I know that a family was taken from there and sent off to be killed."

Heinrich shook his head. "It's Leopoldstadt, Alex. Families were taken from every building in the district." He rubbed at his temples, then clasped his hands together and held them to his chin. "Can you promise me that you will leave the city today?"

"Definitely not."

He stood up, walked over to his door, and opened it.

"Then we have nothing left to discuss. Goodbye, Alex. I

am very sorry our association has ended this way."

I walked out and looked for the nearest phone to call Johanna. I was certain he would lie to her about me, if he hadn't already. Her phone rang and rang, but no one picked up. I stepped out of the phone booth, turned the corner onto a small side street, and passed by a blue awning. A shadow flickered for a fraction of a step before a sudden and intense pain exploded into the side of my head, followed by the cold grit of concrete on my cheek. Time slowed while thick, warm blood pooled around me. I reached about, foolishly, and heard mumbling from strangers crouched above me. They repeated something, far away, but I couldn't understand it. The metallic tang of blood filled my mouth as an unmistakable sweet musk filled my nose—a red wine of some type, maybe a merlot. I had been hit by a bottle of red wine. The light dimmed, then went black.

Unfortunately, my next memory was not convalescing by a warm, sunlit window in a hospital with Johanna by my side. I awoke, to some degree, a few minutes later, then faded in and out of consciousness over the next few hours. Partial images are all I remember: a grey ambulance with blue wires dangling from the ceiling, pieces of my teeth in my hands, men in orange lowering me onto a gurney. Tears down my face, vomit on my shirt. Swelling, cuts, bile, confusion. Each awakening became more painful than the last as I surrendered to the fates and the Austrian emergency medical services. Many hours later, in the cool of the evening, time knitted itself back together, and I found myself lying on a thin mattress in the corner of Vienna's largest hospital, the Allgemeines Krankenhaus. A wrinkled, beige vinyl curtain was all that separated me from an old man coughing furiously eighteen inches away. I tried to find a comfortable position to rest, but there was none. I couldn't sleep, and somehow I ended up lost in a trance replaying the day my professor insisted I withdraw from school. The first two or three hours after leaving his office, I felt relief. I had wanted a break from everything, and dropping out provided it. By night, the relief morphed into despair, and I went to his house on an oak-lined block in downtown Palo Alto. I got the address from our TA, and when my professor answered his door, he was not happy to see me. Away from campus, he allowed his face to twist fully into anger and disgust. "Get the fuck out of here," was all he said, and so I did. I withdrew the next morning.

Sometime before dawn, the beige curtain beside me was pulled back, and a doctor appeared with an oval, silver-rimmed mirror and explained my condition. A moment's glance in the mirror made things clear. Someone had struck me above my right eye with a full bottle of wine. I had suffered the highest-grade concussion, the area around my eye had swelled into a plump, blackened pillow, and two upper molars had been dislodged completely, damaging their sockets to the point that they didn't believe I could have an implant for months, if ever. They had also noticed and attended to my right hand. My last two knuckles were fractured and my wrist sprained. They reset the knuckles' positions and wrapped everything in a soft sling. My concussion warranted admission for two nights' stay in this tired, dim room if I felt so inclined. I did. Then, the doctor brought the mirror close and leaned in. I could feel the heat of his breath. He placed his fingers onto the corner of my mouth, tracing two thick blue lines of plastic holding my perpetual wound together. They had noticed the odd spot there and gone ahead and addressed it with stitches and surgical superglue. I nodded without verbal response, and he left.

As I lay, throbbing pain lessened by the steady drip of paracetamol, my thoughts oscillated between Heinrich and Johanna. I vomited often into a silver metal bedpan, and once my stomach became completely bereft of its contents, I convulsed and retched into the air. Beneath my discomfort, a feeling of peace welled. I should never have taken the job, but I did, and now I suffered. Order and justice had been upheld. It was clear now that what lay between Heinrich and Emil was worth investigating to its conclusion. An elderly nurse came in and injected some antinausea medicine into my IV from a red syringe. It worked, and I slept with some sense of purpose.

The next morning, the pain returned. I continued going in and out of consciousness. Images of my father flashed through my mind, memories mixing forward and backward. Life became one long stream: relentless and without discrete moments. Without breath. I'm not sure how long I was under or when I came out, but eventually, the feel of time's passage returned. An orderly gave me a cognitive test. I passed. Then, she wrapped her arm around my waist, helped me out of bed, and led me to small room in which a dark-haired doctor sat behind a metal desk. Before him lay a stapled stack of papers and a jade plastic cup the size of a child's glass, partially filled with coffee. I sat down, and he motioned towards the papers. I picked them up. Signatures, diagrams, disclaimers. Clearly, thought had been put into my care by someone, somewhere. Doctors' handwriting is illegible in every country, it seems.

"Do I, um—do I owe anything?"

He licked his thumb, reached over, and flipped to the last page.

"Forty-five schillings, but if you complete papers to prove hardship, it could be waived."

It was about the cost of a slice of cake at a café in the first district.

"I can pay. Do you think I could have one of those?" I asked, pointing at his coffee.

"Certainly." He downed the remainder of his cup, tossed it into a trashcan, and stepped out. From the hallway echoed the thunk of two coins sliding into a machine then a loud buzzing, followed by two more coins and a buzz. He returned with two cups, one for each of us. We drank them in silence interrupted by periodic sips. The white of morning shone in through the windows. The beauty and insanity of the moment overwhelmed me, and a tear slipped out before I could wipe it away. I took a deep breath in through my nose and tried to look unaffected. The doctor cleared his throat, then softly spoke,

"San Francisco, right? We found your passport in your bag."

"Yes."

"Went there once. Beautiful city."

"Yeah, thanks." I wanted to be back home.

"Tell me, why are all the power lines running in the sky everywhere? Why don't they bury them?" He turned his palms upward as he spoke. I knew what he meant, and only in that moment realized that Vienna looked different. One Saturday afternoon, I had taken a great photo of Hank while we waited for the bus at Haight and Fillmore. I shot from hip level with the aperture wide open, and the tangle of wires running high over the intersection formed the perfect, creamy bokeh. I wanted to offer an insight or factoid that only a native would know, but I had nothing.

"Earthquakes," I said.

He squinted and then nodded.

"You were quite lucky that your brain didn't swell more."

"Sure."

"If you feel unwell, sitting in a room with the shades drawn may help."

"Ok."

"Here is some medication for nausea and for pain. You should take them as needed. The instructions are on the box." He handed over a brown paper bag containing foil blister packs of orange and red pills. "I also have a note that was left for you." My heart stung: could it be from Johanna? He handed over a folded piece of light-green paper with my name scribbled on the outside in blue pen. They were masculine, hard letters in an unrecognizable script. I didn't want to open it in front of him, so I placed it into my lap and folded my hands over it.

"Did you have any questions for me, Alex?"

"Do you know if the police have any information about the attack?"

His head tilted up, "Ah, yes, sorry." He turned, ruffled through some papers behind him, and then rotated back, handing me a white piece of paper with a watermark of a large bird.

"There is your case number, A03434. I believe if you go to the station, they can help you with that and provide more information."

"Thank you."

I settled the bill, changed, gathered my things, and walked out onto the street. It was late morning, and the sunlight stung my eyes as I headed towards my apartment. I ducked into an entryway around the corner and opened the note left for me.

> Alex,
> When you didn't show for drinks, I had a hunch
> and called around and found you here. I dropped
> by but they wouldn't allow visitors. Let me help
> you. Vienna can be a cold place.
> —Markus

I put the note away and hopped onto a Straßsenbahn. My legs were unsteady. I stared out the window to avoid eye contact with the other riders. Whenever I turned my head, my vision swam and blurred and took a second to align. I needed caffeine and food. I bought a couple sandwiches from the bakery across the square from my apartment and longed for my bed as I rode the elevator up to the top floor of my building. Waiting, taped to my door, was a formal eviction notice. It said I hadn't paid rent, which was a lie. My key still worked, but the apartment was empty. All of my clothes, suitcases, and books were gone. The money, photos, and notes I had taped under the kitchen sink were gone. On the nightstand beside my bed was a white envelope with my name written on it in Heinrich's trademark handwriting. Inside was a ticket for a United Airlines flight to San Francisco leaving that night. I sat down on the corner of the uncovered mattress and carefully pried open my key ring, working free the keys for the exterior of the building and my apartment door. I placed them onto the nightstand beside me. I didn't really feel shock. Each step that had brought me to this moment seemed inevitable, like a damaged ship taking on water until it was swallowed by the sea. I ate my sandwiches, staring out the tall, floor-length windows onto the square. Heinrich wanted me to leave Austria and was willing to do almost anything to make it happen. He couldn't have known the wine bottle wouldn't kill me, so there were no longer any rules to our conflict. I picked up the phone and called Johanna.

"Hallo?" Lisi answered.

"Hey, is Johanna there?"

"Alex?" There was an edge in her voice.

"Yes."

"She's not going to take your calls. Her grandfather told us what you did."

"What did I do?"

An exasperated breath puffed through the phone line. "You stole from him."

"I didn't steal anything."

"Alex, please don't call, and don't come by. It's over." She hung up.

I closed the shades, locked the deadbolt with my key left inside, and dragged a bookshelf over in front of the door. Then, I laid down onto my bare mattress and fell into a restless half sleep. When I woke, it was dark. I decided to call Hank. It was still morning in California.

"Hank?"

"Hello—Alex!?"

"Hey."

"Hey dude! What the fuck? Are you alive?"

"Barely." Hearing his voice took the air out of my chest. All of the homesickness I'd managed to compress for the past three months expanded at once. I cleared my throat and tried to sound like myself. "What's up at home?"

"It's good man. You aren't missing anything. You ok?"

"Yeah, yeah. What's the weather right now?"

"I dunno, fifty-five, sixty? Kinda sunny. Is it snowing there?"

"All the time."

"That's so cool!"

"It is at first, but after a while, I'm not sure. It gets black and dirty."

"Man, I'd love to see snow. How's Vienna? What's it like? Did you get my letter?"

"Yeah, thanks. I sent you a postcard, but it might be a while before it gets out there. Vienna's cool. I, um, I don't have a lot of time 'cause I'm calling with a stupid phone card. I just wanted to apologize about Janet. I was a dick."

"Oh, yeah?"

"Yeah, I didn't—well—I kinda fucked you over. I only went for her because you liked her, and I went *way* harder when you asked me not to."

"Palo Alto, man! It can change you!"

"I know."

"I'm just messing with you. I know you were a little shady. Rose gave me the play-by-play while it happened."

"Oh right—Rose. I'm sorry, man."

"We're cool. Thanks for calling. I didn't have the right to claim her anyway. That's not who I want to be. What happened with Stanford? They kicked you out?"

"Yeah. I got caught cheating on a paper."

Hank laughed. It was the first time I'd heard his laugh in months. I'd forgotten it. He has a carefree, rolling, nasal laugh. I've spent most of my life trying to draw it out of him.

"Forget about Stanford. What's it really like in Europe? Any good music?"

"Definitely. I went to a concert that was cool, and there's this crazy pirate radio station here that broadcasts late at night. People love it."

"Sick."

The line cut out for a moment, and Hank was replaced with a recording of a British woman insistently stating, "You have three minutes of talk time remaining."

"Hey, I only have another couple minutes before my phone card goes out. Don't tell my parents, but, if I don't call you in—fuck, what day is it?"

"It's Tuesday."

"Ok, if I don't call by Thursday, noon, your time, I need you to call the embassy here. I'm kinda mixed up in something."

"For real?"

"Yeah. A guy here, Heinrich Trost, is—well, call the embassy and ask them to look into him if you don't hear from me. Trost. Like trust, but with an o."

"Ok. Fuck dude. Be careful."

"Yeah, for sure. I should be ok, probably. Let me go, before this thing cuts out."

"Cool, call me soon. SF misses you."

"Thanks."

We hung up. Tightness throughout my body released, and I lay down and cried. Heaving, shuddering crying. The time from when I boarded the plane at SFO until that moment had been like one long, surreal day, and hearing a real person, someone who knew me, made it clear I still existed in the actual world and the danger around me was legitimate. As I cried, the swollen areas around my eye and wrist throbbed with the beat of my heart. My tears burned when they ran down into the stitched corner of my mouth. Then, my phone rang.

"Hello? Alex?" It was Markus.

"Hey."

"Are you alright?"

"More or less."

"The doctors said you were pretty well damaged."

"Yeah, I'm fucked up, but I'm ok."

"Wonderful. Let's meet. Are you at home?"

"I am, but let's not meet here because I'm pretty sure I'm being watched. Do you know any place that's out of the way?"

"Of course. Should I come over to walk with you?"

I pushed the tip of my tongue into the void in my mouth where a molar used to be. It felt puffy and tasted the way a dime smells.

"You probably should, but I have an idea how to safely sneak away."

"Ok. There's a bar outside the Gürtel in the sixteenth. Vlado's. There's a back room I have access to. They don't let in strangers, and I'm sure your old boy doesn't have any friends there. I'll call ahead and get you cleared. Just walk up to the bar and say you are looking for *šipak*."

"What the hell is šipak?"

He laughed warmly.

"It's Vlado's codeword. He's Croatian. A Herzegovinian Croat, which is the most Croatian of the Croatians. Šipak is rose hip. I believe Vlado has fields of it back in Herzegovina."

"What the hell is rose hip?"

"Don't you Americans know anything about the natural world?"

"Nothing. Everything we eat involves a can and a microwave."

"I thought so. We'll get you some rose hip. It's healthy. It's the fruit of a rose."

I'd never considered the life of a rose before it arrived cut and wet in Safeway's refrigerated flower section.

"Ok. What time?"

"Ten p.m. Ottakringerstraße and Kalvarienberggasse."

"Ok, until then."

"Ciao."

I hung up and checked the time. It was six p.m., and the plane ticket was for a flight that left at 10:30 p.m. I closed the door to my apartment for the last time and walked down towards the first district. Snow had begun to fall. Flakes stuck to the bruised area around my eye and then melted, providing brief touches of relief. I was certain Heinrich had someone following me, so I trudged with shoulders slumped and tried to look defeated. It wasn't hard. I had to stop a few times and catch my breath. My legs were weak, and a persistent, fuzzy hiss rang in my right ear. I went to the lobby of the first hotel I came across, Palais Hansen. The bright lights disoriented me, and I swallowed some of my antinausea and pain medication with palmfuls of tepid water from the bathroom sink. Then, I asked the concierge to call me a cab for the airport. The ride unsettled me further, and I lay down in the backseat, taking deep, measured gasps, trying to level my equilibrium. Four seconds in, four seconds hold, six seconds out. I wondered if Markus really ran the radio station, and what kind of help he could give me. I didn't really know him. It was possible he worked for Heinrich, or was just some useless, random dude. At the airport check-in desk, when I slid my passport and ticket over the counter, a woman in a navy, formfitting dress gave me a look of fear and concern.

"No bags?"

"No bags."

"On a one-way ticket?"

"Yes."

"Are you ok, sir? Your eye looks—"

"Yes."

She typed loudly on her keyboard for an incredible, irrational amount of time. Ocean swells of typing that expanded and contracted in speed. Eventually, she handed me a boarding pass.

"Do you require assistance to the gate?" She had wide, grey eyes. Her name tag said Laura.

"I'm ok."

After security, I wolfed down a spongy piece of bread and a lukewarm bratwurst with a nondescript airport Helles they had on tap. It was the worst meal I'd had yet in Vienna, but it was still pretty good. In the soft brace I found my right arm useless, so I practiced drinking with my left. For dessert, I bought a Manner waffle, the official cookie-like substance of Vienna: a dusty hazelnut wafer block; the recipe dates to 1898. They are dry and taste like the cover of an old comic book, but I enjoy eating them and imagining a time when life was difficult enough that eating Manner was a pleasurable act. After finishing, I found a bookstore near my gate, Viennese Express, went to the back and skimmed through a photo book on the Habsburgs, a mostly ugly family. Then, I picked up a copy of Kafka's *The Trial* written in its original German. I read the first twenty pages once at normal speed and then again deliberately, with a focus on his word choice and sentence structure. Although I could follow German literature, I wasn't sure how much nuance I missed. I think all of it. It was hard to tell if K in the novel is, despite his verbose protestations, actually guilty. When boarding began for my plane, I bought and put on a thick charcoal hoodie with *Austria* written in small letters down one sleeve and a green-and-white striped knit cap from Vienna's soccer team, Rapid Wien. The hoodie undoubtedly came from the same darkened factory in Shenzhen as the pink San Francisco hoodies sold at Fisherman's Wharf that unsuspecting tourists are forced to purchase when they realize Northern California isn't like *Baywatch*. I left my jacket on top of a garbage can, walked out through baggage claim, and grabbed a taxi back to the city. My assumption was that Heinrich had sent someone to follow me to the airport, and maybe to security, but hopefully he didn't have a way to see if I boarded the plane.

I had the cab driver drop me off where Ottakringerstraße meets the Gürtel. Similarly to Emil's neighborhood, signs and restaurants were more likely to be in Turkish or Serbo-Croatian than German. It was a cold night, and other than a few drunks huddled outside a *kebap* stand, there wasn't much life on the street. Vlado's bar sat on a corner at the crest of a hill, marked by a white neon sign visible from blocks away. From outside, the bar didn't look busy, but when I walked in, I was stunned at size of the crowd and the expansiveness of the place. Every table was surrounded by men talking loudly, smoking, and drinking. Many wore tracksuits; many had sunglasses resting on the top of their heads. A television in a far corner had a soccer game on. I walked up to the bar and approached a gaunt man with black hair and green eyes. He had the worn look of a current or former alcoholic. He was polishing a glass and raised his eyebrows to me. In my new hoodie and hat, with a bruised face, I must have been quite the sight.

"I'm looking for some šipak?"

He nodded and walked down the bar. I followed him, and he stepped out and led me to a closed door. In heavily accented German, he said,

"Please, in here, have a seat."

He opened the door into a darkened, wood-paneled room. No one looked up as we entered. There were no windows, and the only light flickered from neon beer signs hung high on the wall above us. There were four tables inside, two occupied by groups of four men and two empty. He led me towards an empty table in the back corner.

"You are the American?"

"Uh, yeah."

"Have a seat." I sat down into a chair with my back to the wall.

Switching from accented German to worse English he said, "A real American?"

"Yeah, I think so."

"Bruce Springsteen—wonderful," he said with a wide, toothy smile. He was handsome, with a forlorn look. His eyes glowed like that famous photograph of the Afghan girl.

"He's the greatest," I said, nodding.

"My cousin in America. In Pittsburgh."

"Ok."

"He's dead, but in Pittsburgh."

"Ah ok, I'm sorry to hear that."

He squinted. "It's ok, his wife got insurance."

"Ah, that's good, I guess."

He smiled.

"Something to drink?"

"Sure, beer?"

He nodded and walked away. At the other tables, the men smoked and stared off into the distance with stern expressions. When anyone spoke for an extended period of time, their speech accelerated with each passing word until it became a continuous flood. They spoke Croatian, which sounds smooth and vowelless, like an Italian speaking Russian. Those around the table seemed to have a protocol for taking turns. For a few minutes one person held center stage, then someone else would talk over them loudly, increasing in volume until the first person quieted. They spoke with their entire bodies. Hands waving, they often slapped one another's knees, or gripped each other's shoulders. A few minutes later, the waiter reappeared with a tray. He placed a golden beer with a thick white head in front of me.

"*Amerikanac*, what happened your eye?" he asked, tapping alongside his own eye.

I shook my head, and his face showed genuine concern. I slowly mimed a right cross and said, "Bad fight."

He pursed his lips and nodded knowingly. Then, he placed a small shot glass on the table in front of me and filled it with a clear liquid from an unlabeled glass bottle. Judging by the shape and extruded signature along its shoulder, the bottle began its life containing Jack Daniels. He screwed the black cap back on and left the bottle on the table beside the shot glass.

"For pain it's good," he said, opening his hands and gesturing towards the bottle. "*Domaće*... home-homemade," he added, with pride.

"Thank you."

"Nema problema," he answered, smiling, and walked off. I lifted the shot glass to my nose; it stung my eyes before I could smell it. The scent was rubbing alcohol and unripe green grapes. I drank it in one motion, heat scalding my throat at the finish. It was well past eighty proof. I'm certain that if I emptied the bottle into the tank of an eighties Volkswagen Golf, I could crank the engine and drive to Sarajevo and back. I slouched down in my chair, tried to relax my shoulders, and sipped my beer. I didn't have a place to sleep or a plan to get Johanna back. I didn't have a plan for anything, but at least the room felt safe. When I was almost at the end of my glass, Markus entered the room. He stopped at the other two tables, shaking hands and patting people on the back as he worked his way to my corner.

"Quite a grave look you've got on your face there," he said, standing before me, grinning.

"Been a tough couple days."

He craned forward and inspected my injured eye.

"A fist did that?"

"Wine bottle."

"Damn."

He took off his long black coat, hung it on a gold hook on the wall, and sat down in the chair across from me. There were a lot more coat hooks in Vienna than in San Francisco.

"How's the pain?"

"It's ok. I feel pretty lightheaded."

"Do you want some food? They don't normally serve here,

but Vlado's wife can make you something if I ask."

"No thanks, I'm ok. How do you know all these people? Are we the only non-Croatians here?"

He leaned back and scanned the room.

"We might be." Lowering his voice, he added, "I helped them some during their war."

I nodded, then rotated my wrist back and forth, stretching my tendons, and waited to see if he would add any more details.

"Also they're ex-communist, like me, so we understand one another. It was different for them, but similar enough," he said, smiling. The waiter appeared, and in what sounded like convincing Croatian, Markus and he spoke for a while. The waiter left once again before returning with two beers, another shot glass, and a plate of sliced prosciutto and cheese. Markus poured us a both a shot of the clear liquid from the bottle. "This is rakija—it's like grappa, but worse."

"I've acquainted myself with it. What did you do for them in the war?" I asked, without making eye contact.

He leaned back and stretched his shoulders.

"Not too much. They needed guns, and I knew some people who had them. DDR military leftovers and whatnot. It's not something I do regularly, but I grew up with a Croatian friend, Ante, and he needed help."

"Cool."

I couldn't tell if he was minimizing the story to be humble, or as an indirect method of showing off. My first introduction to the Yugoslavian civil war was during the pregame intro to the gold-medal game between Croatia and the Dream Team. Petrović played well. Markus and I each took a shot, and then I proceeded to devour the prosciutto and cheese. The salt of each worked wonders with the beer. The waiter returned with a plate of small puffs of warm fried dough dusted in powdered sugar, freshly made by Vlado's wife for, "the Amerikanac." I updated Markus on the details of the break-in, what I'd seen in the second district, and my conversation with Heinrich. Other than a nod or heavy sigh, he listened in silence. Midway through, he took out a pack of cigarettes and began smoking. As soon as he reached the end of one cigarette, he twisted it down into the ashtray and lit the next. My rakija buzz and postconcussion symptoms merged into one, casting Markus and the room into a pulsing blur. I didn't want the buzz to wear off, ever, so I poured a half shot and sipped it. At the end of my story, we sat for a while. Markus stared across the room, his normally expressive face blank. Without a smile, he looked like a different, older person.

"Fucking fascists," he said, breaking the silence.

"You think so?"

"Yes, unquestionably."

I picked up a wrinkled beer coaster from the table and tried to balance it on its edge.

"Don't worry about Johanna," he said.

"I'm mainly worrying about Johanna."

"Yes, but if you can bring the grandfather down, she'll come around."

"But I don't actually *know* that Heinrich is bad. I don't know that he had me attacked. It could have just been the guy I punched getting back at me. It could be that Heinrich has been telling the truth all along."

"Come on, Alex."

"I don't know. If I'm going to make the case to Johanna, I need evidence. She loves him."

Markus leaned forward and put his face into his hands, then scratched at the back of his neck.

"I think you should go and talk to Emil. Do you still have his photos?"

"Yeah. They took everything from my apartment, but I had his photos on me."

"Does he leave his flat every day?"

"Most days he goes to a bakery near his place."

"Run into him tomorrow. Show him the photographs and see how he reacts. You'll know what to say based on his response." I considered it. It wasn't much of a plan, but I didn't have a better one. "Take main streets and don't walk close to doorways. Look confident, shoulders back, head up."

"Ok."

"I'll think of something for Johanna."

"Yeah?"

"Yes."

"What do you think this whole thing is about?" I asked.

"I think it goes back to the war, obviously. Why else would Emil be looking at maps from back then? The only reason for Heinrich to hire you is if he's trying to hide something from everyone he knows. People don't hide good things."

"True."

"Maybe it's an old girlfriend or some bastard kid or something. I agree that we don't know what it is, but looking at what happened to your face, I don't believe Heinrich is a good fellow, unfortunately."

I ran through a few phrasings in my mind of a question I had for Markus. It was too voyeuristic and infantile, but I wanted to ask it anyway.

"Let's say they did pull a family out of the second district and sent them off to be murdered. How could they do that and then go back to regular life after the war? Wouldn't there be residue, and wouldn't it come out somehow? Did they just pretend to themselves that it never happened?"

"I don't care," he snapped back.

"You don't?"

"No. I don't think it's interesting. I don't want to know the feelings of criminals. It's disrespectful to the victims."

"Sure—I can see that, but it's interesting to me, from, I guess an anthropological or psychological standpoint, or something like that."

"We're not in a university course, Alex. My father was a

member of the Nazi party. A very committed one. Trust me, he didn't have a single interesting thought in his head. There's nothing, and I truly mean nothing, to be gained from gazing deeply into his mind." Markus sat up straight and pointed at me. "At this point, I'm not interested in knowing anyone over sixty in this country or Germany. They were either complicit or a coward, full stop. I'm proud of the fact that my generation are the first Germans in God knows how long who didn't start a war, and I think part of the way we got there was by moving on from navel-gazing about the feelings that fueled my father and his father." He coughed into his elbow, then looked into my good eye. "But don't think that I believe the Americans are really any better than Germans," he said pointing his finger up with a wry smile, cigarette dangling from his mouth. "Hiroshima and Nagasaki were not precise military strikes— and I have family from Dresden."

Two Croatians came by, Mate and Šime, and interrupted our conversation. Markus transformed instantly from a dour arbiter of generational guilt into an affable conversationalist. They spoke together for about twenty minutes in an uninterrupted stream of Croatian. I couldn't follow along, so my thoughts retreated inward. When they left and Markus turned back towards me, he looked drained. I wanted to ask why he was so trusting of me, and to thank him, but I wasn't sure how.

"When did you learn Croatian?"

"We had to learn Russian in school. Moscow was our overlord back then. The languages have a similar root, and I spent a lot of dinners over at my friend Ante's place."

"Awesome. Hey, is Ana connected to this bar?"

He tilted his head to the side and smiled. "She's connected to Vlado, who owns this place, yes. She's his little sister."

I laughed. "What does he think about you two?"

"He loves the idea. They already call me *badžo*, which means brother-in-law."

"Nice. Any updates on her?"

He shrugged. "Well. She's made me an ultimatum."

"Oh, my."

"Yes. She's over my dawdling."

"Well, stop it then."

"Maybe. Do you have a place to sleep?"

"I'm not done asking about Ana."

"That's enough for now."

"Ok. I was thinking of trying the hostel by Westbahnhof."

Markus shook his head. "Save the money you have. Vlado has a mattress in the storage room. He lets drunks sleep there, and it will do for a night or two. I'd put you up, but my flat is quite small, and my cat has a history of peeing on visitors."

"Will there be any other drunks in Vlado's room?"

"I don't think so. It's a first-come, first-served thing, and it's still early."

After a few more minutes of drinking, Vlado appeared, and we both rose to meet him. Maybe five foot six, he walked with a slow confidence that carried an aura of royalty blended with peasantry. He looked very clean—he must have just showered—and wore finely pressed dark pants and a long-sleeve mint Polo shirt, all three buttons unbuttoned. When he shook my hand, he smiled and cradled my elbow with his other hand. He continued to hold my hand as he introduced himself to me, speaking in Croatian, which Markus translated. He spoke for quite some time, looking into my eyes and nodding.

"He said he's very glad to meet an American. A *real* American."

"Thank him for his hospitality."

Vlado smiled and shook his head. Deep wrinkles around his hazel eyes revealed years spent in the sun. "He says, anything for a friend of mine. And if you need help with whomever did that to your eye, let him know, and he has friends who are taller than him who can help." As Vlado waited for Markus to translate the joke, he looked expectantly at me, smiling. We all laughed, and Vlado reached up to signal a tall person, then clapped me on the back. We chatted for a few more minutes, then Markus and Vlado let me down a series of hallways into a narrow storeroom with a barrel for distilling rakija, stacks of crates of beer, and a pink twin mattress on the floor. From the ceiling hung a stiff grey wire, at the end of which was a yellow bulb. I offered some money to both Vlado and Markus, and they absolutely refused. I made plans to meet Markus in the afternoon at a café behind the Votivkirche. The storeroom's door closed tight, and when I pulled the chain for the overhead bulb, I entered into total darkness. I shuffled my way to the mattress, and after a few minutes lying there, I lost sense of where the walls and door were located. The thought of panic occurred to me, but a few deep breaths later, it subsided and I fell into an enveloping sleep, free from dreams and sobriety.

X

I remained in the deepest stage of sleep until Vlado's wife, Vera, opened the door late the following morning and placed a tray with Turkish coffee and twelve coconut-flake-covered chocolate cake cubes just inside the room. If she hadn't done so, I might have slept forever. I exchanged pleasantries with her and Vlado on my way out. She implored me to use their shower. I must have looked terrible, but I resisted. I didn't have any clean clothes anyway. They gave me a key and told me to come back and think of the storeroom as my apartment until I had somewhere better to sleep. When I reached the door, they saw I no longer had a winter coat, and they forced a spare of Vlado's upon me. I was thankful and ashamed.

On the way to the bakery near Emil's, the hat I had purchased at the airport began to itch and rub above my eye, so I threw it into a trash can. At the bakery, I bought a coffee, then took the high table in the corner to the left of the entrance. Before me, I placed the stack of Emil's photos with the three pictures of the central apartment building on top. I covered the photos with a copy of *Der Standard* and waited. I arrived about an hour before Emil normally did, so I had time to read the entire paper twice. My wrist twinged in pain with each page turn. The separation between my senses blurred, and the sunlight streaming in from behind me created a persistent static in my right ear and the sensation of pins pushing into the back of my eye. The pain overcame me, and I put my head down and took slow breaths through my nose until it subsided. I realized my time in Vienna had been defined by bouncing from the care of one random foreigner to the next: first Johanna, then Markus, and now Vlado and his wife. Although the emotional barrier between people on the street was broader than in San Francisco, once invited into someone's life, the intimacy was different. Relationships were free of the latent fringe of competition that had burned at the edges of every interaction I ever had at Stanford. Maybe it was because I was a temporary visitor, or American, or injured, or some combination of all three.

A few minutes before expected, Emil walked into the bakery and up to the glass display case. It was an unusually cold morning, and he wore a heavy, dark-green wool coat with a long brown scarf wrapped around his neck. Although the lines of yarn in the scarf were solid, the loops varied in tightness. It was homemade, maybe by his late wife. I sat up straight and cleared my throat. My pulse raced, and a burning pain ran through my right temple. After paying for his usual loaf of *Bauernbrot*, he turned, bag in hand, towards the exit. When he was about five feet from the door, I mumbled, "Excuse me."

He stopped and looked towards me kindly. At the moment he recognized me and observed my battered face, his color faded, and he stood alert.

"Yes?"

As friendly as I could, I said, "Hi it's me—the American from the Leica shop."

"What happened to you?"

I made sure my newspaper was covering his photos.

"I was mugged."

He stepped forward towards the door.

"I'm very sorry to hear that. I must be on my way."

"Emil?" He looked into my eyes. He hadn't told me his

name when we met. "Emil, I just picked up a roll of film, and although most of them didn't turn out, this one has something to it." I moved my newspaper and tilted his photo towards him. He glanced at it, then back to me. His arms hung heavy at his sides. He wobbled an infinitesimal amount before regaining his balance and stepped towards me. I tensed for a struggle, but then I saw the resigned sadness in his face.

"Where did you get that photo?"

"I took it from your apartment. Someone has been paying me to investigate you."

"Who?"

My instinct was to lie, to say the police or the Simon Wiesenthal Center. But it was too late for that.

"Heinrich Trost."

He placed the brown paper bag containing his bread onto the table in front of me, then leaned his elbow into the chair across from me. He clenched and unclenched his jaw.

"Heinrich?"

I nodded. The bakery cashier, a woman with badly dyed red hair, began to stare in our direction.

"We should go somewhere more private to discuss," I said. He nodded. He didn't appear to be fully present. I gathered my things, and we stepped out into the sunlight. I had no idea where to go. "Is your apartment ok?" I asked. He looked at me and said nothing, so I walked towards his place. We proceeded without words, the sound of our steps relentless and unbearable, like a dripping faucet. I became hyperaware of the color of the sunlight, my breath, my muscles, his face. He moved in a trance as he unlocked his gate, then his door, and we walked into his living room. We sat down across from one another at his coffee table. Light streamed in from the windows. The apartment was different than it had been the other night. More peaceful, quiet. A wave of pain flashed behind my eyes.

"Could I have a glass of water?"

He didn't respond, so I found a glass, filled it, and drank it completely. Some of the color in Emil's face returned. I took out his photographs and placed them onto the table in front of him.

"Can you tell me what your connection is to the buildings in these photographs?"

He leaned over and studied the top photo.

"Who are you exactly?" he asked.

"That's not important," I said. He shifted in his seat.

"How do you know Heinrich?" he asked in a low, focused voice.

"I don't really. I'm an independent contractor."

He flipped through the photos, meticulously removing the topmost and sliding it beneath the bottom. It occurred to me that I had no actual leverage over him. The room was so silent that I became overconscious of my breathing and started to feel light-headed. I walked over to a window and cracked it, letting in a rush of cool air and street noise. I took off my coat, slowly freeing my injured arm, and sat back down across from Emil. He was still wearing his hat and overcoat. I realized he'd never seen the roll developed. I wondered if the excitement of discovering how your photos turn out, even in a setting like this, endured. Markus thought I would know what to say when I confronted Emil. I didn't. Once Emil reached the last photograph, he looked up at me, and a connection formed between the two of us. He had the face of a man in a confessional booth.

"They're nice photos, all well exposed. I like the one odd picture taken from street level, with the Straßenbahn tracks in the foreground," I said. He didn't respond. "Heinrich has made some decisions lately that have led me to sever my relationship with him. Normally, that would be the end of my involvement, but I have suspicions that the conflict between the two of you is a matter of interest."

"A matter of interest to whom?"

"To me." I paused. I was out on a ledge. "And to the many people with an interest in the crimes of National Socialism." I tried to sound legalistic. It was my second time this week accusing old men of being Nazis. I was getting better at it. It's important to place the action at an impersonal distance. Even then, saying *Nationalsozialismus* aloud in German bittered the tongue. He looked down and shook his head. "I have corroborating evidence beyond the photos, but in cases like this, I prefer to let individuals speak with me directly before I go to the authorities. This is your opportunity." My neck tensed. He sat back in his chair. I had the feeling of lifting open a cellar door and standing above a darkened staircase.

"I have not spoken with Heinrich in almost fifty years. I haven't even heard his name in almost that long." He paused to cough into his elbow. "We grew up together. We were practically brothers for a time. Our families lived across the hall from one another."

"In the 1930s?"

"Yes."

"What did Heinrich do during the war?"

"He was a soldier in the East. I believe they had him running alongside a tank."

"And you?"

"I worked in the Augarten. At the Flakturm. Stacking crates mainly. What did Heinrich ask you to do?" He spoke with a hesitant, halting rhythm.

"He wanted me to watch what you were doing day to day. He was concerned you were planning something."

"Was he?"

He'd looped through the stack, and the photo of the apartment building lay on top once more. Street noises—the distant honking of a car—filtered in the room through the cracked window. He didn't say anything. I tapped onto the photo.

"What happened here?" I asked. He looked at the photo without moving. I wanted to endure the silence and make him speak next. A long time passed. A minute, maybe two. Time slowed.

"How is Heinrich?" he asked, his voice wavering.

"In what way?"

He shook his head and his eyes sharpened. "Maybe you can help me," he said.

"How so?"

"Well. We took people from this house into the Augarten, shot them, and buried them in a ditch. I would like to help them be reburied properly, but I cannot remember where we left them. I've walked the area in hopes of recovering the memory, but I can only recall a few images and the sensation of pushing my shovel down into the earth."

His blue eyes were reddened and his face waxen. I had a confession, finally. It felt hollow, weightless. I'm not sure what I'd expected to feel, but this wasn't it.

"After all these years, why worry about them now?"

He stood up, took off his hat and coat, and hung them on a hook on the wall behind him. Turning back towards me, he rubbed at his eyes and then clasped his hands together.

"At the end of September, a friend of mine died, so I went to check in on his mother. She's ninety-seven and lives in this building." He placed his hand onto the top photo. "I had not been in the district in decades. When I turned onto her street, I saw a man on his knees with a saw, cutting a square into the sidewalk. I asked him what he was doing, and he presented me a brass plate with the names of a Jewish family taken from there. They weren't the family that we removed. It was a big building, I suppose. I hadn't seen it since that night. The outside had been repainted, the door replaced, but I recognized it immediately."

"What was the name of the family?"

He left the room, came back, and placed a Junghans wristwatch onto the glass tabletop. It had a small round silver face, and an oiled, black leather band. He flipped it over. The underside had the name Josef Blume engraved across it in shaky freehand. The watch ticked beneath my fingertips. It showed the correct time. He must have wound it every day.

"I don't know why I took that," he said and coughed again, clearing his throat.

"But you said you were just working at the Flakturm?"

He closed his eyes a moment, then opened them. "Yes, I was. I was part of the Volkssturm with the other leftovers in the city. In the war's closing days, Heinrich's division returned to defend Vienna. We ran into one other in the Augarten when his unit came to resupply. I hadn't seen him since he left in the winter of 1942. He was much thinner. We spoke for a while about people we knew, and his brother, who had died."

"Erich."

He looked at me strangely, as if I'd woken him from a dream.

"Yes, Erich. Erich was much older, and a father in many ways to Heinrich and me. That night, we spoke about my boredom of being trapped in the city while the war went on elsewhere. He left to his post, and late in the evening, while I was eating with the rest of the Flakhelfer, he returned. A report had come in of some Jews hiding in this building." He motioned towards the photo on the table. "The report came direct from the Gauleiter of Vienna, Baldur von Schirach. Schirach was hiding out in the Wienerwald, but somehow word of a hidden family reached him, and he wanted the apartment investigated. Heinrich's commander was angry; they needed to wire the Floridsdorf bridge to explode in case the Russians advanced, but Schirach demanded the dispatch of men to the apartment. Heinrich told his commander that he knew someone who could help, which would allow them to leave someone back to work on the bridge. He knew I longed to do something outside the Augarten, so it was his favor to me. At the time, I was grateful."

"Why would Heinrich's unit be assigned something like

that?"

He gave me a bemused look. "Heinrich served in the *Schutzstaffel.* They were capable of such things." My temple stung with pain, and I massaged it with my palm. "Heinrich did this to you?" he asked, pointing towards my eye.

"Not himself, but at his direction, I think."

"He wouldn't want the bodies found. He's had a good life."

"Why do you want them found?"

He sat up and shifted his shoulders.

"It's selfish, really. I don't have any children, so it's easy for me. I'm not—" He stared for a moment, with his lips parted. "My life is over in many respects. I see this as an erasure of myself. At least, as much as is possible."

"You went to the archives. I saw the map you checked out. It didn't help?"

"No."

"Why not just go to the press, and then let them start digging?"

"I believe it is my responsibility. And I don't know whom I can trust. Many people prefer to leave things from that time in the past."

"What's your plan now?"

"Keep looking until I find the location, and then dig. But if I am already being watched—" He shook his head. I wanted to understand him. Not to empathize, but I had heard about Nazis my entire life. They had always been there. In Indiana Jones. In the background of my grandfather's stories and photographs. I'd read *Night* and *The Diary of Anne Frank*; and *This Way to the Gas, Ladies and Gentleman*; and *Die Blechtrommel* and *Ansichten eines Clowns*, and now before me at maybe five foot eight and sixty-nine years old sat the real thing, but like with my own grandfather, a void stretched between us. I didn't know what information could transfer from him to me, and I didn't how to make it happen. So I stared, and my headache pushed against the inside of my skull as my stomach tensed and bitter acid washed up into the back of my throat.

"Excuse me." I went into his bathroom, opened the window, and took deep gulps of winter air. Then, I went back into the living room. Emil hadn't moved.

"I'll help you. I'll be back tonight. We'll go there together. I've studied the map from the archives, so I have a rough idea of the areas that were fields back then."

He blinked, then made eye contact with me.

"Ok."

I needed some aspirin and coffee.

"When you got to the building that night, how did you find the family?"

"We knew where to look. From the neighbors in the building."

I squeezed my hands opened and closed. I wanted to ask about the shooting itself, and the last moments of his victim's lives, but a block within me prevented it. Maybe it was wrong to know, or I knew my curiosity was laced with voyeurism. If it was my family killed, I wouldn't want people to rubberneck at the details.

"Ok, I'll be back at seven," I said.

"Let's go well after dark, in case Heinrich is watching. I will meet you at eleven p.m., in the Augarten, in front of the old porcelain factory."

"Ok."

I walked out of the apartment, down the hall, and out onto Neulerchenfelderstraße. Transitioning from the quiet pressure of Emil's apartment to the open street left me floating for a moment. I walked across town to meet Markus, as planned. He was in the back of the café, legs crossed, reading a newspaper. I sat down and the waiter approached. I ordered two coffees and a plate of scrambled eggs. Then, I told Markus about Emil, pausing awkwardly when the waiter returned with my coffee, then my food. When I finally reached the end of the story, Markus craned his head up to the ceiling, stretching the thick tendons in his neck, then leaned forward and placed his elbows onto the table.

"This will be difficult for Johanna."

"Yeah."

I hadn't even thought about how to tell her, or about her at all since meeting Emil.

"Some old guys killed Jews—that's barely a half-page article deep inside the newspaper here. If you stick a shovel down anywhere in this city you will hit something from one pogrom or another." He paused and scratched at his forehead. "But for Johanna, it's obviously something else. When I found out about my father, I was relieved. My worst fears were all confirmed. Knowing that, I didn't have to worry anymore. Unfortunately from what you've told me, she's had higher expectations."

I nodded and took a sip of my coffee. Past the window behind Markus, a mother and toddler walked alongside the back of a cathedral.

"And I don't see any reason to trust this repentant fascist or help him feel better. We should find the bodies and put him in jail, but I don't think he should be part of it."

"Sure, but I'm supposed to meet him tonight at eleven in the Augarten."

"Fuck him, don't go."

"No, I think the odds are better I'll find something with his help. I understand what you mean, but maybe I can help jog his memory."

Markus leaned back and sighed.

"Ok, but before then, you have to tell Johanna. Just go to her place at nine thirty and I'll get you in."

"How? Her roommate wouldn't give her the phone, and if I show up at the door with my eye like this, they'll call the cops."

He smirked. "You said she likes Radio Seven right?"

"Yeah."

"I'll play something to change her mind about you."

"I knew you were the fucking DJ."

He shrugged. "It's the best job I've ever had. Don't tell anyone."

"You get paid?"

"Not at all."

"What if she doesn't believe the stuff about her grandfather?"

"She's a grown woman, that's up to her. I think she will though."

"Ok."

"You should take a nap. You look terrible."

"I took some medicine, but it hasn't helped." I placed my box of ibuprofen onto the table. Markus inspected it and then pushed out eight pills, four times the recommended dosage. I swallowed them with the dregs of my coffee.

"How did you process your dad's past?"

He leaned back and crossed and his arms. "Oh, it wasn't a surprise. Not really. It came out over dinner one night. He worked for the party as a bureaucrat, pushing papers that increased the efficiency of the liquidation of the mentally infirm. His beliefs about the value of people didn't change after the war, so like I said, confirmation was a relief. It made me hate him, of course, but it clarified my identity to know that my family participated. They weren't swept along, they were willing, and their roots run up into me. That means I contain the possibility to alter a diseased family tree. It was far harder for friends of mine that loved their parents and were truly surprised." He bit his lip and narrowed his eyes. "Just tell Johanna the news. Don't accompany it with American talk-show psychoanalysis."

"Ha. Ok."

He leaned forward, centered his coffee cup on its saucer,

and looked at me. "I think the thing that Americans don't understand—I realized this when talking with Steve, the Floridian that Julian made me suffer through—is that you feel so proud of the war that you can't understand why we don't feel guilt at the inverse depth. But that's identifying the wrong imbalance. It's Americans that shouldn't feel proud. Your generation wasn't there, and mine wasn't either."

We settled the bill, and I walked back towards Vlado's place on Ottakringerstraße. The pain radiated from my skull to my neck, and whenever I rounded a corner and took an eyeful of sun, it buckled my knees. At Vlado's, I fell into a heavy sleep, and when I woke, I was drenched in sweat and had no idea where I was. I groped about frantically until I found a wall, and then the chain of the light bulb. My equilibrium was gone, and the ground listed like the deck of a ship. I lay back down until it settled. A plate of cold, boiled lamb and potatoes was waiting for me outside the door along with a note from Vera. Salty, heavy, and fatty—it helped. Emil's face from when we spoke replayed in my mind. He looked resigned and defeated, which made sense, but there was more that I couldn't name. Did he accept himself as an aged continuation of the person who shot the family, or did he imagine a break in his timeline? What did he pray about all those mornings during Mass in the Servitenkirche? Forgiveness for himself or rest for the souls of his victims? An uncomfortable reality of completely erasing a group of people is that there might not be anyone left to mourn the dead. It's possible that the only living people that remember Josef Blume and his family are his murderers. At nine p.m., I walked to Johanna's apartment. The night was starless and numbingly cold. Any exposed skin stung immediately. The streets were empty.

On her block, I waited two buildings down from hers and tried to move to keep warm. At 9:36 p.m., the door opened, and she stood at the threshold, barefoot. She wore Carolina blue–Adidas shorts and a white V-neck undershirt, her silhouette backlit by the pale light of the entryway. Her hair was pulled down over one shoulder.

"Alex?"

I walked closer.

"Yeah."

"You do know the DJ."

"Yeah."

"What's he like?"

"He's really cool. Like an East German James Dean."

"What's his name?"

"Markus. I don't know his last name."

"Markus, huh. He played a great song—something by R.E.M. that I didn't know—and then said, 'In the spirit of respect for decent Americans, any Austrian women who are on the outs with an American guy should walk downstairs right now.' Then, he paused and added, 'Just to be clear, I mean women named Johanna.' I almost had a heart attack. Here I am."

I looked left and right, then back to her. "I wonder how many Johannas went downstairs to find nobody waiting?"

She laughed. "Lucky them."

I thought about asking to come inside, but I wanted that to be her decision. I took another step towards her, bringing my face into the light.

"What happened to you!?" she asked, stepping out onto the cold pavement and touching my face.

"Uh, well, it's a long story. Can we talk?"

"My grandfather told me you stole from him."

"I didn't. He's lying. He just told you that to keep us apart." A few buildings down a door opened, and a teenager stepped out with a dog on a leash. Johanna looked at me with a pained expression.

"He said you'd say that too. I'm sorry, Alex, I don't be-lieve you."

"Just give me five minutes to explain, and then I'll leave,

ok? I promise."

She stepped back, pushed her door open, and stood to the side.

"Come in."

We walked inside, and she sat down onto the broad bottom step of the stone stairwell. A hundred years of residents going up and down had smoothed its lip from a hard edge into a gentle slope.

"Let's talk here, my roommates are all home. Lisi didn't want me to come down."

"Ok. Aren't you cold?" Her legs prickled with goosebumps.

"I'm fine. What's your side of the story?"

"Well—when I was working for your grandfather, I wasn't organizing his files like I said. I was at first, but then he asked me to spy on a friend of his, Emil Eder. He was concerned that Emil was planning something dangerous. I like your grandfather, so I agreed to do it. I mainly sat in coffee shops outside of Emil's apartment and followed him down to the bakery and back. Then, your grandfather asked me to break into Emil's apartment. I did that too. A lot of things happened from there, and I started to suspect your grandfather's motives were not good. I ended up getting into a fight with someone he sent to follow me, which is why I showed up at your house the other night with a broken hand. And then that same person, I think, attacked me and did this to my head."

She stared blankly. My words echoed in the stairwell, forcing me to listen to my own voice.

"Anyway, I confronted Emil today. He told me your grandfather and he killed a family together at the end of the war. A Jewish family. They were ordered to do it. Emil has been trying to locate where they buried them so he can confess, and your grandfather must have found out somehow. I guess that's why he had me follow him."

She began to take shallow, tense breaths.

"Do you have any proof?"

"Just Emil's confession. The family was buried somewhere in the Augarten. I'm going to meet Emil there in an hour to search for them."

Her eyes flashed for a moment, and she opened her mouth to speak, then closed it.

"Johanna?" I asked.

"So you've lied to me from the beginning," she said in a flat whisper.

"Yeah. But that's what he wanted me to do."

"That's no excuse." She sat, staring forward, motionless. "I have to call my father. Wait here."

"Ok."

She turned and went up the stairs. A long time passed. I'd spent an inordinate amount of time in Vienna waiting. I wasn't the driver of any situation. I was just an observer of other people living lives fuller than mine. I heard a door open and shut above me, then the steady tap of footsteps. I sat up, only to be disappointed when an unknown middle-aged woman came trudging down the stairs, giving me a wary glance. Eventually, Johanna appeared on the turn in the staircase just above the first flight. She wore a long grey coat, a burgundy knit cap, and a tightly wrapped scarf. From her hand dangled a black wool hat. Her eyes were red, their lower lids swollen.

"Can you take me with you to the Augarten to meet Emil?"

"Yes."

She descended, walked past me, opened the door, and waited. We stepped into the night, and she pulled the black wool hat onto my head and gave me a sad look. She led the way, and we walked in silence, our feet crunching on snow. We boarded a Straßenbahn and stood once again at the rear, as we had a few days before, the last time under better circumstances.

"My father believes you. He's going to drive here in the

morning. He's about three hours away in Upper Austria." The Straßenbahn stopped, and a few people got on the first car. "I'm sorry, Alex. I couldn't have known."

"It's no problem."

"I'm sorry about your face. I cannot believe it." She rubbed her eyes roughly with the palm of her hand.

A group of men, staggering and smelling sweetly of beer, stood near us, so we walked up the car until we found an empty row. We sat alongside one another with her leg just akilter enough for our knees to touch. It sent a current through me. Then, she pulled her leg away. I began to ramble to her about the last week, my time at the hospital, my migraines, Markus, everything. I spoke in a whisper, it was difficult to put the right words together in German, so I spoke stiffly and plain. When I told her the details from Emil about the night of the killing, she tensed. We rode in silence for a while, and then she said, "If you respected me at all, you would have told me sooner about what you were doing."

"I didn't want to ruin your image of your grandfather before I knew for sure."

"Alex, I'm not a child." She took a deep breath, then said, barely audible, "I know where they're buried."

"What? How?"

"We went to the Augarten once when I was nine or ten. My parents and my grandparents and me. We had a picnic, and after we ate, my mother and I wandered off to a clearing in a grove of trees. I guess they called for us, but we didn't hear them, so they came looking. When my grandfather stepped into the clearing, he yelled at us for running off and demanded we leave immediately. My mother told him to relax, and he stepped towards her and told her if she didn't take me from there, he would. I didn't understand. My mother glared at him without moving, so he grabbed my wrist, jerked me up, and dragged me away. I'd never seen him like that. They must be buried there."

The Straßenbahn clicked along the tracks, weaving towards the Donau canal and the second district. I wasn't sure what to say. Markus had advised not to offer analysis, so I didn't. I stared forward, and she rested her head against the window, fogging it with her breath. People stepped on and off, and the ride continued. We crossed over the canal, black and shapeless in the dark. A few blocks later, we stepped off into the cold. Johanna looked over at me, eyes weary, and asked, "Can you believe he really did something like that?"

"It's hard to imagine, but I guess so. I'm sorry."

We walked along the street past darkened storefronts. We were only about ten minutes from the park. Johanna walked with strong, quick steps. The patches of ice and metal plates slickened from the cold made my steps uncertain but didn't seem to affect her.

"Accepting that he is a murderer is one thing, but that his entire life as my father's father and as my grandfather came after he murdered people—"

She wiped her eyes and continued forward. We reached the edge of the Augarten. Closed at night, we worked our way around the gate and into the darkness. The former porcelain factory sits on the southern side of the park. It's wide and hanger-like, with a long array of symmetrical windows lining its front. Gravel and snow shifted beneath our feet as we walked around its periphery. Standing near the entrance, at the start of a long path lined with squat, cone-shaped trees, was the silhouette of a man. When we approached, a flashlight shined in our direction, blinding us, sending white pain bursting into my eye. I hunched over, and Johanna put her arm around me.

"Are you ok?"

"Yeah, I'm fine. I'm sensitive to light from the concussion."

"Should you be at the hospital?"

"I'm fine."

The man walked over and stood beside us. It was Emil. He wore his thick grey coat and his familiar brown hat. "Good evening. And you are?" he asked, towards Johanna. Here I was, at night, in winter, introducing a woman I loved to the man who murdered people with her grandfather.

"I'm Johanna Trost. Is it true about my grandfather?" Her voice cut through the night air.

Emil adjusted his hat, then nodded.

"Was it only the one time? Or is that who he is, completely?"

Emil flicked his flashlight back on, casting a pale-yellow beam down the path, between the trees, and deeper into the park. In the distance, the Flakturm loomed. Unlit, its outline was visible as it stood blacker than the night sky.

"I'm not certain. For me, it was."

He coughed into his elbow.

"I have an idea where to look. May I?" she asked, extending her hand. He passed over his flashlight. We walked into the main body of the park and towards the large field surrounding the Flakturm. Without a wasted step, Johanna paced along the edge of the field before taking us across a few paths and into a dense thicket of lime trees. They both wisely wore boots, but the snow seeped into my sneakers, freezing my toes. Johanna paused, then continued on, before suddenly stopping in a small clearing. She placed her hand onto the wide, gnarled trunk of a maple.

"Here."

Emil took the flashlight, walked a slow arc around us, and shined the light up on the trees.

"Some of these are planted since the war, you can see by their height— he said, stepping backwards. He looked down towards his feet, then walked the periphery of the clearing. "I'm afraid this is it. I recognize those four ash trees there, the taller ones." He pointed up and moved his hand from left to right. "There was a tractor parked there with a plow. The ditch ran across this space and was three meters deep. There were additional things buried in it. Refuse and belongings. We'll need a professional crew."

I squatted down and leaned back on a tree. Though frigid, the air smelled thickly of mud, like summertime. I guess there was a family, somewhere beneath us. Without speaking, Johanna turned and walked away.

"Johanna?" I jogged to catch up to her.

"Alex, I have to go see him now."

"Are you sure that's—"

"Yes."

I looked back over my shoulder. Emil was crouched down, shining his light across the base of the lime trees.

"We could wait for your father? He—I mean, for him—it's his father. He might want to be there with you or go in first."

She shook her head. "I don't want to wait," she said and kept walking. We reached a bus stop in front of a bike store. The store had left all their lights on, and the white fluorescents reflected off the fine, almost imperceptible snow that had begun to fall upon us. Johanna studied the bus schedule and map. Her eyes were bright and focused. She pulled off her knit cap, gathered her hair together, and pulled it back on.

"What exactly did your father say on the phone?" I asked.

She looked at me, fully, for the first time that night.

"Your eye looks awful. Can you see?"

"Yeah, it's healing. It's fine."

She leaned in close and placed her fingertips onto my bruised temple.

"I'm really sorry you got hurt. My father said that my grandfather was in the Schutzstaffel, so if I thought that you were trustworthy, I should believe you." She sighed and took a step back. "They only discussed the war together one time. When my father was a child, my grandfather went often to a veterans dinner on Sunday evenings. One Sunday, my grandmother was ill, so my grandfather took my father along. He sat in the corner and pretended to read while he eavesdropped on their conversation. The men didn't talk about the war, or politics, or anything like that. Just football and the weather. On the walk home, my father asked my grandfather what he did during the war, and my grandfather said that he served proudly in the Panzer Corps of the SS. My father was nine, so it wasn't until later that he realized what it meant."

"Your dad never told you?"

"No. He said he was waiting for me to be old enough to understand, but then my mom died, and my grandfather was such a comfort for me that he didn't want to complicate things."

A bus pulled up and we got on. It was empty, and we sat side by side in the front section on hard blue plastic seats. In our reflection in the window across from us, we looked like a couple at the end of a long argument. The bus was warm, and I took off my hat. She did the same. The bus waited at a long red light, and she asked, "What would you have done? If you'd been alive back then, I mean. What do you think you would have done?"

There it was. The only question worth thinking about. Impossible to know. I wanted to say something that would help her, but I wanted to be honest. She pulled off her gloves, then rubbed her forehead and eyes. I looked towards her reflection and said, "I don't know. I probably would have had to be a soldier, but I have to believe I wouldn't have killed innocent people." I stretched my injured arm out and extended my fingers. I knew that her question was, really, how much is Heinrich to blame. I wasn't sure, but people were dead. Historical context wouldn't interest the Blume family. The bus turned sharply, and our shoulders brushed against one another.

"Yeah," she replied.

"Maybe we should just go to the police now or to the Wiesenthal Center?"

"We will, but I want to see him first."

"Ok."

I put my arm around her, and she leaned her head against my cheek and closed her eyes. My head throbbed and my eyes grew heavy. A few minutes later, we got off, walked a few blocks, and stopped in front of the door to Heinrich's apartment. I wondered if we had been followed all along. Being there felt like a risk, but I couldn't imagine him hurting her.

"Alex, thank you for telling me everything and riding with me here, but I think you should stay outside."

"Absolutely not."

She blinked, then scratched at her eyebrow. She pulled a key from her pocket, unlocked the exterior door, and we walked in. When we reached his apartment door, she stopped, removed her gloves and hat, and smoothed her hair back. Then, she took off her coat, handed it to me, and knocked on the door. A moment later, Herinch opened it, dressed in brown slacks and an ivory button-up shirt.

"Johanna—Alex," he said, calmly, looking to her and me. "It's late, how can I help you?"

"Can we come in? I need to talk to you."

"Of course."

For a moment, it all seemed normal. Maybe it had been a twisted, continuous misunderstanding, and all the pieces fit together differently. Johanna walked past Heinrich into his kitchen, poured herself a glass of water, and took a sip. He and I followed and stood alongside his white kitchen counter. It was my first time with the two of them in the same room. I did see a family resemblance. The arcs of their noses and the ovals of their eyes echoed one another. Johanna finished her glass and cleared her throat.

"Alex told me you've been having him investigate an old friend, is that true?"

"Yes, that is true."

"And this old friend, did you and he kill people during the war?" she asked, her voice low and tense.

He chuckled and shook his head slightly.

"Johanna, unfortunately, that's what one does in a war."

"You know what I mean. Did you murder a family? A Jewish family?"

"We may have, yes."

She placed one hand over her eyes and stood still. Then, she wiped her eyes and asked, "Why would you do that?"

Heinrich's face was calm, his eyes bright.

"Well, those were our orders. We were on duty."

"I cannot believe you were part of that."

"We all were."

She began to breathe deliberately through her nose. Deep and even.

Heinrich put one hand on the edge of the counter, gripping it, and said, "It was my goal to keep this a secret in order to spare your father and you the empty hatred of your contemporaries."

"Do you regret what you did?"

He scratched at his neck, then straightened his shoulders.

"There was much asked of my generation, and I do not believe in looking back and rendering judgment."

She refilled her glass, drank it, then placed both hands onto the counter and stared down into the sink. The pressure in the room increased, my pulse thumping in my eardrums.

"That is a very kind way to excuse yourself for murder," she said.

He let out a quiet, exasperated laugh.

"All war is murder, Johanna. I understand that this is beyond you."

She rinsed her glass, placed it upside down on the metal drying rack beside the sink, and looked directly at him.

"Why would you get Alex involved? How could you hurt him like that?"

Heinrich glanced over at me.

"I'm sorry. His injuries were not my intention nor directive. I—well, I had hoped he might be more understanding."

She walked over to the door.

"I'm going to the police now. Will you confess?"

He blinked, then sat down in the chair by the window. His favorite spot. He clenched his jaw and stared for a moment, chest steadily rising and falling.

"If that is what you would like."

"That's exactly what I would like."

"So be it."

She left, and I followed. I had expected a different resolution, Heinrich storming out of the room followed by a single, concussive gunshot, or at least a long argument between them. I guess there wasn't much to say. The facts were now known; it was a story from fifty years ago, and the only thing left was for everyone to decide how they felt about it. I felt nauseous, empty, and homesick. Johanna and I didn't speak on the way to the police station. It was past midnight, and the officer on duty didn't seem too interested. He suggested we come back the next morning during their investigators' normal shift. Johanna insisted on seeing someone that night, so we sat for hours on curved red plastic chairs in the low-ceilinged, windowless room. Every twenty minutes or so somebody rambled in, usually a drunk, and the officer behind the counter morosely scribbled their information into a logbook. Eventually, a tired man in a rumpled suit, obviously pulled out of bed at our request, entered and took us upstairs into an even smaller room. He wrote our statements down on a green notepad. When we were done, he took a sip of coffee, adjusted the cuffs of his sleeves, and asked, "Are you sure you want to go through with this? Your grandfather must be at least, what, seventy years old? He won't ever get out again."

"I'm sure," answered Johanna. He shrugged, nodded, and we signed a few papers. Afterwards, I walked her back to her apartment and then checked into a hotel. I took the first one I came across. It cost all the money I had left. I've never seen a bed with more pillows. With the last joule of energy remaining inside my body, I called Hank collect to let him know I was alive, and that he didn't need to ask the consulate to look for me.

Late the next morning, Johanna, her father, and I rode out to the Augarten in a rusted, white police van. Her father was handsome, a younger, sturdier version of Heinrich, with the same jawline but with rough stubble instead of a cleanly shaven face. As we rode, he held Johanna's hand tightly clasped between his. We sat in the back alongside three police officers and an assortment of shovels, metal detectors, picks, and sifting equipment. It turns out there's a special unit in Austria, the *Sondergruppe,* called to investigate unexploded ordnance, stumbled-upon archaeological sites, and potential mass graves. In the center of Vienna, right outside the Hofburg, you'll find Michaelerplatz, a Roman ruin accidentally unearthed. Beneath Judenplatz, in the first district, lies the remains of a burned Jewish synagogue. The Sondergruppe stays busy.

We drove, bumping down icy paths onto the Augarten grounds while Johanna signaled to the driver which area she recalled having the incident with her grandfather. Markus joined us shortly thereafter; he wanted to meet Johanna and see the end of the story. The three police officers—Franz, Reinhard, and Julia—went to work methodically, sticking probes here and there, taking some soil, putting it into bags, and running some measurements. In the midday sun, the Flakturm looked on without a shadow, its face grey and unchanged. One of the police officers explained to me that the upturning of earth, when done in earnest, was easy to detect fifty, a hundred, even five hundred years later. After breaking ninety minutes for lunch, they began to dig a preliminary hole. The ground was hard, but they persisted. When they hit the first femur, they stopped, taped the area off, and went home for the day. Within forty-eight hours, they called to tell us that it hadn't been luck that they managed to hit bone so quickly. There were bodies everywhere. Heinrich and Emil had undersold their work by quite some margin. By the time the dig was complete, which wasn't until months later, eighty-five bodies, neatly lined in three rows, were found beneath the clearing. They don't know yet which group was the Blume family. There were multiple sets of adults with children, and the problem with DNA is that it requires a relative to be matched against. Many Jewish family lines came to an end in 1945.

The investigator in charge told me that he had explicit instructions from the Austrian government to not search more than three meters beyond the edge of the last found remains. The assumption was that if they ventured far enough afield, they'd hit another site, and before long, the entire Augarten would have to be exhumed. In the last days of the war, the Flakturm had been a civilian shelter from Allied bombing and the Russian advance, and the surrounding area had been long suspected to be a mass grave. Digging through so much black earth would prove expensive and require the closure of a number of playgrounds used several times daily by public-school students in the district. What point would there be anyway? If people had been buried peacefully for fifty years, what harm was there in leaving them there for another hundred and fifty? Besides, the Vienna Boys' Choir has their headquarters next to the park. It would be best to not have their study disturbed by trucks lugging out bones from a regrettable era.

Heinrich and Emil were arrested, and though they pleaded guilty, it appears that their legal unraveling will take some time. They coordinated their story, and they claimed to be the only members of their squad that had fired their weapons that evening. Prosecutors remain unconvinced. The story received a lot of local coverage given Heinrich's history as a journalist, and rival newspapers began poring over his past work, looking for fabrications and political slants. His entire professional life was erased within a week's time. A few days after that morning in the Augarten, Johanna withdrew from university. She decided to take a road trip with her father somewhere distant and warm. They would drive to Portugal in his emerald Alfa Romeo sedan, find a beach, and then go from there. We met for coffee at a cramped, forgettable café in the eighth district the morning she left. We made small talk across a polished black marble table streaked with veins of grey. I sat on a chair with my back to the room and she on a bench, against the wall. Between our first and second coffees, she brought up Heinrich.

"I visited him last week, in jail."

"Wow. How was that?"

She shrugged. I reached across the table and held her elbow.

"He looked older and thinner already."

I nodded. I went around the table, sat next to her, and took her hand. I'm not sure what we talked about after that, but when she left, she gave me a single kiss. She said she'd write me a letter when she gets back to Austria, and I hope that she will. I booked a return flight for a week later, then hung out with Markus a bunch. Late one night, we went over together to Emil's apartment—I still had a key—and we took Josef Blume's silver watch. Markus plans to track down his relatives, if they exist, and give it to them.

Boarding my second international flight didn't equal the feeling of the first. From the window of the plane, as we did a loop over San Francisco before landing, the city looked white and jarring against an expanse of cobalt. My hometown was a strange, remote outpost on the tip of a jutting finger of land at the edge of a broad continent. It's hard to imagine that my ancestors traversed the Atlantic from Europe, and instead of stopping somewhere within earshot of the beach they arrived on, they continued for months across unforgiving terrain until they couldn't proceed any further and then finally called that home.